"Listen, Miss [...]
I suggest you cooperate with me."

Holt planted his hands on the desk and looked her straight in the eye. "Because I can make it very uncomfortable for you if you don't. I'm the chief of police, got it?"

"Got it." A saccharine smile parted her lips.

"I'm glad you have a sense of humor, Miss Westbrook. You may need it before we're through. Turn around, spread your legs and hold your arms away from your body."

Casey stared at him as if she didn't comprehend the command. Her fledgling smirk disappeared. Surely he didn't mean . . . surely he wasn't going to . . .

Dear Reader,

Welcome to the Silhouette **Special Edition** experience! With your search for consistently satisfying reading in mind, every month the authors and editors of Silhouette **Special Edition** aim to offer you a stimulating blend of deep emotions and high romance.

The name Silhouette **Special Edition** and the distinctive arch on the cover represent a commitment—a commitment to bring you six sensitive, substantial novels each month. In the pages of a Silhouette **Special Edition**, compelling true-to-life characters face riveting emotional issues—and come out winners. All the authors in the series strive for depth, vividness and warmth in writing these stories of living and loving in today's world.

The result, we hope, is romance you can believe in. Deeply emotional, richly romantic, infinitely rewarding—that's the Silhouette **Special Edition** experience. Come share it with us—six times a month!

From all the authors and editors of Silhouette **Special Edition**,

Best wishes,

Leslie Kazanjian,
Senior Editor

SANDY STEEN
Vanquish the Night

Silhouette Special Edition

Published by Silhouette Books New York

America's Publisher of Contemporary Romance

SILHOUETTE BOOKS
300 East 42nd St., New York, N.Y. 10017

ISBN: 0-373-09638-0

First Silhouette Books printing December 1990
Second Silhouette Books printing January 1991

Printed in the U.S.A.

Books by Sandy Steen

Silhouette Intimate Moments

Sweet Reason #155
Past Perfect #202

Silhouette Special Edition

Vanquish the Night #638

SANDY STEEN

spent many an hour daydreaming while growing up in the Texas Panhandle. Later, inspired by her husband of more than twenty years and her two children, Sandy decided to put her dreams on paper.

Although her family had some doubts when they first observed her method of plotting her stories—staring into space for endless hours—they are now her staunchest supporters. Sandy herself believes that if she can make a reader believe in the wonder of fantasy and feel the joy of falling in love, then she has, indeed, succeeded.

Underlined places are fictitious.

Prologue

California, 1939

"Hello, movie fans. This is Adelle Adams in Hollywood with all the news that is news. In a few hours Tinseltown will bid goodbye to one of the silver screen's most dazzling silver blondes, when Norah Tanner forsakes Hollywood for the lone prairies of Texas. The always press-hungry star announced her retirement following the scandalous deaths of her director-husband Phillip Tanner and Alex Grant, promising newcomer and costar of her latest and now last film.

"The movie colony, indeed the world, has mourned the tragic loss of Phillip Tanner, the brilliant director of such classic films as *For Heaven's Sake*, *Bound by Yesterday* and *The Reckoning*. Young Grant, Tanner and, of course, the stunning Norah have been headlines since the two men were found dead in the Tanners' hilltop mansion over two weeks ago.

"According to servants, the disastrous love triangle reached its explosive conclusion shortly after Grant arrived unannounced at the Tanner home, demanding to see Phillip Tanner. Servants reported the sounds of a heated argument, then gunfire around midnight. Both men were dead when police arrived on the scene.

"News of the shocking deaths had barely hit the airwaves when Norah Tanner was taken to police headquarters for interrogation. After lengthy questioning of the so-called 'Female Valentino,' authorities released Mrs. Tanner, pending the outcome of the investigation. It was no secret the Tanner marriage had deteriorated, and sources close to this reporter have verified the twenty-year-old star had filed for a divorce from her forty-five-year-old director husband. Norah and Phillip Tanner were one of Hollywood's most flamboyant couples, and their public fights and lavish parties have certainly provided endless copy and conversation.

"Nonetheless, the scandal has sent shock waves crashing throughout the movie community, the effects no doubt to be felt for months, maybe years. Everyone from extras to moguls has an opinion and a verdict, and most of those verdicts label Norah Tanner guilty. If not of murder, then certainly of playing husband against lover with disastrous results. She has brought shame to the industry and to the town that took her to its heart and made her name a household word.

"I have over the last three years had numerous occasions to interview the flamboyant Norah, and for all her beauty and charm, she was always a little too cocky for my taste. But she was news. We may not miss her style but we will miss her talent. Tragedies often mold fool's gold into sterling characters. In this case we can only hope—"

Norah snapped the radio off, silencing the venomous columnist in midsentence, then sighed, taking one last look at the spectacular gardens of the estate. Once she had hoped to be happy here for the rest of her life. Now she couldn't wait to leave. Happiness, she had learned, was a fleeting thing, greatly prized but seldom attained. In retrospect she wondered if she had truly been happy in this place.

In a single motion she turned and scooped a small, black-fox-trimmed hat from a nearby end table. Looking at her reflection in the multipaned window, she fitted the fashionable accessory at a jaunty angle atop her silver-blond curls, securing it with a jet-tipped hat pin. She tucked a black leather clutch bag beneath her arm, gathered the remaining scraps of her dignity and walked out of the room.

The polished marble floor of the massive foyer reflected the crisp black and white of the servants' attire as they stood in line, like chess pieces awaiting a skilled player. A perfect row of perfect servants. Symbols of the world's perception of Norah Tanner's life. The notion of her life as something approaching perfection was so far removed from the truth it was laughable. A slight smile lifted Norah's painted lips as she moved down the line of employees, shaking hands and speaking to each one, expressing her appreciation for their service. The loyalty of these steadfast few had given her strength in moments when she doubted her own sanity, and she would miss them terribly. At least the butler and two of the maids had elected to join her in Texas.

After shaking the last hand, she stepped back, granting the small assembly time to mingle for their own farewells. Bless them all, she thought, wishing she could be assured each had a new job waiting, and hoping their association with her wouldn't hinder chances of finding good positions. Norah knew too well how quickly and cruelly Hollywood could ostracize those who, they considered, had blemished the carefully constructed, glittering facade. In this town you were most definitely judged by the company you kept.

As the last of the servants moved quietly out of the foyer—out of her life—she wanted to cry, but didn't. She wanted to raise her fists in rage to the heavens, but couldn't. In truth, she had been her own worst enemy. Where is it written that life is fair? You play the hand you're dealt. Never bet more than you can afford to lose, and leave the rest to the Almighty.

Sound advice she should have heeded, but hadn't. Instead she had wagered everything on the kind of love that keeps to the grave and beyond....

And she had lost.

True, she wasn't destitute. Phillip had made sure she would never want for money and that she could live in splendor, albeit solitarily, so long as she accepted the terms of his will. Unfortunately, an army of lawyers had failed to produce a single avenue of escape from the outrageously confining document.

Denied work in a town that spoke her name in whispers and refused to return her agent's phone calls, her options had dwindled to none. Even if she could find a job, any job, what employer would put up with constant hordes of reporters and photographers?

Trapped.

If only she had realized how sick Phillip had become, perhaps she could have prevented what had happened. Why hadn't she followed her instincts and gone away with Alex as he asked, rather than insisting on facing Phillip honestly? If only she had known his twisted mind would contemplate first murder, then suicide. The warning signs had all been there, if only she had looked. If, if, if...

Covering her face with trembling hands, she fought back a sob and prayed for the strength to face her future. A future alone and without love.

Chapter One

The imposing mansion came into focus, and Casey Westbrook inhaled sharply, her tongue instinctively making a fruitless attempt to moisten parted lips. Adeptly cradling the two-foot long lens with one hand, she adjusted the focus with the other. *Click. Click.* Nervous, scared and excited, anticipation skated down her spine while the motor drive of her Nikon whirred, the shutter winking like a flirtatious maniac. *Click, click, click.*

Lush, green, rolling hills of an English countryside would have better suited the mammoth brick and cast stone Tudor-style house framed by her lens, yet here it sat in the middle of windblown north central Texas, a few hundred yards from a man-made lake. An aging manor without a domain. *Click, click.*

Slowly Casey lowered the camera and weighty lens, then swiped sweaty palms across the seat of her jeans. She couldn't believe she actually stood less than a half mile from the home of the legendary Norah Tanner.

Everything about the fabulous star—her brief but brilliant career, her infamous off-screen life, the scandal—intrigued Casey. But most of all she was fascinated by the woman herself—the star, the wife, the lover. The murderer? Which one was the real Norah? Or was she all of these?

The Tanner scandal had shocked the world, Casey knew, and its mystique had not only thrived, but grown as the years passed. Possibly because of Norah's fifty-year seclusion. Possibly because no one but she actually knew what had happened that night. And the desire to unearth secrets of such magnitude proved far too enduring to die, no matter how many years they'd lain buried.

Glancing at her watch, Casey realized she had stayed longer than was prudent. It was common knowledge throughout her industry that reporters and photographers were about as welcome in the remote Texas town as bag ladies in a swank department store. Communal protectiveness, plus the fact that the mansion sat on an isolated and well-guarded peninsula of Moon Lake, spelled extreme difficulty for anyone sporting a press pass or a tripod. This was definitely not a photojournalist's dream, and she wondered for the hundredth time how she had allowed herself to be sweet-talked into accepting the assignment.

The sun's heat, warming toward noon, made her bulky sweater, so welcome only a short time earlier, feel unduly heavy. *Now what? You can't camp out here all day. Too risky. And face it, chances of getting a picture that easily would be a stroke of pure luck.* Casey never gave much credence to luck, pure or otherwise.

Well, did you expect fortune to smile sweetly? When has it ever?

No, she hadn't *expected* anything. Hoped, maybe. Dreamed, certainly. But Casey had learned long ago that expectation led to disappointment. Years of being passed from one nanny to another had taught her that the only person she could depend on was herself. A tough little cookie, Ramsey had called her. Only he knew a marshmallow center lay hidden beneath her crisp and rarely sugar-coated exterior.

Casey detached the awkward lens and slipped it into its own case inside the carryall resting at her feet. Most of her equipment was locked safely in the trunk of the rented Volkswagen, but the telephoto lens had been a must. Deft fingers, moving quickly and confidently, withdrew and screwed another lens onto the camera. Concentrating to the point of being oblivious to all else, Casey brought the camera into position, randomly selecting a subject to check her equipment. Habitually squinting, she adjusted the lens until a bright yellow sunflower came into focus. The motor drive purred in the quiet morning.

"Stand right where you are."

The soft, deadly voice, cold as arctic wind, made the hair stand up on the back of her neck. Casey froze.

"Raise your hands above your head. Slowly. And I mean *slowly*. Turn around. And don't even think about running. You'd be dead before you got two feet."

Nerveless fingers released the grip on the Nikon. It would have landed in the dust next to her booted foot and the carryall, but for the worn strap around her neck. Casey's arms shot into the air above her head. Slowly—very slowly—she turned and came nose to barrel with a pistol, not three feet away, aimed between her startled blue eyes.

"Who the hell are you, and what are you doing, trespassing on private property?"

The owner of the gun didn't need a weapon to enhance his authority. Didn't even need the words Chief of Police emblazoned on the badge pinned to the breast pocket of his shirt. Sheer size, plus the timbre of his voice, would have accomplished his purpose without any weapon. His tall, broad-shouldered frame completely blocked her view of the dirt road she'd walked along only a short time earlier.

Casey swallowed hard. She could almost hear the lead-in for the network's five o'clock news now: *Today Cassandra Westbrook, daughter of wealthy International Studios executive Jason Westbrook, pleaded guilty to charges of trespassing. The property in question was none other than the Texas estate of the legendary movie star, Norah Tanner. Film at eleven.*

"I'm, uh ... I was just ..." The gun, the man, the situation, all combined to rob her of logical thought. "My ... name ... is ... is ... uh ..." She swallowed hard again. The usually unflappable Ms. Casey Westbrook of Beverly Hills could barely remember her name, much less think up a reason, any reason, plausible enough to keep her out of trouble. *Stall for time.*

"I, uh, wanted a picture of uh, this ..." Without lowering her hands or taking her eyes from the gun, with a flick of one wrist Casey motioned to the wildflower. "And I wanted to get closer so I could get a better shot—"

"Are you a reporter?"

"No."

"A photographer?"

"Yes."

"Pick up your gear and get your tail over that fence. Let's go."

"Go? Go where?"

"You don't ask the questions here, lady. I do. Now, move your butt back over that fence. Fast."

Casey moved. Taking a step backward, she whipped the camera from around her neck, stuffed it into the bag and retrieved her denim jacket from the gnarled fence post. Why hadn't she been satisfied to look from a discreet distance?

When she turned to face him again, Holt Shelton was momentarily shocked. He wasn't sure exactly what he'd expected, but a face like an angel certainly wasn't at the top of the list.

My God, but she's young. If her innocently youthful face was any indication, she was barely old enough to be out of school, much less mature enough to have spent time on the payroll of some newspaper or sleazy magazine. Her body, on the other hand, was anything but schoolgirlish. She exuded a sweet sort of sexuality that was irresistible to men.

But Holt had seen them looking sweet enough to cause cavities and still be cutthroat cold when it came to getting a hot story. The presence of Crescent Bay's most notable citizen frequently drew reporters and photographers the way Las Vegas drew gamblers, which only made Holt's job more difficult.

"Make it snappy," he barked, angrier at the situation than at her.

She shouldered her equipment with an economy of effort that belied its considerable weight and awkwardness. Holt noted her momentary grimace as her body adjusted to the extra burden, but not so much as a glance in his direction indicated she wanted or expected help.

He watched her swing first one long, jean-clad leg, then the other, over the fence and had to admit she was a cut above the usual, and Lord knows, he was something of an expert by now. He lowered the gun.

A softer version than the rigors of the story-at-any-cost life-style generally produced, she didn't fit the mold, Holt decided and was unreasonably angered that she didn't. Her eyes, now understandably wide with fear, were pale aqua, or maybe an incredibly light shade of blue, a clear and alluring contrast to her dark-as-coffee braid of hair.

"What...what are you...going to do?" His gaze narrowed. His attention was riveted on her voice and mouth.

The husky contralto voice belonged in the body of a born-to-be-bedded kind of woman, totally at odds with her fresh, sunshine-on-dew face. And her mouth. Lord, her mouth. Full, sexy. Naturally sexy. She looked kitten soft.

Innocent.

Innocently trespassing on Tanner property with a camera in her hand? *Not likely. She's trouble.* Holt knew it. He could *feel* it in his gut. With a face sweet enough to defy angels and a mouth sexy enough to jump-start a cardiac-arrest victim, she had to be trouble. He scanned her from head to toe.

Casey watched him watch her, inspecting her the way a lepidopterist might inspect a pinned butterfly. He'd been quietly staring for so long that when he finally spoke, she started at the sound of his voice.

"I said, let's go." The long-barreled weapon dropped into a holster riding low on his hip. The leather creaked a soft protest.

"But where—?"

"To jail."

"Jail! But…but—" Casey struggled to maintain her grip on the bag and jacket. She lost half the battle, and the jacket hit the dirt with a *thunk*. A reprimand she'd expected, even a dressing-down and maybe a fine. But jail? That imagined five o'clock news introduction was dangerously close to becoming a reality. She'd better think of something fast.

"Uh, listen—"

"Move it," he said reaching for her arm. "I don't have the time or patience to play games."

Instinctively Casey resisted his hold. "You can't take me to jail," she blurted without thinking.

"Can and am." With his other hand he scooped up the jacket and shoved it at her. Casey's free arm captured the garment, anchoring it to the carryall, holding on for dear life as the powerful man hauled her along with him.

"But…I…I didn't do-o-o…anything…wrong!" The ineffectual protest skipped like a needle over a record as she was bounced and jarred along, trying to keep pace with his long stride.

"Trespassing, just like the sign says."

"What sign? I didn't see—"

"There are signs posted exactly one hundred feet apart. Couldn't have missed them." He shoved her ahead of him across a dusty, weed-choked hill and down toward the road.

A step or two behind, but easily within reach, Holt surveyed her well-worn and unquestionably well-fitting jeans, oversize sweater, worn-to-pale denim jacket and decided the wardrobe was more practical than trendy. Still, she didn't look like she had done a hard day's work in her life. The word *soft* kept popping into his head.

City born and city bred, from the intricate French braid right down to her butter-soft, taupe boots. He'd bet his badge on it. His sharp-eyed assessment didn't miss the dark twist of hair trailing the neckline of her sweater. The baggy sweater hung to reveal one smooth shoulder. A teal-colored tank top peeked around the neckline and pointed the way to several inches of creamy skin, looking soft as a baby's behind. But when it came to city women, Holt knew softness didn't necessarily equal sweetness, even if such women did resemble Lucifer's greatest piece of temptation.

As the hand on her back directed her body in an arc to avoid a boulder, Casey glanced up and caught sight of a police vehicle, the driver's door panel boldly imprinted with City of Crescent Bay Police Department seal. Seeing the official vehicle drove home the reality of her situation. Mr. Macho wasn't kidding. He was definitely taking her to jail!

The gravity of her predicament resuscitated Casey's fears as she struggled to keep her balance, while trying to formulate a plan to keep herself out of jail. Years of living in a town built on a foundation of make-believe and well-constructed distortion of truth had given Casey more than a nodding acquaintance with lies and liars. Even though she hated Hollywood's fabricated values, she had learned from them. And if ever she'd needed to draw on that knowledge, now was the moment.

By the time they drew even with the car, Casey's fear had flip-flopped into anger. Determination having replaced panic, she faced him with an always effective, don't-push-your-luck glare.

"Take your hands off me, you hillbilly." Casey jerked her arm free, surprised to discover his hold wasn't as tight as she had originally thought. "You don't have to play Dirty Harry. I'll come along...*peaceably*."

Enough sarcasm dripped from the last word to fill a five-gallon bucket. It stoked the simmering flames of Holt's temper.

"I'm relieved to hear it." He opened the car door and reached for her bag.

She clutched the lumpy nylon tote to her chest. "Nobody takes my equipment."

"Lady, you keep missing the point. *I* tell *you* what to do. And I'm telling you, don't give me any trouble, or I'll add resisting arrest to the charge of trespassing."

"And I'll scream police brutality."

Holt gritted his teeth. Apparently she was bound and determined to show the hick-from-the-sticks cop he had met his match. Well, Little Miss City Smart-aleck, you're about to learn just how effective this particular hick can be.

He slid his heated gaze away. Intentionally shifting his body, he negligently hiked a hand onto his hip and sighed. She appeared to answer his telegraphed body language and relaxed. The instant she did, Holt ripped the bag from her grasp and pitched it through the open window and onto the front seat, hardly giving Casey time to take a breath.

"Hey! That's expensive equipment—!"

In an equally swift move he grabbed her right arm, twisted it behind her, yanked a pair of handcuffs from his belt and snapped a ring around her wrist. With a slight tug her body leaned into his, her buttocks flush with his hip. In a deceptively calm voice only inches from her ear he said, "You should have thought of that before you decided to break the law." Holt had intended to cuff both hands behind her back, but something about the way the sweater's neckline drooped to encircle a tank-top-covered breast, as she extended her chest, changed his mind.

Casey tried to move her body away from his, but couldn't. "I didn't know it was against the law to take pictures of *flowers*! And since when did Texas become a fascist state?" Furious, she enlisted every ounce of control she possessed not to give him a detailed summation of his less than admirable personality.

"Photograph flowers until the world looks level, as long as you don't do it on private property. Where's your car?"

"I don't own one."

He glanced down at her boots. "If you're trying to make me believe you walked from town, forget it. The heels of those boots wouldn't last a mile. Now, I'll ask you just once more, where is your car?"

A head toss indicated a spot several hundred feet up the road. "Over there. Behind that clump of bushes." Casey knew the admission didn't help her position one bit.

He attempted to push her through the open rear door of the patrol car.

"Aren't you going to call someone to pick up the car?"

"Why should I?"

"Someone might steal it. It's a rental—"

"Tough." His big hand atop her head, Holt pressed her down and onto the back seat. Quickly looping the handcuffs over a steel bar running the length of the backside of the bench seat, he secured her other wrist.

The click of a lock followed the door's solid whack, and before Casey could settle herself on the seat he had the black and white unit backed out of the trees, turned around and headed down the road.

Great start, Westbrook. How are you going to talk your way out of this one? And you better make it good, or the poor man's Eastwood will probably be more than happy to provide you with room and board, courtesy of the city.

Bent slightly forward to accommodate herself to the metal restraints, Casey barely had time to formulate a plausible story before the patrol car pulled into an assigned space in front of a small, one-story building. The officer unlocked the manacles and hauled her from the car, stopping only long enough to retrieve her equipment.

The police station, situated at one end of the town's main street, was more state-of-neglect than state-of-the-art, but appeared clean. A youngish, uniformed officer, not as tall as the chief, looked up from a desk as they entered.

"Whatcha got, Holt?"

"Trespasser." There seemed to be no need to explain *where* she had been trespassing.

"Caught her red-handed, huh?"

Casey cut her gaze to the other officer. He was leaner than the Neanderthal and sported a snooty, ear-to-ear grin. If she hadn't been scared right down to her toes—not to mention furious—the situation would have been laughable. A small voice inside her head whispered caution. She ignored the warning.

With a none-too-gentle nudge Casey was guided past the deputy and into an office with the words Holt Shelton, Chief of Police stenciled on the door. He plunked her gear bag onto the desk and faced her.

"This all the equipment you have?"

"It's all I need to do my job," she said, rubbing tender wrists.

From the yawning opening of the carryall he withdrew her camera and a paperback-book-sized purse. "Any more film?"

"You're holding the bag. Check for yourself."

He yanked several rolls of sealed film and two exposed rolls from the nylon container. "You sure this is everything?"

"Why don't you search me, if you think I'm not telling the truth?"

"I'll do more than search you, if you're lying."

"Oh my-y-y, you're frightening me, Sheriff."

"Chief. How many pictures did you take?"

"None."

"None?"

Everything about him, the harshness in his voice, the don't-mess-with-me body language virtually shouted, "You're lying through your teeth." In her heart Casey knew he wouldn't give an inch, but old habits died hard, particularly when he had backed her into a corner.

"Which word didn't you understand, Sheriff? None. As in not a single one. *Nada*. Zero." Her bravado would collapse if he checked the frame-counter window of her camera, and she knew it. *Bluff, bluff, and keep on bluffing*.

"What's on these rolls of undeveloped film?"

"Pictures."

Rebellious little brat, Holt thought. Struggling with the rocking lid on his temper, he deliberately lifted her purse into the air, then turned it upside down, dumping the contents onto the desk.

"Look, Miss..." He plucked a wallet from the heap, flipped it open and glanced at her driver's license, rapidly calculating her age. He recalculated. "How old are you?"

"How old do I have to be, Sheriff?"

"Listen, *Ms.* Westbrook, I suggest you cooperate with me." Leaning across the collection of lipstick, compact, address book and other paraphernalia, he planted his hands on the desk and looked her straight in the eye. "Because I can make it *very* uncomfortable for you if you don't. And the title is *Chief* of Police. C-h-i-e-f, got it?"

"Got it." A saccharine-sweet smile parted her lips.

He tossed the billfold onto the desk. For reasons he couldn't fathom, he was relieved to discover she was of legal age. "I'm glad you have a sense of humor, Ms. Westbrook. You may need it before we're through. Turn around."

Casey stared at him, not quite comprehending the command. She felt her fledgling smirk disappear, anger slide into fear. She suddenly realized how far her rebellious temper had carried her. Maybe too far. For the first time her bravado slipped a notch.

"Wh-what are you going to do?" When he failed to answer, she swallowed hard and licked dry lips.

Holt had only intended to intimidate her, but she had called his bluff and smarted off one time too many. She deserved to be taken down a peg or two, and he was just the man for the job. His momentary twinge of guilt for pushing the letter of the law was obliterated by the you-wouldn't-dare look in her eyes.

"I said, turn around." Intense blue eyes hardened to a steely glint. "Spread your legs and hold your arms away from your body."

Her heartbeat keeping time with a hummingbird's wings, mouth parchment dry, Casey blinked and obeyed. Surely he didn't mean . . . ? Surely he wasn't going to . . . ?

Chapter Two

At the first touch of his hands on her outstretched arms Casey's entire body flashed hot, cold, then hot again.

"What are you doing!"

"What does it look like I'm doing, Ms. Westbrook?"

Strong, confident fingers skimmed down her arms, then retraced the path, pushing the sleeves of the sweater almost to her underarms. His hands paraded over her shoulders, down her narrow back. They bracketed her waist, clutching great handfuls of knitted material. Jerking the hem of the sweater high, his hands coasted up her rib cage, dangerously close to her breasts. His thumbs grazed the undersides. Casey gasped.

"Relax, honey, I'm not interested in a cheap thrill."

Cheap thrill! There was nothing cheap about the way her temper was costing her precious bits of pride.

Relentlessly the insolent search continued. Downward. Ever downward. Moving quickly, fingers splayed, he eased both hands over her flat abdomen. Across her hips. The weight of the sweater tugged across her breasts as it dropped back into place. Big hands slid over her buttocks. Around to the front of her thighs. Over knees, then inside her thighs. All the way up to her—

Oh, my God!

Actual contact lasted less than half a heartbeat, but the split second of expectation failed to prepare her for the shock of his touch. It was startling, humiliating.

And sexual. No one had *ever* touched her in such an intimate way.

Tingling electricity shot through her body with the velocity of a high-speed bullet, exploding nerve endings, leaving an invisible trail of heat shimmering in its wake. Leaving her imagination free to manufacture some very erotic and explicit pictures. Casey flinched.

His fingers loosely encircled her calves, gliding down and around her ankles. Slower now, gentler, until finally the search ended.

Clammy perspiration coated every inch of Casey's skin. Her breathing was shallow. Alarm faded into humiliation, then indignation, leaving pure white rage burning in her soul. Mortified, she couldn't decide what had been more degrading, being hauled off to jail in handcuffs, the embarrassing search, or being touched so intimately. And being humbled and treated as a common criminal definitely wasn't at the top of her things-she-wanted-to-do list.

Equally humiliating was the knowledge that an inappropriate and extremely erotic slide show had flashed across her mind while his hands roamed her body. *Get a grip on yourself!*

Staying in control of the situation was essential, as far as Casey was concerned. Luckily, hiding her doubts and insecurities was a habit as natural as breathing. Casey firmly believed in the popular ideology, "Don't let the bastards wear you down," and for her own uses had simply added, "And don't let them back you into a corner." Her technique had provided much-needed protection during her childhood, but had occasionally proven self-defeating in adulthood. Casey knew that if she didn't curb her sharp tongue, she had less than a snowball's chance in hell of getting anything from this man but an escort out of town. She was dangerously close to ruining her chance of a lifetime.

Forcing a frosty calm into her voice, she took a deep, steadying breath and looked the chief of police directly in the eye.

"Am I free to go now?"

"Not just yet. A few questions first. Who do you work for?"

"Nobody."

"Then what newspaper, magazine, or tabloid are you free-lancing for?"

"None of your business." She was a breath away from demanding her one phone call, then telling him to go straight to hell. Death was too good for this, this ... Casey scanned her memory's storehouse of nasty insults in several languages, but decided to fall back on good old American profanity.... Sonofa—

Holt's head snapped up as if he had read her mind. "It became my business the minute you swung your tail over that fence and onto private property. I repeat, where are you from?"

"Dallas." She waited until he began to scribble the word in the appropriate blank of the form in front of him, then added, "Tucson, Seattle, Memphis—and half a dozen others I've forgotten at the moment."

"What the hell kind of answer is that?"

"You wanted to know where I'm from. I'm from all of those places."

"Your driver's license lists your address as Beverly Hills, California." His gaze nailed hers.

The cover story grew more uncomfortable with each passing moment, but she had gone too far to turn back now.

"It's also my parents' address. But I don't *live* there. For the past eight months I've traveled across the country with my camera." She folded her arms across her chest. "Taking pictures. Nature shots, wildlife."

"What's the matter, antisocial?"

"No, antistarvation."

"Starvation," he scoffed. "With a *Beverly Hills* address?" Then he looked at her slender body and saw just *how* slender it was. He noticed the dark circles beneath her eyes, plus the fact that her clothing definitely didn't speak of Rodeo Drive.

"In case you're wondering, *Chief,* I'm an independent businesswoman. I *earn* my living with a camera, and lately the living has been on the lean side."

Her answer was defensive, laced with pride, making Holt wonder if he might be dealing with the black sheep of the family.

"What are you doing in Crescent Bay?"

Casey sighed. He was either dumb as a doorknob or just plain hard of hearing. "Taking pictures."

"You just go around taking pictures, hoping you'll get lucky and sell something?"

"No. I currently have an agreement with *World Magazine* for some—"

"You said you didn't work for a magazine."

"I'm not on their payroll or anybody else's. I am a freelance photographer. It just so happens that *World* is, uh, doing a 'Day in the Life of America' sort of thing, except with nature and wildlife. Several photographers from all over the country are contributing. I'm only one of many." Desperate, she mixed half truths and imagination.

"So they could vouch for you?"

Casey glanced away, gnawing the inside of her cheek. Ramsey would back her story, but she had to get to him first. Calling him now was risky, particularly if the call had to be made within earshot of the chief of police. She looked back at the lawman. "I've only dealt with one guy. He probably interviewed a lot of photographers. He may not even remember me."

Holt straightened. Resting a hand on the butt of the gun riding his hip, he said, "Let me see if I understand, Ms. Westbrook. You have an address, but you don't live there. You work, but not at a regular job. The man at *World Magazine* hired you to take pictures, but may not even remember you. Does that just about cover it, Ms. Westbrook?"

"More or less."

"I'd say less." Returning his attention to the forms on his desk, he said, "Ms. Westbrook, I've decided to be lenient. This time. I'm letting you off with a one-hundred-dollar fine and a warning."

"A hundred dollars! But that's almost all the cash I have!"

Holt experienced a stab of regret, but the fine was out of his hands. "I don't determine the amount, Ms. Westbrook. It's preset by a judge."

"What if I can't . . . or won't pay the fine?"

"If you *can't*, then I'll have to add vagrancy to the charge of trespassing and place you in a work program. If you *won't* . . ." He shrugged. "Either way, Ms. Westbrook, a visit to the Wise County correctional facilities would be in order."

She hated the way he kept saying her name, the same way a high-school principal addressed a truant student.

"Perhaps *World Magazine* would be willing to foot the bill," he said.

"I'd rather not bother them."

To describe the smile he gave her as self-satisfied would qualify as the understatement of the decade. He collected the items strewn across the desk and dropped them into her purse.

"If you'll follow me to the clerk's office, she'll take care of the paperwork." He turned and started down the hall.

"What about my things?"

"You can pick them up...on your way *out* of town, which I recommend happens shortly after you leave this office."

In less than ten minutes Casey retrieved her belongings and was on the way back to her rented car, courtesy of the police department. The return trip to the edge of the Tanner estate, sans handcuffs, was made in total silence. The young officer who dropped her off gave her a half-hearted salute as he watched her drive down the road leading from the posted property.

By the time Casey closed the door to her motel room, she was rip-roaring mad. Not only over the chauvinistic attitude of the chief of police and the treatment she had received at his hands, but at her own carelessness and inability to control her temper. Again. One slip had almost cost her dearly. The current objective was to emerge from the encounter with what little dignity remained intact. Dignity? What was dignified about this outrageous assignment? Or about the fact that she was and always had been putty in the hands of one H. A. Ramsey, tenacious editor, whip-cracker extraordinaire, and . . . surrogate father.

"Ah, Ramsey." Casey plopped onto the too-soft bed and kicked off her boots. "You did it to me again." Actually, Ramsey wasn't totally to blame and she knew it.

From the day her parents had purchased the Tanner Beverly Hills estate, Casey had lived with the legend of Norah Tanner. Playing dolls on the rolling lawn and hide-and-seek in the gardens, watching movies in the small theater, so stamped with the star's personality that it seemed haunted, those were the boundaries of Casey's world. She loved the house and idolized its famous former owner. But unlike Casey, her parents treated the mansion and its unearthed treasures with a proprietary arrogance, as if living in *her house* somehow gave them ownership of the legend.

Jason Westbrook, vice president of International Studios, and Cinnamon Westbrook, former top agent to the stars, were the epitome of Hollywood's rich and famous. Legends, past or present, dead or alive were chic. And the Westbrooks thrived on chic, glamour and the spotlight.

All except Casey.

Growing up in a goldfish-bowl atmosphere, displayed among her mother's finery like the latest piece of jewelry, had been more than Casey could handle. So she'd found her own style—tomboyish, outspoken and unspoiled. Plain and shy, she'd been her parents' greatest disappointment—and they hers.

Now, having turned her back on the ornate, California estate, Casey wondered what her parents would say if they knew she had almost been arrested for one glimpse inside Norah Tanner's Texas home.

A hundred-dollar glimpse.

A check of her wallet revealed one twenty-dollar bill and forty-five cents in change. Credit cards, of course. Thank God for plastic, or she would really be stuck in this one-horse town. Casey looked down at the stack of cards in her hand. Stuck was exactly where she wanted to be. She smiled. "Brilliant. Why didn't I think of—"

The ringing of the phone jarred her concentration.

"Hello."

"Hiya, sweetheart. How goes it?"

"Badly."

"How badly?" Casey could almost hear Ramsey's thick brows draw together in a frown.

"I thought about calling you an hour ago...from jail."

"Jeez, what the hell happened? Do you need a lawyer? Did they take your camera—?"

"Slow down Ramsey. I'm in my motel room. With my camera. And no, I don't need a lawyer. Yet."

"I don't like the sound of that last word."

Casey sighed and shifted the phone from one ear to the other. "I've got a few more for you. Try search, humiliation, hundred-dollar fine and get out of town."

"Sounds like you've had a very busy morning."

"Very."

"But was it productive?"

"You're all heart, Ramsey."

"It's a living. Now you want to tell me how you got your sassy little rear into so much trouble?"

"By letting you convince me to become part of the wild-goose chase in the first place. How could I—?"

"Whoa, cookie. If memory serves me correctly, and it usually does, I didn't drag you kicking and screaming into this thing."

"No, you manipulated me, played on my generous nature and tapped into my sense of guilt."

"Well...besides that."

"You always did have such a way with words, Ramsey."

"And you always were a smart-mouthed brat. Don't know why I put up with you. So tell me, cookie, have you got a Plan B?"

"Maybe," she said, thinking about the idea that had begun to take shape when Ramsey called.

"By the by, just how did you talk your way out of spending the night in jail?"

"Lied. At least partially. And I may need you to back me up."

"Don't I always? Have I ever given a boyfriend, the IRS, or your...*anyone* one syllable of info I wasn't positive you wanted released?"

"I don't exactly have a male harem waiting for me, and you, of all people, should know I don't make enough to cause the IRS a minute's concern." They both knew the undefined "anyone" was a periodic inquiry from a Westbrook lawyer or accountant, or occasionally her mother's secretary, checking to make sure Casey's current life-style or circle of friends wouldn't embarrass Jason or Cinnamon.

Ramsey always played the game by Casey's rules. Since the first day she had started working at the magazine, whenever she asked about messages, the unspoken question was always, had her parents called. Invariably the answer was no, so they had fallen into a kind of code of asking, without really asking.

"Well, if the occasion ever arises, I'm prepared—"

"You're a treasure."

"Ain't I just. Now, you want to tell what happened?"

"I was caught on the Tanner estate, camera in hand and had to come up with a story, so I said I'm a free-lancer, working to contribute to an article you're doing."

"That's not a lie."

"But the rest is. I told the sher—chief of police, the article is a sort of A Day in the Life, et cetera, et cetera, only with nature and wildlife. I work my way around the country while I shoot."

"So what's the angle?"

"There is no angle, Ramsey. I told you before I left L.A., the chances of getting this picture were slim and none."

"And I told you the picture had to be got...if not by you, then by someone else. The time is right, and the demand is enormous."

"I still don't understand why you think I can accomplish what no other photographer has been able to in almost fifty years."

"Because Casey Westbrook is the ultimate Norah Tanner fan. And because Casey Westbrook will bust her butt to do the dignified, professional piece we talked about."

There was a long pause, in which Casey thought about hanging up and packing her bags. But she knew Ramsey was thinking about his next line of attack to convince her to stay.

"I'm not so sure." Her uncertainty had more to do with the basic disquiet nagging at her than the day's hassles.

"About Plan B or the whole deal?"

"You've been reading my mind again."

"Nothing to it. Don't forget, I'm the guy who sent you to shoot a suspected killer and wound up with egg all over his face, when you helped prove the guy's innocence."

"Oh, I don't know, Ramsey. It sounded so right when we discussed it in your office, but out here, just a stone's throw from the real thing..." Her voice trailed off.

"Listen, cookie, nothing has changed. It's been over thirty years since a reliable shot of Tanner has surfaced. You've practically worshiped this woman since you were big enough to walk. Now, here's your opportunity to do a first-class photograph on a classy old broad who is still front-page news, fifty-plus years after her last movie. It doesn't get any better than that."

"Don't call her an old broad."

"Okay, okay. Ageless star, how's that?"

"Better."

"So when does Plan B go into action?"

Casey sighed and rubbed her temple. She hadn't eaten all day, and a headache was blossoming behind her left eye. "I'm, uh, supposed to be broke, so I thought I might look for a job so I can hang around."

"Doing what?"

"Maybe working in the motel office, or there's a convenience store on the main highway and a restaurant connected to the motel."

"Have you ever waited on tables or worked in a kitchen?"

"Sure."

Ramsey laughed. "When?"

"Every summer at camp I helped out in the kitchen."

"You're putting me on. Those high-dollar kiddie spas you attended probably had the meals catered from the Beverly Hills Hotel."

"Nope. Besides, the staff liked me, and I didn't have to spend all my time talking about the last movie my father's studio cranked out and how much money it made. Or the last shindig my mother threw or charity bazaar she organized. They let me just hang out."

"All right, so you can flip a pancake or grill a cheese sandwich. That doesn't mean you can make it as a short-order cook."

"Oh, ye of little faith. A minute ago you were trying to talk me into keeping this assignment. Now it sounds like the opposite."

"Naw, just playing devil's advocate."

"Well, put away your pitchfork. I'm staying."

"Good girl. You need anything?"

She thought for a second, then asked, "Did you call the kennel?"

"They called *me*, complaining that damned miniature horse you call a dog was eating them into the poorhouse and trying to get to the poodle in the next cage. Randy bastard. So I picked him up and brought him home with me."

"Thanks, Ramsey. Give Sugar a big kiss from me."

"Not bloody likely."

Casey laughed. Ramsey was good for her ever-sagging confidence, and she knew he cared almost as much as she did for her affectionate but goofy Great Dane. Anger and the traces of defeat she'd experienced after her close call with the law gradually faded.

"Just don't let Sugar near your Haagen-Dazs chocolate-chocolate chip. Like you, he doesn't know when to stop."

"Very funny. Why am I paying long-distance charges for this kind of abuse?"

"Because I'm the closest thing to a family you've ever had and, at the rate you're going, are ever likely to have."

"Yeah, well." He cleared his throat. "Stay out of trouble and let me know how Plan B goes."

A moment later Casey said goodbye and sat staring at the phone, wondering what in the world she would do if Plan B failed, because she sure as hell didn't have a Plan C.

Chapter Three

"She was a looker, wasn't she?" Arms folded across his chest, a grinning Deputy Bensen leaned against the door-jamb of Holt's office.

"She was trouble." Holt didn't have to ask which *she* his deputy was referring to. Wayne Bensen had stumbled all over himself at the chance to drive their attractive tres-passer back to her car.

"Yeah, but trouble sure did look tempting."

"It's supposed to."

"Never seen eyes that color before. Kinda blue but not really. And did ya get a gander at those eyelashes? They musta been a mile long and black as midnight in a coal bin. Did ya see that hair? I'll bet when it's loose, the stuff nearly comes to her waist. And she wasn't married. I looked at her ring finger."

Holt tried to keep his mind on the departmental budget figures in front of him, tried to keep Wayne's words from summoning the unprofessional images that had paraded along the edges of his consciousness ever since his hand accidentally brushed the underside of Casey Westbrook's breast. The soft underside. But memory turned traitor, recalling smooth, warm flesh, a tiny waist dipping to nicely rounded hips, eyes the color of the sunlit Caribbean and a mouth sexy enough to tempt a saint. Holt Shelton was no saint, and at the moment he was having a great deal of difficulty reminding himself to shove thoughts of this morning's arrest into a mental file marked Closed.

"Did ya see—?"

"Did *you* see the stack of damage reports on city property I put on your desk early this morning?" Holt insisted, forcing himself to concentrate on his job. "The storm was a month ago, and the insurance adjuster is screaming bloody murder."

"Sure, I'll get to 'em," Wayne said, apparently oblivious to Holt's rigid posture. "Boy, you were on her like a duck on a June bug. Don't think I've seen you that steamed since those kids blew up the water tower, Fourth of July, two years ago. For a minute there, I thought—"

Holt's gaze met Wayne's and held. "And I thought you had work to do. In case you've forgotten, this is a police station, and we are paid to uphold the law, not the quota of gossip."

"Well, hell, Holt. You don't have to get so riled. Gotta admit she was a notch above the usual newspaper trash we get. And a damned sight better lookin'."

Crescent Bay wasn't exactly the epicenter of crime, but it had its share of lawbreakers. After dealing with numerous female "media representatives" with an eye toward making a buck from the Tanner legend, Holt couldn't dispute Wayne's statement. Their attractive trespasser was definitely a cut above the usual. What galled him was the way his young deputy had practically drooled over Casey Westbrook from the moment she walked into the station. That he himself could so readily recall her name drove another nail into the wall of irritation that had so far structured his day. She was just another photographer, so why should he remember her name out of an endless list of similar cases? *Because she was soft? Because she got under your skin?*

"Ridiculous." Holt didn't realize he had answered himself out loud until Wayne responded.

"I don't know about that, Holt. If that's how they grow 'em in the city, I just might have to take me a trip to Dallas, real soon."

Fingers massaged the tension at his right temple. "You do that, Wayne."

Sadie Boatwright, city secretary and police dispatcher, stuck her head around Wayne's shoulder. "Miss Willingham just called. Her cat's up in that big red oak again. Way up."

"Wayne's free," Holt said without taking his eyes from the column of figures.

"But those reports—"

"You can do them as soon as you get back. Better take the sixteen-foot ladder. The last time she called, the little pest was all the way to the top."

"Okay," Wayne agreed on a sigh. "Log me out, Sadie."

As soon as they disappeared, Holt walked across the room and closed his office door against further interruptions. If he didn't do a better job of eliminating distractions, he would never finish the projected budget for next year; and even though it was one of his least favorite responsibilities, it still had to be done.

His three terms as chief of police had been fulfilling, but time-consuming. And time, or the lack thereof, had been on Holt's mind a great deal lately, along with a restlessness he had been unable to shake, a need to hurry toward some nameless destination.

By the world's standards he had made it. After years of hard work and saving, he was right where he wanted to be—

on his own hundred-and-twenty-five-acre, quarter-horse ranch outside town—doing exactly what he wanted to do.

Then why aren't you happy?

Strange, Holt thought, *happy* was a word that seldom crossed his mind. Was he basically happy and didn't even realize it? Or was it a subject to be avoided, because he might not like what he found? Possibly. Was he having a midlife crisis at age thirty-four? Doubtful. People in Crescent Bay didn't have midlife crises; they just got wrinkles. Whatever the answers, after years of life with a hard edge, a core-deep instinct was telling Holt he was ready for softness.

Kitten softness.

A vision of aquamarine eyes and a plait of velvet-brown hair sprang to mind. Casey Westbrook definitely fell into the soft category. Holt reminded himself he had no business dwelling on such things as her eyes, the way her body felt, the way she filled out her jeans, the way her mouth glistened, moistened by her small pink tongue, or . . .

Enough!

Maybe *he* needed to take the trip into Dallas Wayne had suggested. How long had it been, he wondered? The last time he had held a warm and willing female in his arms was . . . He couldn't remember.

"Too damned long," he said out loud, quickly tagging his self-imposed abstinence accountable for the effect one very sexy photographer was having on his body. Abstinence plus restlessness drove a man to do things he might not otherwise consider. Such as think about a woman who was trouble, even if she did look soft enough for a man to sink into and gladly die from the pleasure.

Whoa, cowboy. She's not your type. Besides, after this morning, you probably top her dirt-bag list.

As much as Holt hated to admit it, he had treated her a bit roughly. He *could* have skipped the search, he reminded

himself. The book-procedure pat-down was often a judgment call on the part of the arresting officer.

*So she rattled your cage, and you enjoyed going by the
book. So what? You're only human.*

He tunneled his fingers through his hair. Unaccustomed
to questioning his motives, Holt's honest self-appraisal of
his encounter with the lady photographer yielded an un-
avoidable fact. He had taken out several days of irritation
on an unsuspecting target. Casey Westbrook appeared to be
exactly as she presented herself, while he, on the other hand,
had not enhanced the image of his office. All of which sub-
stantiated the something's-just-not-right discontent that had
dogged him of late.

"Ah, hell," he said. At this rate he would never finish the
damned budget. So far, his entire day had been a series of
nit-picky interruptions strung together to form a very frus-
trating shift.

He plopped into the 1940s-vintage, leather office chair
that had long ago given up resilience and checked his watch.
The hands on the black face confirmed the message his
stomach had been growling for the last hour, namely that he
had missed lunch. Reaching for the phone, he punched out
a number.

"Hey, April. Too late to get a special delivered?"

When Casey strolled into the diner attached to the Bay
Motel, the young woman behind the counter was on the
telephone, taking an order. The girl looked up, smiled at
Casey and waved her to a seat.

The stools perched in front of the serving counter looked
like chrome-stemmed mushrooms, and Casey climbed onto
one, the urge to twirl on the padded seat coaxing the corners of her mouth upward. The smile broadened as she
glanced around the interior of the café. A vision straight out
of the fifties, complete with black-vinyl-upholstered booths

and black-and-white swirled Formica with tabletop juke-boxes.

Pencil flying over an order pad, the young waitress laughed aloud at something the caller said, then hung up a few seconds later.

"Hi." She automatically picked up a half-full coffeepot and a clean mug as she headed in Casey's direction. "Coffee?" she asked, the container already poised over the lip of the cup.

"Thanks," Casey said. "I need it."

Pot still in hand, the girl reached for a menu and flopped it onto the counter.

"Tough day?" the waitress asked.

"Yeah. A real Bad Day at Black Rock."

"Excuse me?"

Seeing the blank expression on the girl's freckled face, Casey smiled. "Old movie," she said. "Before your time."

"Oh." She shrugged. Straight, ash-blond hair framed her cosmetic-free face and brushed across thin shoulders. She looked at Casey with brown eyes Bambi would have killed for. "Can I get you something to eat? Today's special is meat loaf, green beans and new potatoes. Corn bread and iced tea come with it."

"Sounds wonderful." Casey ran a finger down the printed menu. "Can I have just a minute to decide?"

"Sure thing." She smiled, her pink polyester uniform swishing softly as she walked away. When she returned a few moments later, Casey ordered a sandwich, then added, "By the way..." She glanced at the name badge pinned on the breast of the waitress's uniform. "April. Do you have a copy of the local newspaper?"

"*The Register* only comes out once a week, on Fridays."

Casey was disappointed. "Then could you tell me how a newcomer goes about checking employment possibilities?"

"Ever done any waitressin'?"

"You mean...here?" Casey asked, surprised.

"Well, we *are* shorthanded. But you'll need to check with the owner."

"Can I speak with him?"

"Her," April corrected. "The lady who owns the restaurant is Grace Malone, and I reckon she'll talk to you."

"Thanks," Casey said, wondering why fate seemed so willing to substantiate the web of lies she was constructing.

Sipping the strong, hot coffee, Casey glanced around the café at the dozens of photographs covering the walls, displaying a pictorial history of the town and its citizens, even of the world. Everything from a World War II group shot of marines, prizewinning fish, cheerleaders, school bands, sports teams, to front-page headlines of Kennedy's assassination and the moon landing.

As a photographer, Casey was impressed. As a person whose own history fell short of the solid, no-frills permanence so evident in the pictures, she was envious. And uncomfortable.

If she got her picture, how would it affect the people who lived and loved in this small, friendly spot on the map?

Several minutes later, April slid a well-stacked BLT, snuggled on a platter with hot, curlicue French fries in front of Casey and asked, "What's your name?"

"Casey Westbrook."

"Okay, Casey, I'll tell Grace. Check back in about an hour."

"Thanks again. You've been a big help."

"No sweat," April said with a smile.

Leaving the café, Casey's feelings flip-flopped between encouragement and discouragement, and she didn't understand either. On one hand she was glad she might actually have the opportunity for a once-in-a-lifetime photo, but on the other, it all seemed too... easy. She didn't like the idea of how easily her lies had fallen into place.

* * *

Casey immediately spotted the owner when she walked back into the café an hour and a half later. The description April had provided earlier was accurate, down to the wide mouth lipsticked in bright coral. Casey quickly realized that when April had volunteered with a sly smile, "Oh, you can't miss Grace," she hadn't been joking.

The words robust, jovial, *vital* sprang to mind the minute Casey saw the plump proprietress with the dimply smile. Looking scarcely older than fifty—although her pearl-gray hair appeared to be on intimate terms with the just-a-hint-of-blue rinse older women favored—Grace Malone looked like every kid's idea of Mrs. Santa Claus.

As Casey approached the counter, the woman was inserting sheets of paper into the menus' see-through plastic holders. Her uniform duplicated April's, only in a much larger size, and she hummed as she worked.

"Excuse me. Are you the owner?"

The woman glanced up from her task, but kept on working. "Owner, bookkeeper, part-time cook and full-time busybody. Hell, I do a little bit of everything, honey. Name's Grace Malone. What can I do for ya?"

Casey couldn't help but smile. *Strike the Mrs. Santa image, and substitute Ma Kettle.*

"I, uh, was in earlier and talked to April—"

"You the one looking for a job?"

"Yes."

"Where ya from, honey?"

"Los Angeles."

Casey saw a dark gray eyebrow rise slightly. "Long way from home, ain't ya?"

Casey shrugged.

"Ever wait on tables before?"

"Yes." Only, she thought, if Girl Scout camp counted.

"Ever handle a cash register?"

"Yes." Casey justified the lie by asking herself how difficult it could be.

Grace propped a hand on her ample hips and grinned. "You don't exactly look like your average hash slinger, honey. How come you want a job?"

"I'm broke," Casey replied, hoping she sounded more convincing than she felt.

"And just how do you pay the bills when you're not broke?"

"I'm a photographer."

Grace Malone's grin solidified, and her eyes darkened to burnt umber. "Why would a reporter want to work as a waitress?"

"Photographer," Casey amended. "Because I need money to pay for my equipment and supplies, not to mention an occasional cheeseburger and clean bed. I'm twenty-five...." She ticked off the information from pinkie to index finger. "Single. Healthy. Reasonably intelligent. And," she ended with her thumb pointing up, "I've answered the obligatory questions once today for your local sheriff—the one possessing the *disgustingly sweet* disposition *and* the last of my cash reserves, because of some ridiculous fine for trespassing, when I had no earthly idea I was on private property in the first place." Casey ran out of words and air at the same time. She inhaled deeply and looked the other woman straight in the eye. "I think that about covers it."

"Whoa, there, girl. Don't get your dander up."

"I'm sorry." Casey cursed herself for allowing her frustration to spill over into the interview.

"I was just curious why a city-bred girl wouldn't just call her folks to bail her out of a jam."

"I *never* ask my family for money." Regardless of what lies or half truths went with this assignment, despite tight squeezes or near misses, for Casey that one, single truth never changed. She would steal before she asked her parents for money.

"You say somethin' about a fine?"

Casey sighed. "Yes, ma'am. I was trying to shoot one of your spectacular Texas wildflowers and—" she shrugged, "—wandered onto private property. I had no idea climbing over a little barbed-wire fence was such an offense. Your sheriff—"

"Sheriff?"

"Excuse me, chief of police—"

"You had a run-in with Chief Shelton?"

"More like a head-on collision."

Grace's chuckle reverberated through her well-endowed chest. "Uh-huh."

"The man was . . . impossible, unreasonable."

"Sounds like Holt."

The familiarity in Grace's voice stopped Casey cold. "Is . . . is he a friend of yours?"

The throaty laugh came again, deeper, stronger. "You might say that. I've known Holt Shelton since he was born."

"Oh." Murphy's Law, thought Casey. Just her luck to be voicing a less-than-complimentary opinion of the local law to a longtime friend of his. *You are definitely having an off day, Westbrook.*

"Don't worry, honey. I may love Holt like he was my own, but I sure as hell know his faults, too. And few and far between they ain't. You must have been close to the Tanner place."

Casey glanced at Grace's expression, relieved to see an absence of suspicion or censure. "If it's that house that looks like it belongs in a remake of *Wuthering Heights*, then yeah."

"Taking pictures?"

"Yes. But you'd have thought I was an assassin with a high-powered rifle, instead of a harmless Nikon. He handcuffed me and hauled me off to jail like a common criminal."

"Sounds to me like you caught Holt on a bad day. He's not usually so hard on trespassers, but we've had a lot of folks pokin' around lately, and I reckon he's had his fill."

"Well, he should pick on someone his own size," Casey said. "Like Godzilla."

Grace threw her head back and laughed. "That oughta do it."

"I admitted my mistake. There was no need for him to act as if I was about to steal the crown jewels. What's the big deal, anyway?"

"Well." Grace swiped at moist eyes as her laughter slid into chuckles. "Reckon you might as well hear this now, since you're gonna get an earful, anyway, when the customers find out how green you are." She patted her cheeks dry with a paper napkin. "Does the name Norah Tanner mean anything to you?"

Casey's heart skipped a beat. "Sure. I love her old movies."

"I'd think a young 'un like you wouldn't appreciate a has-been like Tanner."

"A couple of years ago I attended a festival of her films. Terrific stuff," Casey said, trying to control the surge of excitement coursing through her.

"Yeah, well, she left California and moved out here, 'long about '39."

Casey widened her eyes and let her mouth fall open. "You mean *that*'s where she lives?"

"Absolutely."

"No kidding?" Casey whispered, stretching her acting abilities to their limit, ashamed that they stretched as far as they did.

"Now maybe you can understand why Holt assumed you were after a picture of somethin' other than flowers, and why he got so bent outta shape. A rash of reporters and such shows up every so often, and folks 'round here are sorta protective when it comes to Norah Tanner. They don't take kindly to anyone, particularly outsiders, nosin' around, trying to take pictures and make up stories for those trashy tabloids. Holt takes his job real serious where the Tanner place is concerned, 'cause he's partly responsible for the security up there. You see, we all kinda think of her as one of us, a friend, you might say. And 'round here we treat our friends with respect. You're gonna hear customers joke about Norah and her fine house, but they won't be cruel or envious, just good-natured.''

"Does that mean I've got the job?" Casey crammed her instinct to pursue the topic into a far corner of her mind.

Grace's grin dimpled chubby cheeks and added another wrinkle. "You're quick. I like that. Yeah, you got the job. I need someone to wait tables and help April, till that fool Connie gets off crutches. They're my regular girls, and that's where my loyalty lies, so you'd only be temporary.''

"That's all I need.''

"Pays minimum wage. No personal calls on my time. Whatever you do after work is your business, long as it don't interfere with doing your job. You treat me right, and I'll do the same by you.''

"Sounds more than fair to me." Casey extended her hand and Grace grasped it firmly. "Thanks. I really don't know what I would have done if you had turned me down.''

"Don't mention it, honey," Grace said with a wave of dismissal. "Way I figure it, broke's broke. Don't matter much how you got there, so long as you can get out. By the way, where you stayin'?"

"I've got a room at the motel next door," Casey answered.

"That's mine, too, so you tell Jake behind the desk you're my new waitress. He'll know what to do. Long as you work for me, the room's fifty dollars a week. That okay with you?"

"Fantastic with me."

"Good enough." Pointing to Casey's jeans and sweater, she said, "That all the clothes you got?"

"I travel light. One dress, one suitcase." And two sets of principles, a small voice added. The same small voice Casey had been steadily trying to shove aside, but was fast losing ground to.

"Come on back to the office. I've got an extra uniform." Grace eyed Casey's slender frame. "We might have to take a tuck here and there, but it'll do."

After twenty minutes of trying to make a size-twelve uniform appear merely baggy instead of outrageously sloppy on Casey's size-eight body, Grace gave up and offered to make the necessary alterations. Casey gladly accepted. Her travel wardrobe was scrupulously light—two pairs of jeans, some shirts, one sweater and an extremely simple, packable, wine-colored silk dress. Until the uniform was ready, jeans and a cotton shirt would have to do, even if she had to wash at night to wear during the day. Casey suddenly visualized the horror on her mother's face at the idea of wearing the same clothes in the same month, much less two days in a row. But then, a lot of things her daughter did horrified Cinnamon Westbrook, the least of which was traveling *anywhere* with only a single suitcase.

Casey spent the rest of the afternoon following in Grace's impressive wake. "Just watch me, honey, and you'll be an old hand in no time."

Casey seriously doubted she would ever be able to take food orders, bus tables, shuttle platters of steaming food and joke with customers, all practically at the same time, the way Grace did. The woman was the quintessential waitress, making the entire process appear as natural as breathing.

For Grace Malone, everything was "easy as pie," and everyone was "a honey."

When April reappeared, late-afternoon sunshine slanted through Venetian blinds, striping the café's interior in golds, reds and oranges. During the afternoon Casey had developed a new level of respect for anyone who worked in the restaurant business. The next time she ordered so much as a cup of coffee, she would remember to express appreciation, verbally as well as monetarily.

"Looks like you've met the waitress business up close and personal," April said as she stepped behind the counter and tied an apron around her waist.

Swiping errant strands of hair from her cheek, Casey sighed. "I've hung upside down from trees with a camera dangling from my neck, and worked my way through a Mount Everest of dirty clothes during a piece about the owner of a Chinese laundry. I've stood for hours in the heat or rain or both at Wimbledon, and been thrown from an airplane—with a parachute—for a skydiving article, but none of them can hold a candle to the last few hours. Is it always this hectic?"

"Hectic?" April asked, feigning shock. "Today was as easy as falling off a log. Now tomorrow you'll get a taste of a normal day."

"Normal?" Twisting the lid of the last sugar shaker, Casey wiped sticky hands on her apron and scooted the glass container to the end of a long line of newly filled self-servers.

"Yeah. You'll barely have time to go to the bathroom."

"Great."

At Casey's less-than-enthusiastic response, April laughed out loud. "Oh, boy, I can't wait until the wild bunch get a look at you."

"Wild bunch?"

"Uh-huh. The guys that come in here for lunch are the biggest bunch of teasers and braggarts this side of the Mississippi. And they're at their best when they got someone new to pick on."

"So I should come to work prepared for the worst, right?"

Her hopeful expression clearly said she would prefer to be wrong.

"You got it. But don't worry none. You'll do just fine, so long as you give as good as you get. A couple got roamin' hands, but once you set 'em straight, you won't have no trouble. They like a woman with spunk, just so long as she doesn't get sassy."

Casey shot April a cautious glance. "Why do I get the feeling tomorrow is going to be a very long day?"

April only smiled. "Don't worry. They're all harmless enough."

"Even the chief of police?" Why such a question had popped into her head, Casey didn't know, and why she'd voiced it was even more of a mystery.

"Who, Holt? Ah, he's not too bad. But don't take my word for it...." April pointed across the room. "Ask him yourself."

Chapter Four

Holt couldn't have been more stunned if he had walked into Grace's place and found a little green man with three heads standing behind the counter. What the hell was *she* doing here?

Casey stared at the broad-shouldered chief of police, surprised and apprehensive at his appearance. Had he decided her story had too many holes? *Don't be paranoid, Westbrook. He probably wants a cup of coffee, not your head.*

"Hiya, Holt," April called out.

Without taking his eyes from Casey, he said, "Hi, April. Where's Grace?"

"She left soon as I came back. Said she needed some pink thread to fix a uniform for Casey, so she drove into Decatur. And she usually stops by the market when she goes...." April looked from Holt to Casey, then back to Holt. "Uh, you staying in town for supper?"

"Depends." Holt crossed the room and sat down on a bar stool directly in front of Casey, calmly folding his arms on the smooth Formica counter. "I didn't expect to find you here, Ms. Westbrook."

Casey's earlier humiliation suffered at Holt Shelton's hands, lingered like a bad taste in her mouth and his presence triggered a defensive anger. "Surprise." Her smile was a shade less than sincere.

April's eyes widened. Her gaze ping-ponged between Holt and Casey.

"At the risk of sounding melodramatic, I believe I *recommended* you leave town. Why didn't you?"

"Funds," Casey said succinctly.

"Funds?"

"As in busted. Flat broke. And since my cash reserves have recently been *depleted* . . ." She gestured with a sweep of upheld hands. "Voilà. You see before you the newest employee of the Moon Lake Café."

"Grace hired you?"

"No," Casey said flatly, sliding her hands into the back pockets of her jeans. The gesture stretched the cotton fabric of her shirt, Holt noticed, accentuating the outline of her breasts. "I have a fetish for rotating bar stools. One look at these, and I was overcome."

Holt leaned over the counter until he was less than a foot away. His mustache crawled up at the corners in a dangerous grin. His voice, though every bit as cool and deep as the first time she heard it, held none of that earlier animosity. "Do you lay awake nights, thinking up smart-ass comebacks, or does it come natural?"

The grin altered his whole face and her perception of him.

In the space of a smile, Holt Shelton went from policeman to just plain man. Make that man with a capital *M*. The abrupt change was unsettling and, in a way Casey couldn't explain, threatening.

"L-let's just say I've developed a talent."

"Overdeveloped." Unconsciously his gaze dropped to her chest, then quickly returned to her face.

Realizing her mistake, Casey jerked her hands from the back pockets of her jeans and folded her arms across her chest. They were close enough for breaths to whisper over cheeks. Close enough to see more than they intended and not as much as they wanted.

Holt decided Wayne needed glasses. Her eyelashes were blacker than a thousand midnights, thick and...

Breathtaking, Casey decided. At close range his eyes were nothing short of breathtaking. The color reminded her of the exquisitely perfect sapphire she had once seen adorning the slender neck of a sultan's favorite wife. Stunning, compelling, difficult not to look at.

They drew away at the same time, the close proximity threatening to breach some imaginary barrier both instinctively knew existed, yet fought to ignore.

"Some..." Casey cleared her throat. "Sometimes I, uh, have a tendency to shoot first and ask questions later," she said, her voice sounding far from normal to her.

"Shoot?"

"My mouth."

Against Holt's better judgment his gaze went to that sexy spot.

"Uh, shoot my mouth off. You know, let my temper get the best of me."

Holt nodded.

"Sorry if I gave you a hard time."

"I think I deserved it on a couple of occasions."

"So...so, now that I'm gainfully employed?"

"Officially..." Holt, too, cleared his throat. He squelched the urge to loosen his tie, until he remembered he wasn't wearing one. "I have no objections to your staying."

"Thanks," she acknowledged, her voice barely above a whisper. "Truce?" She offered a weak smile and her hand.

"Truce."

Her hand disappeared in his, and a warm tingling immediately scampered from her fingers to her neck, her earlobes registering the delicious thrill more sensitively than she would have thought possible.

Holt thought how small and frail her hand was inside his, like a tiny, frightened bird within his grasp, and he was suddenly caught in an ebb and flow of sensations. One second he wanted to protect her and the next he wanted... It was best not to think about the wants that came to mind.

Protectiveness won out as the mouth he had tagged as tantalizingly sexy favored him with a uniquely childlike smile. Holt decided it was one of the most appealing he'd ever seen. His heart did a funny little quickstep when she withdrew her hand.

Casey licked her lips nervously. "Well, I'm, uh, glad we got that straight."

"Yeah." He looked so deeply into her eyes, Casey couldn't blink. "So am—"

"Hello, darlin'," came a drawled interruption from behind them. A gust of warm, humid air shot into the room as Grace bustled through the door, a grocery sack nestled in each arm.

Holt turned toward the voice, moving as if coming out of a trance. Then he shook his head and hurried across the floor.

"You should have called for help." Gathering the sacks in one fist, he relieved Grace of her burden. "How many times have I told you, I don't like you carrying heavy bags? There's always a man or two around here. If I hadn't come by, you'd have carried these groceries upstairs yourself, wouldn't you?"

"Nag, nag, nag," Grace teased. "I may not be a spring chicken, but I'm still strong enough to warm your backside."

"You're a stubborn ol' broad, you know that?"

Grace smiled up at him. "But you got a thing for ol' broads, don't you?"

Holt grinned. "I got a thing for you. You're the only decent cook west of the Mississippi and the only—"

"Woman who'll put up with your baloney," she finished, just as he bent and kissed her cheek.

Casey was dumbfounded by Holt's reaction to Grace. The zing she'd experienced as he held her hand ricocheted, and the returning warmth again caught her unawares.

The chief of police was no longer the brittle personality Casey had first encountered, and she had to admit Holt Shelton was not altogether unattractive. In fact, some might pronounce him a good-looking man. Her trained eye took in the thick, taffy-to-chestnut-colored hair that looked in need of a cut, the blue eyes, and a fine webbing of lines at the corners, proclaiming him to be past his youth, but certainly not his prime. And of course, there was the mustache.

Casey had always favored mustaches on men and fancied herself something of a connoisseur by virtue of the countless photos she had taken. Holt Shelton's mustache was a prizewinner, if ever she saw one. A shade darker than his hair, it drooped slightly to parenthesize his mouth.

Fascinated, she watched as he followed Grace toward a door at the back of the diner, which, she assumed, led to the upstairs apartment April had told her was Grace's residence. Pausing at the door, Holt glanced over his shoulder, met Casey's gaze for a second, then stepped through.

"Well, I'll be damned," Casey said when the couple disappeared.

"They joke around like that all the time," April said, already back to business as usual, clipping an order to the wheel used by the cook. "Must run in the family."

"Family?"

At Casey's puzzled look, April said, "Yeah. Didn't Grace tell you?"

"She mentioned she had known the chief all his life."

April laughed. "I guess so. He's her nephew."

Casey instantly felt twice as bad about voicing her ear-lier, frustration-based and hastily formed, opinion of Holt. Not only because he was the boss's nephew, but because it was no longer valid. Reminding herself not to forget she had a job to do, Casey vowed to be less judgmental in the fu-ture and much more cautious where Holt Shelton was con-cerned. Still, she couldn't help envying the love she'd seen reflected in Grace's eyes as she gazed at her nephew. Casey wondered for the millionth time how she could miss some-thing she'd never had so badly that it was difficult not to hate the fortunate ones who did.

Upstairs Holt kicked the apartment door closed with the heel of his boot. "I didn't know you were looking for a new waitress."

"She needed a job, and I needed help. Simple as that."

"I thought the objective was to discourage newspaper people from lingering in Crescent Bay."

"She doesn't work for a newspaper," Grace corrected.

"Aren't you splitting hairs?"

"Naw. If Casey was interested in invading Tanner's pri-vacy, you wouldn't have nabbed her so easy."

Holt frowned. Grace's logic followed the trail of his own. "I see you've heard her version of the story."

"Is there more than one?"

"Don't think so," Holt said, trying to still the last, al-most minuscule, scrap of doubt about Casey Westbrook.

"Then why the frown?"

"I'm not sure. Her story sounds plausible, and it's sure enough easy as hell to check." Holt rubbed the back of his neck. "There's something about her that makes me—"

"Uncomfortable."

"I hate it when you finish sentences for me."

Nutmeg-colored eyes twinkling, Grace grinned. "You hate it when you can't pigeonhole people. How many times have I told you?" An age-spotted finger poked at his broad chest. "Lighten up. People don't always fall into just two categories. You can't label everyone either a white hat or black. Some people don't *wear* hats."

Out of sheer orneriness he asked, "Could I have a translation, please?"

"Don't get smart with me, young man. And don't—" Grace stopped emptying sacks long enough to wag her finger at him "—give my new girl a hard time."

"Me?" Holt tried to look offended and knew he'd failed.

"You."

"Hey..." He held up both hands as if to ward off her offense. "As long as she keeps her nose clean, she's nothing to fear from me."

Hands on ample hips, Grace shook her head. "Well, if that ain't the unfriendliest attitude I ever heard."

"Unfriendly?" Holt groaned. "If you had seen her in my office this morning, you wouldn't be so quick to jump to her defense. I have a feeling your new employee is a scrapper."

"Gave as good as she got, huh?" Grace nodded her head in approval.

"And then some."

"Yeah, well, you know very well you can be a real pain in the putooty, when you put your mind to it."

"That's what I love about you, Gracie. You never let prejudice cloud your vision," he teased, ripping open a bag of potato chips and helping himself.

"Mind your manners," she warned.

"Need I remind you? Sometimes accepting everyone at face value can get you—"

"A lot of disappointment. And sometimes a lot of joy," she replied. "Aren't you judging all women against one who didn't have the brains to recognize a good man when she found him?"

Grace's look told Holt he was in for a lecture, and sure enough . . .

"Darlin', you got burned, and you're understandably cautious. But females from the 'city' aren't all cut from the same cloth any more than those from right here in Crescent Bay. You've let a bad experience color your thinkin'."

"I wouldn't call almost marrying a gold-digging liar a bad experience," Holt retorted. "More like a nightmare."

"There, you see? That's precisely the attitude I'm talking about. When you first met what's-her-name—"

"Monica."

"Right. You thought she was perfect."

"So, I made a mistake."

"Your mistake," Grace informed him, "was in thinkin' you could decide to put a woman in your life, the same way you add a brood mare to your stock. Time came, you looked around and decided you needed a wife. Monica was smart, pretty . . . Hell, what man wouldn't have wanted all that frosting, no matter how the cake tasted? But we both know your judgment was less than sound when you offered the sexy lady architect your heart, only to discover she was more interested in your land."

"Hitting below the belt, aren't you, Gracie?"

She reached out and patted his arm. "No, honey. I'm just remindin' you things and people aren't always what they appear to be. You failed to look past a beautiful smile and a designer wardrobe to the woman beneath. To your credit, you recognized your mistake before permanent damage was done."

Holt smiled sheepishly. "With a little help from my dear, sweet guardian—"

"Who loves you very much."

"How did you get so wise?" he asked, still as proud of and awed by this remarkable woman as he had been in childhood. The years had only served to enhance her wisdom.

"When you've lived as long as I have and seen as many people come and go across that counter downstairs, you get an education in humanology. You learn to listen to your own heart."

Holt glanced at his boots. "Haven't had much luck doing that, have I?"

"Only because you're so all-fired hardheaded. And . . ." Though she hesitated, Grace didn't mince words. "Because your mama left you without a backward glance, you figure women in general are a sorry bunch."

Holt's lips curled into a tender smile. "Except for a certain endearing, but nonetheless nosy relative of mine, I don't have much proof to the contrary."

Grace sighed. "Darlin', I know we settled the subject of your mama years ago, but I think the past still gnaws at your gut. Like it or not, you're part of her, and understanding her helps you understand yourself."

"We did settle it, and sometimes it does bother me," Holt admitted. "But I'll never allow my attitude about my mother, good, bad or indifferent, to color my opinion about something as important as picking a woman to love. I know who I am and what I want out of life."

"You don't *pick* 'em, honey," she said, adding, "It just sorta happens. Usually when you least expect it."

Uncomfortable with the subject matter, he tore into a package of Oreos and removed half a dozen. "What has all this got to do with Casey Westbrook?" he asked, popping a cookie into his mouth.

Grace cut him a sly glance. "Maybe nothin'. Maybe everything."

"I still need a translator."

"To make it short and sweet, boy o' mine, you've shown more interest in my new waitress in one day than you have in any woman in months. Now why is that, do you think?"

"Probably because I'm not gettin' any—"

"Holt!" Grace gasped.

"You asked."

"And got a smart-mouth reply. You're either not listening or you're avoiding the subject."

Holt looked closely at the only real mother he'd ever known, the woman he trusted above all others. "Avoiding," he said around another cookie.

"Why?"

"She's too soft."

"Pardon?"

"Nothing," Holt replied, wondering why he couldn't shake the image of a helpless kitten every time he thought of Casey Westbrook. And wondering why, after years of professing an allergy to the two-legged variety of felines, he was suddenly so attracted to a feisty she-cat photographer with claws.

Chapter Five

Casey's first thought the next morning was that she had survived her first day working in the diner, and her second encounter with Holt Shelton.

Her second was that the nightmares had started again.

Random pockets of torture left over from her growing-up years occasionally waged a round-robin battle for possession of her sanity. The nightmares came to her in varying shades of blackness, depending on the scenario.

One replayed a lonely Christmas Eve when she was five. Deep gray. Another chronicled endless "parent appreciation events," where she would be seated alongside two empty chairs. Charcoal. And of course there were the corners. All her nightmares had corners. Dark places she was forced into by an intangible, unseen horror so terrible that even as a child Casey had known she must fight it or die. Even now, fully grown and independent, the memories tugged, pulled her backward in time, backward into black....

* * *

Ruffle upon ruffle of handmade, imported Belgian lace whispered secrets as Casey tiptoed down the carpeted hallway. Secrets she shared only with her dolls and the life-size panda bear in her room.

Today she was seven years old. Almost grown-up. Even Mrs. McCarthy, her newest nanny, had said so while helping the fidgeting birthday girl on with her finery. And today was the day of her party, the event she had secretly longed for, as far back as she could remember. Always before, according to her mother, Casey had been too young to appreciate parties or too rambunctious or too...something. But not today. Practically every boy and girl she knew had received an invitation, but for Casey the most important guests were her parents. Never in Casey's life could she remember being so absolutely giggly happy.

Ignoring strict instructions to remain in her room until the guests arrived, Casey simply couldn't sit still another minute. Drawn by the sound of voices coming from the master suite and anxious to show off her beautiful dress, she slipped unnoticed into the dressing room connecting her parents' individual bathrooms. Out of sight, but able to see past the partially opened door, she peered into her father's bedroom.

"For God's sake, Cinnamon. Don't you think this damned affair is ridiculously ostentatious, even for you? It's a kid's birthday party," her father said. Walking toward his closet, Jason Westbrook yanked the tie from beneath his shirt collar and tossed it onto the bed, then began unbuttoning his shirt.

Her father was angry. Casey could always tell when he was mad, because he always cursed.

"Don't fling your clothes about," Cinnamon Westbrook insisted. "This isn't a college dorm." Casey could see her mother, her hair perfect as was the black silk dress she wore. She was lying on a chaise lounge on the other side of the room. "And this affair is *not* ostentatious in the least. Only last month the vice president of MGM staged a Wild West show for his son's birthday."

To Casey, her mother was the most beautiful woman in the world. People said she had an unforgettable smile, though Casey had rarely had the opportunity to judge for herself.

"So, you rented an entire circus?" her father mumbled, head bent, buttoning and tucking a fresh, white shirt into his suit trousers. "I can't believe you'd spend so much money on a child."

"*Our* child."

Jason faced his wife. "At least we know you are her mother."

Casey saw her mother rise, so smoothly that she almost seemed to flow to her feet. "And you are her father." She crossed to a credenza, plunked several ice cubes into a glass, then poured herself a drink.

"I wish I could be so sure."

"You can be."

"Why, because you say so?" he said sarcastically. "You lie at the drop of a hat."

Casey shrank from the door. She wanted to run, wanted to hide from the meanness in their voices and the anger on their faces. But most of all from their hurtful words.

"Careful, my dear," her mother said sweetly. "Your Midwest upbringing is showing." She raised her half-empty glass in mock salute.

"And your trashy morals are showing. Who are you trying to impress with that dress cut nearly to your waist? Surely not me."

"How dare you preach morality to me!" Casey heard Cinnamon shout angrily. "You and your cheap, big-breasted starlets."

"Well, we certainly can't accuse you of being cheap, now, can we?"

"No wonder you were always so anxious for me to have a kid," she sneered. "You thought I would be tied to a runny-nosed brat, leaving you free to chase every whore—"

Casey receded farther into the corner. The walls of the dimly lit dressing room closed in, her mother's stinging words repelling every bit as forcibly as a slap across the face. With each step Casey felt her slender frame take another blow, her heart suffer another wound.

"Why should I go look for something I've always had at home?" she heard Jason snap.

"Bastard." Casey heard someone move, the sounds of ice cubes falling into a glass.

She longed to get as far away as possible, yet her feet refused to answer her brain's command to run. They called each other such hateful names, and all over *her*.

"Since you've arranged this little gala and, I assume, informed every newspaper columnist and photographer in town, don't you think you could stop drinking, before you make a fool out of yourself?"

"Go to hell."

"I thought that's exactly where I was, *my dear*." Jason glanced at his watch. "Where's Casey? It's almost time for this farce to begin."

"How should I know?"

In a tone of audible disgust he said, "So do *we* have a present for her?"

"I sent Mrs. McCarthy out yesterday. I'm sure she came up with something suitable."

"For crying out loud, Cin. Couldn't you even take the time to buy gifts yourself?"

"Preparations for today took up every waking moment. You know how meticulous I am. I simply didn't have the time."

"Then get off your overpriced rear and at least pretend to be the doting mother. God knows, the way you lie with a straight face, this shouldn't be a stretch."

"Did you know she talks to herself?"

"Who?"

"Cassandra. Gives me the creeps."

Desperately clutching the hem of her lovely dress, Casey scooted farther still into the shadowy corner.

"Maybe you should take her to a psychiatrist," her father offered.

"And have every gossip columnist in town breaking their necks to put it print? No, thank you. Face it. No amount of expensive clothes or coaching can change the fact that she's mousy and plain. I'm living for the day she goes off to boarding school. The child is smart enough, I suppose, but she has no personality. She's boring."

"She's a child. Children aren't put on earth to entertain and amuse," her father retorted.

"Don't be flippant. I mean, she's just not very... lovable."

Her tiny shoulders wedged into the V of the wall, Casey continued to retreat, grinding her little body against paint and plaster in an effort to get away from her mother's tormenting words. She covered her ears, trying to shut out their voices, trying to block the pain. Mousy. Plain. Not lovable, boring, not lovable, not lovable....

Clutching the edge of the mattress in a white-knuckled grip, Casey shook her head furiously, dislodging the nightmarish memories and sending her hair spilling over trembling shoulders.

Mustn't dwell on the darkness. Think about light. You're not seven anymore.

Turning her gaze toward the window, she searched the fading darkness for the first rays of dawn.

Concentrate on the sunrise. Sweet, warm light. No more corners. No voices. Just the light.

Instead of the familiar mental picture painted with the promise of new-day reds and oranges, a picture that never failed to banish the dark dreams, Casey visualized only one color. Sapphire blue. The blue of Holt's eyes.

The image was so real it took her breath away.

Where did he come from? she wondered, feeling as if he had somehow physically slipped into her room instead of her subconscious. His presence slowly filled her mind, crowding out painful memories, pushing murky colors into light, bringing her safely into the present. Even her skin, always chilled after the hellish nightmares, felt warmer than usual.

Needing protection more than warmth, Casey dragged bed covers to her chin, struggling with the foreboding that she had somehow allowed—no, invited—Holt's presence. She tried to expel thoughts of him from her mind. But try as she might, the vision of intense blue eyes and a coppery-brown mustache, curled upward in a smile, refused to vanish.

This is ridiculous.

Casey threw back the covers and commanded wobbly legs to carry her to the shower. *The man is so far out of your league, he might as well be on the moon.* Twisting both taps fully open, she stepped beneath the stinging spray.

He's probably got women waiting in line for him. What could he see in a little girl still afraid of the dark?

But as hot water sluiced over her shaking body, she couldn't deny he had been close enough to invade her dreams and powerful enough to change darkness to light. Something no one had ever been able to do for Casey.

A half hour later, with persistent thoughts of Holt Shelton still on her mind, Casey stepped outside her motel room and saw a Rolls-Royce. Glistening polished ebony in the morning sun, the classic vehicle appeared to be circa late forties. Without demanding attention, the elegant car honored its recognition with a simple, sleek statement of class, good taste and ageless beauty.

Where in the world did such a grand old—? Casey's thoughts skidded to a halt. Who else in this part of the world but Norah Tanner would own such an obviously outdated, but well-kept car? The Rolls *had* to belong to the legendary movie queen. Casey frowned. Most of the English-speaking world knew Tanner was never seen in public. Casey cautioned herself against jumping to the wrong conclusion. There's no way THE recluse of the twentieth century is sitting inside the Moon Lake Café, having breakfast. Funny, Casey thought, until she saw the car she had almost forgotten why she came to Crescent Bay in the first place.

Casey picked out the driver the moment she stepped from the kitchen into the busy restaurant. In a sea of Western shirts and cowboy hats his handsome black livery stood out like a bad habit at a church picnic. The gray-haired chauffeur sat alone, leisurely enjoying his morning meal.

April and Grace were already hip-deep in the breakfast rush, with customers entering and exiting to the point that Casey couldn't tell which waitress was which.

"Mornin', honey," came Grace's smiling greeting. "Will ya grab a pot of coffee and do refills? They're drinkin' faster than we can make it."

"Good morning." April whizzed past, balancing an armload of platters piled high with fried eggs, bacon, biscuits and grits.

Casey's responding, "Good morning," and smile were for April, but her thoughts focused on the solitary customer. Heart banging against her rib cage, Casey tied a starched, white cotton apron over her altered uniform and picked up a freshly brewed pot of coffee. Nonchalantly she worked her way from table to table, making sure she started away from the chauffeur. Halfway through the customers she returned for another full, hot carafe.

"See that guy sitting by himself?" April said, reaching around Casey to slap three more tickets onto the stainless-steel order wheel.

Casey almost dropped the empty glass container. She cleared her throat. "Which one?"

"Over there, in the black uniform."

"Oh, yeah," she replied casually.

"He likes his coffee hot enough to burn the skin off his tongue, so give him the first cup from the fresh pot, will ya?"

"Sure."

"Thanks," April said, plunging back into the din of demanding customers.

Casey wiped moist palms on the apron and firmly grasped the handle of the glass urn. The man was engrossed in a copy of the *Wall Street Journal* and didn't notice her approach.

"Good morning." She offered her warmest smile. "Would you like me to freshen your coffee?"

He glanced up, smiled and repositioned his cup from one side of his half-empty plate to the other. "Please, thank you."

"Could I get you anything else?" *Easy does it. Just polite conversation.*

"No, thanks, I'm fine." He brought the now full cup to his lips, sipped and returned his attention to the newspaper.

Arms loaded with steaming food orders, Grace brushed by Casey without giving the solitary customer a glance.

"My Lord, you'd think none of them's eaten in a month," she said over her shoulder. A customer two tables away raised his empty cup and waved it in the air, snagging Grace's attention. "Hold your horses, Ollie, she's comin' with the java."

With a forced smile, Casey forfeited her opportunity to talk to the driver.

Time zipped by in a flurry of noise and activity as the customers, mostly working men, consumed the mountains of food flowing from the kitchen in an endless stream. Grace and April were everywhere at once, with Casey racing to keep up. When, at last, an entire ten minutes passed without a call for more butter, honey, gravy or coffee, Casey glanced up and realized the uniformed driver was gone. She should have felt disappointed. She was in Texas to do a job, after all, and a golden opportunity had just slipped through her fingers. Yet she was relieved.

Billy, the cook's helper, was busing tables, and April was ringing the last ticket at the cash register, when Grace poured herself a cup of coffee and motioned to Casey and the others to take a well-earned break.

"Lord o' mercy," Grace sighed. "Sometimes I think those boys are going to eat everything but the silverware. My body's gettin' too old to withstand this kinda punishment." She patted the stool beside her. "Take a load off, honey."

"Thanks." Casey's leg muscles vehemently protested the morning's abuse. "Is it always this noisy?"

Grace laughed the warm, throaty laugh Casey now identified so completely with her boss. "Round here everybody knows everybody else. Besides, we're what ya might call a nosy bunch. Always interested in what the other fellow's doin'."

"I gathered as much."

"Man, I'm bushed." April rounded the counter and reached for a mug. She filled her cup, then returned the urn to its warming pad at the end of the counter closest to her tired companions.

"Amen to that," Grace agreed, turning her attention to the young waitress. "By the way, I didn't see that wild Indian, Jody Lee Thomas, in here this morning," she added as April claimed a stool.

"He had to go into Dallas at the crack of dawn to pick up some supplies for his daddy." April smiled shyly. "But he's taking me to supper tonight at the Trail Dust over at Denton."

"Long way to drive for a steak."

April ducked her head, and Casey saw a rosy blush touch her cheeks. "Gives us time to talk ... and stuff."

"Stuff? That what they're callin' it these days?" Grace said teasingly, at the same time delivering a gentle poke to April's ribs. "When I was a girl it was sparkin'.... Say," she added, turning to Casey. "Speakin' of 'stuff,' you ought to go to the dance."

April leaned over the counter to talk around her employer's ample profile. "That's a great idea. Bet Jody could get you a date."

"A date?"

"Yeah, for the dance tomorrow night. Didn't you hear a word I said? There's a dance every Friday night over at the Community Center. You wanna go?"

"I don't know...." Never comfortable in social gatherings, Casey automatically began thinking up plausible excuses to decline. "Maybe it's not such a good—"

"Aw, come on, Casey. It's fun. Me and Jody Lee go all the time. And he's got a cousin. Not much on brains, but he can dance like a dream. Whaddya say?"

Smiling, Casey shook her head. "I'm not much on parties or blind dates." Or dates of any kind, truth be known. "Besides, I don't have anything to wear to a dance."

"We could go shopping," April said excitedly. "Please, please, say yes."

"Friday-night dances are a regular institution round here. Everybody goes," Grace said.

"And I do mean ... *everybody*," April chimed in.

In spite of herself, Casey had to laugh. "Even the chief of police?" *Now where in the hell did that come from?*

April and Grace exchanged looks. "Holt rarely misses one," Grace said. "But I got the impression you two were barely civil to each other."

April grinned. "They made up."

Casey shot her a halfhearted, mind-your-own-business glance. "You make it sound as if we had—"

"A lover's quarrel?" Grace finished, brown eyes twinkling.

"Yes."

"And that's the last impression you want to make, right?"

"Right." Then remembering Grace was Holt's aunt, Casey quickly added, "Not that he's unattractive, he's just—"

"Not your type."

"Exactly."

"And what is your type?"

Casey looked at the faces of the two women, both waiting for her answer. "I'm not sure I have a *type*," she said truthfully.

"Well, for crying out loud," April said eagerly. "What kind of guys do you usually date?"

The conversational twist knotted Casey in its center, its very personal center. She felt an urgent need to change the subject. "Uh, speaking of dates, who is Jody?"

April breathed an exasperated sigh. "You *didn't* hear a word I said, Jody is my—" Wisps of straight, blond hair flew across April's flushed cheek as she turned her head, apparently afraid of being overheard. "Jody Lee Thomas. A boy I, uh, like."

"Now there's an understatement." Grace rolled her eyes.

"Grace," April warned.

"Don't 'Grace' me. I'm too old to pay much attention to anybody's opinion but my own. And you know what I think about all this sneakin' around you and Jody been doin'. If Emmett Thomas had more than two brain cells to rub together, he could see his son's crazy in love. And if *you*—'' a finger jabbed the airspace in front of April's nose "—had any brains at all, you'd accept Jody's marriage proposal and tell Emmett to take a flying leap.''

"I can't marry Jody." April's voice lowered, her expression sobered.

"The hell you can't," Grace insisted. "Why, even a blind man could tell that boy's so head over heels in love with you, it's pitiful. April—'' Grace's softly wrinkled hand touched April's shoulder "—honey, you deserve to be happy same as anyone, but you can't just sit back and wait for happiness. Sometimes you've got to reach out and grab it with both hands. Don't be afraid to take a chance.''

An unsmiling April pushed her mug away. "It's not me that's takin' a chance," she whispered, then slipped from the stool and disappeared into the kitchen.

On a frustrated sigh Grace turned back to Casey. "Sorry. Sometimes I just can't keep my mouth shut. April's real touchy on the subject of her and Jody. I embarrassed her by talking about it in front of you. And I ought to know better.''

Vastly relieved to have the spotlight's glare focused on someone else, Casey said, "I won't say anything.''

"Ah, hell. My urge to mother April gets outta hand sometimes, that's all. I've known Jody Lee Thomas since he was a twinkle in his daddy's eye and a smile on his mama's lips. And even though I've known April a damned sight less, those two belong together like sunshine and flowers. If only April weren't so all-fired stubborn.''

"Stubborn?" Casey had seen only a sweet, gentle girl-woman.

"Honey, if that girl had been on the Titanic and been told to jump, she'd've stayed and sung. I reckon she's been that way all her life. She walked in here about a year ago, told me she was broke and hungry, and if I'd give her a job, she'd work her butt off and never complain. Not a day has passed she hasn't been true to her word.''

''First April, now me. Do you make a habit of taking in strays?''

Tilting her head to one side, Grace's right eyebrow rose a fraction as she said, ''You weren't a stray.''

''But April was?''

Grace stared at her for long seconds. ''Yeah,'' she said finally. ''She looked like the ragged end of nowhere when she showed up here. Came to the back door.'' Grace shook her head in visible dismay. ''To the *back door*, mind you. Said she would wash dishes all day in exchange for one meal. Nearly broke my heart.''

''What about her family?'' Casey asked, feeling a kinship with the young woman.

''None I know of, but then she's so shut-mouthed about herself, who can tell? Anyway, I learned a long time ago a person's past is just that…past. Whatever they did or didn't do can't be changed, only learned from. Yesterday don't mean diddly squat. It's today that's important.''

Too bad the rest of the world doesn't share your point of view. Casey thought of the countless times her yesterdays had intruded on her todays and would probably influence her tomorrows. Had April's past, as hers had, formed a woman of determination from a child of despair?

''Only trouble with April is, Jody's father makes her feel inferior. Thinks she's not good enough for Jody. If you ask me, it's the other way around.''

''One of those can't-live-with-them, but can't-live-without-them relationships?''

Grace shook her head, then lifted the cup to her lips and took a deep drink. ''They get along just fine, till Jody starts pushing for a preacher. Don't get me wrong. He's got the makin's of a fine man, he just needs a little seasoning.''

''And April?''

A smile, part melancholy, part joy, touched Grace's brightly painted lips. "She's a tough little cookie, but deep down, no different from the rest of us. Just needs somebody to love her, and scared spitless that kind of special feeling won't last. I think she figures, why risk the hurt?"

Images of childhood leaped from a dark corner of Casey's memory. The ecstasy and agony of waiting days for one small gesture of love from her parents, yet dreading it all the while, knowing the moment of joy would be so brief. How many times had she gone to drink from that particular bittersweet well of emotion, only to learn the brackish taste of loneliness lasted far longer than the flavor of hope? Too many times, until finally Casey had locked away the hopeful child inside herself and turned her back on Cinnamon and Jason's unpalatable brand of caring.

"That kind of attitude doesn't take root without being fed by years of pain and disappointment," Casey whispered. "She must have been hurt very badly."

"I suspect so," Grace said softly, watching Casey's face. Instinctively she covered Casey's hand with her own and gave a tiny squeeze. "And usually by people we love."

Casey looked up into the soft brown of Grace's eyes and saw gentle understanding, listened to the sound of her voice and heard genuine caring. Two souls, one old and scarred, one young and still stinging with hurt, recognized each other. There was no need to identify the emotion flowing between them. It was enough to know a bond existed.

The cook stuck his head through the kitchen door and called to Grace, interrupting the weighty moment; Casey blinked, and saw Grace's too-bright eyes do the same.

"Guess I better go see why Cook's got himself in a tizzy. He's yelling his fool head off," Grace said at last, her voice raspy with emotion. Without waiting for a reply, she gave Casey's hand a final squeeze, then headed toward the kitchen.

For several seconds Casey stared at the kitchen's double doors, which were swooshing back and forth in Grace's wake. She glanced down, surprised to view her own hand through watery vision. A blink dislodged a single, fat tear that splattered against the counter top. Unaccustomed to such displays of affection, Grace's simple gesture had touched a long-hidden need, a need Casey tried hard to ignore, but couldn't. She sniffed, reminding herself that emotion was a luxury she couldn't afford. It simply wouldn't do to become involved in the lives of these people. It wouldn't do at all.

Casey replayed the conversation several times during the rest of the morning, and each review weakened her resolve to remain detached. How could she hold herself apart from the kind of warmth and compassion she experienced from April and Grace?

April, strange mixture of child and woman, suffered from a state of mind Casey knew all too well, one of low self-esteem and self-doubt. And she would bet her best lens April was a runaway. Grace, sage, collector of strays, seer of souls, had enough strength and security for several Aprils.

Working with the two women, the friendly interaction with customers and the homey atmosphere of the café all had the makings of a personal entanglement. And even knowing such involvement was the death blow to maintaining a professional distance, Casey hesitated to step away. Thoughts of Grace's warmth refused to be relegated to a far corner of Casey's mind. The image of April's sweet smile rejected all attempts to erase it.

They touched her in a way few people ever had. But Casey was afraid, scared to death of opening old wounds, giving rein to old wants and needs.

She kept telling herself she could be polite and friendly without losing her precious professionalism. But later, when April resurrected the campaign to get her to attend the Community Center dance, Casey found herself inexplicably drawn to the idea of spending an evening of music and fun, surrounded by the very people she was supposed to be keeping at a distance. Her mind reasoned that refusing to go would seem strange, even rude, to the open and honest citizens of Crescent Bay. What could it hurt to pretend, for a short while, that she *was* here because she wanted to be, free of ulterior motives?

You could forget it's just pretend.

Pretense wasn't her style, and dishonesty certainly wasn't in her nature. But she was up to her neck in both.

The lunch crowd arrived all at once, forcing Casey out of her own thoughts. Again, forever it seemed, the café was perpetual noise and motion. Casey had poured, sliced, ladled, smiled and joked her way through the bulk of the rush when she looked up and found Holt seated at the counter.

"Hi," he said in a slow drawl.

"Hi," she answered, her voice more breathy than she intended.

"I'll have the special."

Holt smiled, and Casey's stomach took a two-second roller-coaster ride. To have such warmth directed at her was...unsettling. *Maybe you need to be unsettled once in a while, if this is what it feels like.*

"You, uh, don't even know what's special— I mean, you don't know what's *on* the special."

"Doesn't matter. When Gracie's at the stove it's all good."

"How did you know Grace was cooking?"

"Simple deduction. She's not gabbin' with the customers and she's not in town...so she must be in the kitchen." His shoulders lifted in a nothing-to-it shrug, and she was again reminded of their breadth and power.

"Very observant," she said, wondering what it would be like to observe those shoulders bare except for a sheen of healthy sweat....

"Not really. I phoned her about an hour ago, and she told me she was pinch-hitting for the regular cook."

His smile widened, and her blood unexpectedly trip-hammered through her veins. Yesterday's confrontation had been a threshold of sorts, one he had crossed without realizing its importance.

Shaking her head, Casey tried, but failed, to hide her own smile. "They warned me about you."

"Who did?"

"April and Grace."

"April is a brat, and you should never believe everything Gracie tells you, especially if it concerns me. What did they say?" Elbows propped on the counter, he leaned closer, as if her answer were the most important words he would hear all day.

"That you weren't as bad as some and worse than others." Her voice dropped an octave, boosting Holt's blood pressure several points.

"Exactly what am I going from bad to worse about?"

"Teasing. They, uh, warned me hazing went along with the job. Your name was mentioned specifically." She had no intention of telling him she had been the one who mentioned it.

"Guilty," he said, staring into her eyes.

They were light blue, Holt decided. No, gray. They were both and neither. Azure, maybe. Yes, and no. He couldn't decide, and it suddenly seemed vital that he know for sure. One thing was for certain, no one in his right mind would ever describe her eyes as pale anything. Holt wondered if she knew her eyes were so clear and compelling that a man had the feeling they could see right straight through his soul. And he wondered if she had any idea how enticing such a prospect was to a man with a soul-deep hunger.

"You're, uh, probably hungry," Casey whispered; she was having difficulty finding her voice.

"Yeah," he said softly, then after seconds of silence, added, "My belly is rubbing against my backbone."

The word "rubbing" suddenly took on a whole new connotation. Casey's hand went to her midriff and she inhaled deeply. "I guess I better turn in your order."

"Guess you better."

Watching her move gracefully away, Holt felt magnetized, pulled along in a trance, for endless seconds. Finally the clamor of the noisy restaurant rushed in, as though an invisible volume knob had clicked from Off to somewhere just below deafening. He shook his head.

What the hell are you doing, cowboy? Yesterday you were ready to run the woman out of town on a rail, and today...

What was he ready to do to her today?

A few moments later Casey set a steaming plate of chicken-fried steak, mashed potatoes and green beans in front of him.

"Can I get you anything else, Chief?"

"Holt." He smiled. "H-o-l-t. Got it?"

"Got it," she said, fascinated by the way his mustache did a slow crawl up one side of his mouth, then the other, to form a smile.

Did he realize what a smile such as his was worth on the open market? Casey wondered. She personally knew women who would kill to have such a smile directed at them and advertisers who would be willing to lay out staggering sums of money to place it alongside their product. Life is fun, the smile said. Come join me and you won't regret it.

Nervously she wiped her hands on the hem of her apron, then patted the fabric across her hips. "Well, if you need anything, let me know."

"Thanks." Hands tented above the plate, he made no move to begin his meal.

"Uh, you're welcome." She turned away.

"Casey?"

"Yes?"

"I just wanted you to know I thought it took a lot of guts for you to apologize the way you did."

"I *was* wrong."

"And *I* was a bully."

"Yes, you were."

He laughed. "You don't give an inch, do you?"

"The trouble with giving inches is the taker always wants miles."

"I'm not interested in taking anything. Didn't your mother teach you how to accept a compliment gracefully?"

"Guess she thought it was a waste of time," Casey said, shrugging narrow shoulders. "Like I said, I was wrong. No big deal."

Holt watched her walk away and wondered who had taught her not to be an inch-giver. Wondered why someone as beautiful as Casey hadn't received enough compliments during her life to fill the Superdome. And if she hadn't, there was a basic injustice in the world desperately in need of correction.

That evening, as a very tired Casey brushed her teeth, preparing for bed, she decided the best thing for her would be to take the picture she came for and leave as soon as possible. Things were becoming complicated.

Things? Don't you mean feelings?

All right, feelings...thoughts...

Relationships?

Casey realized she had friends and acquaintances, even enemies, but no relationships. There was Ramsey, of course, but that was different. He was a friend—more than a friend—a substitute family.

Family.

She rinsed the inside of the toothpaste tube lid and the tube itself, then replaced the cap. Tidy. Exactly the kind of thing her mother would do, and one of the few personal habits Cinnamon had actually taught her daughter. Casey quickly put away the toothpaste, turned out the lights and crawled into bed. Lying in the dark with only her thoughts, she resented the time, any time, spent dwelling on her family. And she had spent more time doing just that today than she had in months.

"Go to sleep," Casey ordered herself, determined to corral the disturbing thoughts galloping around in her head. They ignored her.

Her parents' images swirled across her mind, insistently bringing with them memories, pain. She knew precisely what their reaction would be if they had even the vaguest idea where she was and what she was doing. But, of course, vague ideas were the only ones they'd ever had of her. Her father would probably dismiss her attempt to photograph the reclusive movie star as impractical, expensive and therefore inadvisable. Her mother would declare Casey's plan too flawed, and flawed meant untidy. If there was one thing her mother worshiped, it was neatness. Perfection appropriately described everything about Cinnamon Westbrook, her beauty, her position, her entire life.

Everything except her only child.

Perfect was not an adjective Cinnamon had ever used to describe her daughter, and in not doing so she had wiped it from her child's list of adjectives, as well. Delete "perfect." Replace with "imperfect, flawed, defective. Unlovable."

Alone in the darkness, Casey fought tears. What good did it do to retrace one's steps? What good did it do to reopen old wounds? Pain, once inflicted, had a way of riding just below the surface, waiting for a summoning word or gesture. Casey had worked long and hard to bury her hurt layers deep.

Punching the pillow beneath her head with the intent of a heavyweight contender, she berated herself for dwelling on the past. *Sloppy, Westbrook, very sloppy. Think about something else.*

Such as the dance.

Who says I'm going?

Afraid you'll run into you-know-who?

Put a sock in it.

But socked or unsocked, her thoughts immediately conjured up the image of Holt Shelton, outrageously broad shoulders, devilishly attractive mustache and all. He wasn't like any man she had ever known, not that she had *known* many. At least not in the biblical sense. One, actually. But he had certainly been more than enough. Her single venture into a sexual relationship had definitely left a lasting impression. Only the memory was not a cherished one. Even after five years, the memory was as painful as the actual experience had been. Tony Edwards had used and manipulated her in a way her parents had never dreamed of; but they had been, as they always were, at the heart of her torment. That one brief, soul-rending encounter had convinced her beyond a shadow of a doubt that whatever talents, intelligence or strength she possessed were not enough to attract a man, and never would be. Although Tony failed to completely kill her dreams of love, he'd succeeded in inflicting a near-fatal wound. One so deep that Casey had never fully recovered.

That was long ago and faraway, Casey reminded herself staunchly. Tony had been a deceptively charming boy, but a far cry from a man like—

Casey groaned into her pillow. *That's all I need.*

Maybe you do.

No, thanks. I've been around that block. A second trip doesn't interest me.

But Holt Shelton does.

Does not.

Then why do you tingle all over when you remember the way he looked at your breasts?

I don't!

And why does the idea of dancing with him, very close, keep flirting with your imagination?

Shut up.

Not until you admit he's attractive, sexy and someone who interests you.

Holt *was* interesting. And dangerous. He had almost thrown her into jail and had definitely thrown her for an emotional loop. What difference did it make if she *did* find him attractive? What could she offer Holt Shelton, or anyone else, for that matter? He was a man, and she was a crazy-quilt excuse for a woman, patched by her own guts and determination but still, always, failing to blanket the cold loneliness.

So admit it.

All right, all right. He's attractive.

And?

And sexy.

And?

And don't push your luck.

Chapter Six

By noon the following day Casey was forced to admit she could justify her reasons for going to the dance until hell froze over. The simple truth was she wanted to go. But by the time she heard April's knock on the door that evening, her lack of experience and self-confidence had whipped up a fine case of nerves.

"Hi," April gushed the instant Casey opened the door. "You ready to...? Good grief!"

"What? Don't I look okay? Is it the blouse? April, you promised it wasn't too—"

"You look..."

"What?" Casey cried, unable to interpret the astonishment on April's face as positive or negative.

"Fabulous," April breathed.

"Oh, April, are you sure? Maybe this evening wasn't such a good idea, after all."

"My Lord," April exclaimed, still wide-eyed over the transformation in Casey's appearance. "Your hair."

"It was a mistake to wear it loose, wasn't it? It's so thick. Without the braid the damned stuff just sort of goes..." Nervously she touched the dark, curled tresses that spilled and tumbled across her shoulders. "Everywhere. Maybe I should—"

"Stop fidgetin'. You look like a million bucks. Every man at the dance will be dying to get you on the floor, just so he can put his arms around you. Turn around."

Pivoting slowly, Casey held her breath, awaiting her young friend's stamp of approval.

Their frenzied, late-afternoon shopping spree had produced a new pair of shoes for April and an entire outfit for Casey. An outfit unlike anything she had ever worn. For years a love-me, love-my-jeans attitude, born of teenage rebellion, had been her fashion identification. Like her favorite attire, Casey thought of herself as durable denim and unadorned simplicity. The impulse to buy the white cotton blouse with its elasticized neckline and deep ruffle of matching cotton eyelet came out of nowhere and surprised her with its tenacity. In a soft fabric and an old-fashioned style, it was the perfect mate for the mauve and indigo, gored skirt that now swirled around her calves. But the finishing touch—a pair of huge, golden loop earrings—brought the ensemble together with stunning results. The consummately feminine and uncharacteristic purchases had been such a spur-of-the-moment urge that she barely remembered handing the clerk one of her seldom-used charge cards. The decision to leave her hair unbound had flowed from the same secret well of untapped femininity, and now Casey questioned all decisions, not to mention her current state of mind.

"One problem," April added, eyeing Casey's blouse.

"What?"

"You need to take off your bra."

"Take off my—why?"

"Because," April announced, hands on hips, "that style is meant to be worn off the shoulder, and for that you gotta ditch the bra."

"Oh." Casey hesitated. "Can't I just—?"

"Nope. Only wallflowers and old ladies wear the elastic all the way up on the shoulders."

"You're sure?"

"Positive. Hurry up, Jody's waitin', and he's already fit to be tied."

"What's wrong?" Casey asked as she removed her bra and shoved the filmy scrap of nylon into a drawer.

"Same ol' thing," April sighed. "He and his daddy had another one of their knock-down-drag-out arguments. Jody always gets in a kinda blue funk afterward."

"Do they argue a lot?"

"Just when my name comes up." She gave a so-what shrug that didn't fool Casey for a moment. Apparently April and Jody's relationship had some rocky ground to cover before they could hope for a smooth road.

"Now c'mon," April urged. "Let's get moving."

Despite Jody's "blue funk" moodiness, he and April had eyes only for each other. In fact, the young cowboy's gaze strayed from the road so frequently that Casey was concerned for their safety. Finally they arrived at the Community Center in one piece, and Casey discreetly lagged behind, giving the sweethearts time for several quick kisses.

The trio entered the cavernous building vibrating with people, music and the sounds of a good time. Everywhere Casey looked, she recognized one of Grace's customers. But scanning the crowd, she failed to see the one specific customer she hoped would attend.

And what makes you think he would pay any attention to you if he was here?

Wishful thinking?

"You weren't kidding when you said this dance was probably the closest entertainment for fifty miles," Casey said after Jody had seated his "dates" and gone for refreshments. From the number of couples on the dance floor and the press of bodies around the bar, it did indeed appear that *everyone* in Crescent Bay was under one roof.

"Every Friday night, regular as clockwork. These folks work hard all week, and this is the only night they got to howl."

"What's wrong with Saturday night?"

April shook her head. "Church on Sunday morning."

"I keep forgetting I'm in the heart of the Bible—"

The six-piece band hit the first strains of an upbeat tune, and the volume drowned Casey's words.

"Whatdaya say?" April yelled.

"Never—" Jody suddenly reappeared, plunked three frosty bottles of beer onto the table, grabbed April's hand and pulled her with him into the stream of bodies flowing toward the dance floor. "Mind," Casey finished to the now empty space.

She stared at the spot where April and Jody had been swallowed up by the crowd. *Now what?* Was this a sign of how the evening would progress, watching while everyone else enjoyed themselves? She shouldn't have come. Fighting the familiar tug of loneliness, she quickly stuffed the feeling into a closet in her mind and locked the door. Wondering why the key to said closet kept turning up at inconvenient times, Casey absently smoothed folds in the cotton skirt.

She eyed the long-necked amber bottles, and noted Jody had neglected to provide drinking glasses. The flavor of beer always reminded her of soured bread dough, and she'd never developed a taste for the popular beverage; but the thought of anything cold and wet was too appealing to ignore. Raising the bottle to her lips, she took a sip, closing her eyes as she tilted her head back to allow the cool liquid to slide down her parched throat. Her brow wrinkled into a frown at the biting aftertaste.

"I'd offer to replace it with champagne, but we're fresh out."

Casey's eyes flew open, to find Holt Shelton close enough to touch. One booted foot rested on the rung of the chair next to hers, and a half-empty bottle dangled from two fingers of the hand resting on his bent knee. She almost choked on her last swallow of the yeasty-tasting brew.

"I—" she coughed "—didn't see you walk up."

"I noticed."

Holt didn't add that he'd noticed her the minute she came through the door, or that the sight of her, looking like a gypsy beauty, had stolen his breath. He didn't add he'd watched her from a discreet distance ever since, or that she interested him as no other woman had in a long time. The inner voice he had come to depend on as an alarm system against involvement with city women, no matter how beautiful or enticing, was less audible than usual. For the present he didn't ask why.

Casey noticed his uniform and badge had been replaced by faded jeans, Western-cut shirt, boots and a decidedly friendly sparkle in his eyes. The pulse at his throat drew her attention, and she wondered what it would be like to place her fingertips there and feel his heart beating against her skin, drumming. . . .

"Enjoying yourself?"

Her gaze darted to his face. "I, uh, we just arrived."

"We?"

"April and Jody Lee."

"I see." All he was really interested in seeing at the moment was her exquisite face.

They stared at each other.

Casey was the first to break the stare—and the silence. "I, uh, like the band." The pad of her thumb worried drops of condensation from the bottle, while her brain searched for conversation. "Are they a local group?" Why was he looking at her as if she were something tall, cool and wet and he had been out in the sun too long?

"Mostly." Why couldn't he look at her without imagining the feel of her mouth beneath his, her body beneath his?

"They're quite good. Do they play here regularly?" *Go away, Holt Shelton. You make me nervous.*

"Yeah."

The bottle he had been unconsciously twirling between his fingers abruptly stilled. He settled the glass container on the table as if making a decision to leave, but he stayed. He heard her toe continue to tap out the beat. His fingers lightly drummed against faded denim.

They fell silent again, watching the dancers. Watching each other watch the dancers.

Forcing her gaze away from Holt, Casey allowed her photographer's instinct to take over, cataloging the angles of bodies, tilts of heads, facial expressions, all swirling together, with the music creating a fascinating kaleidoscope of color and rhythm.

"You know there's something earthy and basic about country-and-western music," she said, completely enthralled. "It's not just the hard-drinking, he-done-me-wrong lyrics. But an elemental way the music makes you feel. Maybe because the words and tunes deal with basic, gut-level feelings. Real feelings—"

"Would you like to dance?"

If he had asked her to jump into the middle of Moon Lake stark naked at high noon, she couldn't have been more shocked. He must have thought she was angling for an invitation.

"To . . . to—?"

"Dance."

Holt was stunned at his own request. As a rule, he avoided "eligible" partners at the Friday night dances in favor of Grace's contemporaries, or occasionally the wife of a friend. He couldn't figure out what scrambled part of his brain had produced the invitation, or what malfunctioning cells had allowed him to voice it. For fleeting seconds he contemplated backing out. Then she looked up at him and smiled.

Too late.

Holt didn't like the way his libido went into Fast Forward every time he was around her. So she was a beautiful woman. So it *had* been a while since his ego—or anything else—had been stroked by anyone soft and female. So what? *So just remember, cowboy. City girls are long on looks and short on morals. Fight the urge.* Holt had never felt less hostile in his life.

"Ever do any boot scootin' and belly rubbin'?" he asked in that soft, slow drawl, obviously designed to drive women insane. The thought of rubbing bellies with Holt produced a strange flutter in the pit of her tummy. Strange, yet warm.

"Is . . . is that what you call it?" Casey murmured, deciding the voice technique had worked. Why else was she seriously thinking about stepping into his arms?

"If you want to get technical, Cotton-eyed Joe, two-step or schottische, but when you cut to the chase, it's leather to hardwood and belt buckle to belt buckle. And easy. Even a city girl like you can pick up the steps in no time." Maybe, just maybe, if he kept reminding himself where she came from, he could put a check on his hormones. Maybe.

City girl? For some reason she couldn't fathom, Holt felt the need to attach labels. He probably thought she didn't know the difference between Johnny Cash and petty cash. Maybe he even thought she might embarrass them both. Well, he was in for a surprise. "Then by all means, let's cut to the chase."

"Don't worry." Holt held out his hand. "I'll take you slow and easy."

His hand on the small of her back guiding her toward the dance floor, Holt fought the images his own words conjured, images of Casey's soft, sweet body yielding even sweeter secrets, while he gave new meaning to "slow and easy.'' He could control his erotic thoughts and did to some degree. Controlling his body fell somewhere between maybe and forget it.

Eyeing the way the blouse's neckline encircled her creamy shoulders didn't help. He kept fantasizing about slipping his fingers beneath the elastic, sliding the ruffle down, down until all of her smooth, warm back was displayed for his hungry eyes.

Working his way through the dancers, Holt found a spot on the crowded floor and swung her around to face him. He took several deep, *controlling* breaths before his right hand slipped beneath her hair to lightly embrace her slender neck. The other curled around the fingers of her right hand as he drew her to him. A dip of his head brought his mouth a breath away from her ear.

''Relax.'' He was having one hell of a hard time taking his own advice.

At his touch, the idea of relaxation became as foreign as a Volkswagen trip to Mars. Beneath his hand her skin tingled and grew warm, just like the spot in the pit of her tummy. She had never experienced this same kind of—her mind struggled for a word, rejected several and settled on *intimacy*—with the nice young bronc rider who had taught her to dance to George Strait's mellow tunes.

Holt smiled down at her. ''Okay?''

How not okay could you get? The few men who populated her life were buddies, colleagues. She was out of her element and knew it. Dancing was one thing. Dancing with Holt was another.

''I don't want to make a fool out of myself.'' She didn't realize she had voiced her thoughts until a laugh rumbled from his chest.

''I've never seen a less likely candidate. You're very graceful.''

Her left hand instinctively sought the denim belt loop at his waist. He was talking about the two-step, and she was talking about a giant step into a totally unfamiliar situation—a man-to-woman situation.

"Rest your left arm over my right," he instructed, the words spoken so close to her ear, his breath warmed her skin.

Casey complied. The movement brought his oversize, oval-shaped belt buckle into her midriff. Deliciously warm sensations welled up like underground springs in several places other than her stomach.

"Okay, take three steps backward." She followed his movement as he spoke. Bodies brushed, creating a delicious friction. "Now we step to the side and a little touch step—"

"A what?" Concentration was difficult, knowledge of past lessons stored somewhere in her brain suddenly inaccessible.

"It's a hesitation. Like this." He demonstrated and again she followed.

"Very good."

"Thanks."

"Now, just go with the flow. You'll develop your own rhythm."

"How am I doing?"

"Fine. Just fine." At the next intermission he intended to ask the manager to crank up the air conditioning. A film of perspiration tickled the skin beneath his mustache.

"You're very good. Smooth."

"Thanks." Was that throaty sound her voice?

Her voice made him think of cool water tumbling over rocks in a Colorado stream—slightly husky, soothing, very sensual. That voice made him think of sudden thunderstorms on hot, listless summer nights. It made him think of many things he shouldn't, such as forgetting his rule to never again become involved with a city girl. Holt reminded himself she wasn't right for him.

Then why does she feel small and delicate in your arms? And very, very right?

She should tell him the steps weren't new to her, that she was merely a little...dazzled. By what, his presence? Her own response to being near him?

All of the above.

The last strains of the slow song ebbed, moving quickly into a lively version of Cotton-eyed Joe. Whistles shrilled while dancers cheered, clapped and stomped their approval. The entire crowd seemed to move at once, carrying Holt and Casey along with them. He switched gears and steps so quickly that if Casey hadn't known what was coming, she would have ended up in a heap at his fast-moving feet.

Holt almost missed a step when he realized she'd not only kept up with him, but was actually singing along with everyone else. Surprised, he glanced down into her upturned, smiling face about the time the lead singer in the band called the obligatory, "Whaddya say?" The crowd's collective and equally obligatory, "Bullshit!" boomed across the room in answer.

"Oh, Chief!" Casey laughed. "You should see the look on your face."

Momentarily surprised that she was obviously well acquainted with the dance, he quickly recovered. Joining in the laughter, he swung her around to join other dancers in forming a line. When the music ended, she was still smiling.

"You're a fraud," he said as she led the way back to the table.

Casey stopped so quickly that Holt's body collided with hers. "Hey." His arm automatically encircled her waist. "Thought I was teaching you to dance, and all the time you were the expert." *God, but she's soft. Soft skin, soft voice...soft everywhere?*

"Hardly." Turning to face him, she laughed uneasily, relieved the accusation had been a tease and disturbed at the sudden spear of panic over the juxtaposition of their bodies—her hips to his fly. Glancing into his face, she longed for the cool finesse to deal with this man and the feelings he invoked.

"You felt...looked like you'd been two-stepping all your life." Holt's smile faded, the spark in his eyes changing from laughter to a glow of a different nature.

The embers of a seductive heat brightened, then flamed, a wildfire flash between their bodies, threatening to trap them hopelessly within its fury.

He released her. "This place could use a few thousand fans."

"Yes." Casey lifted her hair and held it high to help disperse the heat.

His gaze went immediately to the vulnerable column of her neck. Another fantasy—his lips against her skin, a kiss starting behind her ear, his tongue tracking a path down that enticing flesh all the way to her—

"How...how about something tall and cold?" His voice was slightly hoarse.

"Wonderful." She fanned the back of her neck. "But—"

"No beer," he finished.

"Please."

"Two soft drinks, coming up." With a grin and a wave that belied the coiling tension in his body, Holt headed toward the bar.

As Casey approached the table, April and Jody appeared to be in the middle of a serious discussion.

"Maybe your daddy's right. Maybe you should find yourself another girl and—"

"He's wrong. Dead wrong. And I've *got* a girl," Jody insisted. "The only one I want." He reached across the table and took April's hand in his. Then, apparently realizing their conversation had been overheard, he said, "Casey, will you tell this hardheaded friend of yours that she's makin' mountains outta molehills."

"Jody, he's never gonna change his mind," April insisted.

"I don't give a damn if he does or not. And if he doesn't get off my back, he can find himself another foreman . . . and another son, for all I care."

"You don't mean that."

"Yes, I do, April. If he makes me choose between him and you—"

"Jody! He's your family." April dropped her head and whispered. "You don't know how lucky you are to have someone care enough to worry about you."

He sighed and glanced at Casey as if to say, what am I going to do with her? "I'm sorry, darlin'," he said at last. "Guess I'm just tired of all the fussin' and fightin'." His gaze darted around the noisy hall. "And I've had it with this racket. Let's you and me go somewhere private."

"But we can't—"

Jody rose, downed the last of his beer and reached for his hat. "April I *can* and *will* do what's right for us. You trust me, don't ya?"

She looked up into his eyes and smiled. "Course I do."

"Then let's get the hell outta here."

Holt joined Casey as the young couple rounded the end of the table. "Can you see Casey home?" April hollered over her shoulder.

"No! I—" Casey started to speak.

"No problem. I'll see she gets back to the motel safely."

"But, but . . ." Casey stammered. The thought of being alone with Holt sent a bolt of panic through her.

"Thanks." Wrapping an arm around April's shoulder, Jody grinned widely.

"See ya Monday mornin', Casey." A smiling April waved as Jody maneuvered her through the crowd.

"But…" A frown furrowed Casey's brow as she watched the young couple disappear through the door.

"Casey?"

She turned to find Holt's deep blue eyes searching her face. "Casey? Is there a problem?"

You scare me silly and thrill me at the same time. I'm out of my depth with you. Yes, there's a problem. Me.

She shook her head. "No."

"Do you want to leave?"

"N-no."

"Then would you dance with me again?" Holt held out his hand.

Gazing into his eyes, seeing the flame of desire spark in cobalt depths, should have shocked her back to her senses. It didn't. Even as inexperienced as she was, Casey knew standing too close to this particular flame was a mistake. She was courting a third-degree, heart-deep burn. All the while her mind screamed, *No, you might never survive the hurt,* her heart prayed, *Please, maybe Holt Shelton will be different.*

She took his outstretched hand.

Once again she found herself in Holt's arms, gliding across the hardwood floor. The band had taken a break, leaving the jukebox to substitute. Someone's quarters took a stroll down memory lane, while one Patsy Cline tune after another drifted over the swaying couples as they moved to the sensual rhythm. The tempo was slow, and he held her close, her body gathered against his in a warm, wonderful embrace.

"Where did you learn to dance?" He wondered *who* had taught her and what kind of relationship they'd shared, and if the relationship waited back in California.

"At a Phoenix rodeo two years ago. I was shooting a sports magazine layout." She wondered how many other women had danced with him. Was there a special one, and if so, where was she tonight?

"I see." Where her temple rested against his jaw, he felt her pulse against his skin, felt her heartbeat, surprised that it beat in time with his. Pleasantly surprised. "No ex-husbands, lovers or fiancés lurking around?"

Breath feathered over the sensitive top of her ear, the timbre of his voice sent pleasure curling deep inside her. "Not a one."

"Not even an occasional boyfriend?"

"N-no," she said, her own voice paper-thin.

His embrace tightened slightly. "I'm glad."

Ms. Cline's achingly sensual voice sang of sweet dreams that wouldn't come true, and Casey gave herself to the music and the man who held her. His embrace was heaven, if only as long as the song lasted. She relaxed and pretended that she was the kind of woman Holt would find attractive.

And that he was the kind of man she could trust.

When the dance ended and Holt escorted her toward the table, Casey realized the pretense was over; she had been a fool to indulge herself, even for a few seconds. Reality was the world she occupied. She knew who she was and where she fit. And it was *not* in Holt Shelton's arms.

"Can you take me home now?"

"If that's what you want."

I don't know what I want when you're close, but I know what I should do.

"Yes."

Chapter Seven

Whispers of coolness borne by the evening air caressed Casey's skin as they stepped outside the Community Center a few moments later. Casey breathed deeply, letting the fragrance of wildflowers fill her nostrils and clear her head.

Holt, too, took the opportunity for some deep breathing and to put some distance between them. The brush of her unbound breasts lingered, haunting his memory. So did the sweet way she'd nestled against him while they danced. She'd felt so good in his arms. *Too good. She's deliciously sweet. And you're hungry. Dangerous combination.*

"Here." Holt cleared his throat and pointed to a sleek-black and shiny-chrome pickup truck.

When they stopped beside the truck, Casey avoided the assistance he offered and hiked her skirt to climb into the front seat.

Walking around the truck bed, Holt needlessly adjusted his belt, ran thick fingers through already rumpled hair and nervously knuckled his mustache. *Face it, cowboy, the lady is ringing your bell.*

Bell ringer or no, intellectually Holt knew he should avoid any further physical contact with the delectable Ms. Westbrook. *Hold that thought,* he commanded himself, also knowing full well he would rather hold her.

The moment he climbed into the front seat of the pickup and closed the door, an uncomfortable silence engulfed them. Uncomfortable for Holt, because his concentration centered on the gentle sound of her breathing. His own breath was decidedly less gentle.

He should take her straight back to the motel.

She should go straight back to the motel, but didn't want to.

She should stay as far away from Holt as possible, but didn't want to do that, either. Being with him was disturbing on several levels, some of which she dared not examine too closely, yet she couldn't deny she was attracted to him.

Holt started the engine, glancing at the digital clock on the dash. "It's, uh, still early."

Casey offered no response, because her train of thought so closely paralleled his. Ending the evening now was undoubtedly the wise choice, yet neither of them seemed eager to do so, regardless of words to the contrary.

"You sure I couldn't talk you into a drive around the lake?"

You could probably talk me into a lot of things. Casey knew she was tempting fate, pushing her luck, all the clichés describing an error in judgment exactly like the one she contemplated. Her mind asked why? while her heart answered, why not?

She looked at him and smiled. "I suppose a drive would be all right." A compromise, but wasn't life full of them?

"Would you like some air?" he asked. Without waiting for her reply, Holt reached across the seat, grasped the window crank and turned. "This handle is a little stubborn."

"That'll be fi—" His elbow nudged her breast, and a rapid-fire tingling scorched a path from the point of impact, exploding tiny bursts of sexual energy inside her body—frightening, exquisitely thrilling explosions.

Cold sweat sheathed Holt's entire body.

"Sorry." He swallowed hard.

"It's okay." She held her breath.

"There."

"Thanks."

"Cooler?"

"Fine."

He yanked the gearshift into Drive and took off.

The Texas night was warm, but thankfully the slight breeze was cool. Its sweet scent rushed through the cab, whisking away some of the tension.

"Oh, how lovely!" Casey exclaimed a few moments later as they rounded a bend in the winding road, and a spectacular panorama of one side of Moon Lake came into view. Moonlight skipped hand in hand with the breeze along the surface of the water, shimmering silver on inky black.

"This is my favorite spot. Would you like to get out and walk around?"

"Please."

Casey helped herself out of the truck. Scattered with loose gravel, the uneven ground was treacherous. She had taken only three strides toward the lake when she lost her balance, instinctively throwing her arms outward as she swayed.

Holt grabbed for her. "Here. Hang on to me."

Gladly, Casey thought, her hand resting on his Greek-god-sized shoulder.

"Watch your step."

Good advice, she told herself. *Oh, yeah? Then what are you doing taking a moonlight stroll by the lake, instead of going back to your motel as you should?*

Good question. She had no answer. At least not a sensi-
ble one. Senses, good or bad, momentarily operated on a
purely tactile level. The refreshing breeze, the warmth of his
hand against her waist, moonlight, the fragrance of his spicy
after-shave, all assaulted her mind and body. Casey was
dizzy with sensory input. So much so that when he finally
released her on more stable ground, she fought the urge to
reach out and steady herself.

"You okay?"

Not trusting her voice, she merely nodded.

Hooking thumbs into his belt loops, Holt drew a deep
breath of night air. "I can taste the air's sweetness. There's
nothing better except maybe the smell of the earth right after a spring rain. Great, isn't it?"

"Great," she agreed, settling for a breathy version of her
own voice.

"Yeah. I'll stack this against a California sea breeze any
day of the week."

"You wouldn't be one of those bragging Texans I've
heard so much about?" Glad of a safe topic of conversation, Casey took her first steady breath since the instant his
arm had slid around her waist.

"No brag." Slowly folding his hand into a fist, he
knuckled one side of his mustache in a blatantly devilish
gesture. "Just stating a fact, ma'am."

"And so modestly."

"Gracie taught me never to shy away from the truth."

"What else did she teach you?" Casey asked, grateful
that the earlier slow smoldering she had seen in his eyes had
been replaced by amusement.

"To study hard, say my prayers, wash my hands after
using the bathroom, and keep my britches buttoned."

"Y-your—?"

"Britches buttoned. As in—"

"I get the picture." And she certainly did, only not of Holt as a little boy. In her mental snapshot he was fully grown and every bit a man. *So much for safe topics.*

"I'll bet you were a holy terror," she said with a laugh, thinking that he had easily terrorized her, with a little help from her own insecurities.

"You'd win."

Holt's deep growl of a laugh joined hers, and she thought how wonderful it must have been to be able to enjoy such a seemingly normal childhood. Now she could visualize him as a small boy, tousled brown hair, charming grin, maybe even a freckle or two, and Grace scolding him—but not too sternly—for a lapse in his behavior. Then Casey realized Holt had never mentioned his parents, and, strangely enough, she had never connected him with anyone but Grace.

"Sounds as though Grace had your number. You must have spent a lot of time with her when you were growing up."

His laughter slowly died. "I spent all my time with her. She raised me."

"Oh, I, uh . . . didn't mean to—"

"It's all right," he said softly. "I never knew my father, because he didn't marry my mother. And I never knew my mother because . . ." He looked out over the lake, and when he continued his voice held a harder edge. "Being a parent was too ordinary and dull for her. Certainly not worth sacrificing the fun and adventure of bright lights and big cities."

Casey tried to conjure up an image of her own mother forfeiting so much as a trip to the dentist in favor of parenting. She couldn't. And she understood Holt's bitterness because she shared it, only in a stronger dose.

"B-but still you loved her—"

"I was too young. I loved a dream."

Didn't we all, she thought, and without asking knew his dream, like hers, had died a slow and painful death.

"She never came back." Her words were a statement rather than a question.

Gazing at her, Holt shook his head. "We got word when I was about nine or so. She had hooked up with some rich-guy jet-setter. They were both killed when his sports car went off a mountain switchback in the Alps."

Casey's soft, subdued gasp was almost carried away by the breeze.

Holt heard it and acknowledged her response for what he hoped it was, not pity but genuine sympathy. She'd recognized his pain.

"Hey," he said, turning toward her. "Don't take it so hard. *I* didn't."

"Yes, you did." Never had she intended to speak the truth she felt in her heart, but the willful words somehow slipped out.

His hand brushed a wind-tossed strand of hair from her cheek, and she retreated from his touch. "You got a license to operate that crystal ball, little girl?"

The tag she normally found highly offensive sounded like an endearment on his lips.

"Well, you're right," he continued. "But not many people take the time to look, much less *see*. My mother's going left a gap in my life. But thank God, I had—"

"Grace," Casey whispered.

"Yeah," he said tenderly. "I could have grown up hating my mother. And I can't deny there's some bitterness, but Grace taught me how to deal with it, to live life on my own terms. She said life is full of raw deals, but mine were no worse than anyone else's unless I made them so. Sort of a lemonade out of lemons philosophy."

As he gazed into Casey's upturned face, lemonade and philosophizing suddenly fell to the bottom of his list of important items. And soft blue eyes and even softer lips jumped into first place. Holt wondered if she realized how beautiful she was. A sweet, wild, innocent beauty that shot straight through his heart and pierced his soul like sunlight slicing through clouds.

"We've, uh, gotten into some pretty heavy stuff here. I didn't mean to bore you with my life story." How long had it been since he had wanted to share so much of himself with anyone? Forever, it seemed.

Casey wanted to tell him she understood and why, but pride, always her staunch ally, prevented her. But, oh, how she longed to be able to tell her own story in such simple terms, to be able to share herself as he had. What she wouldn't give to banish her personal demon, the way Holt obviously had his. Such freedom could change lives.

But Casey had risked too much and received too little to be in any hurry to expose her heart again. Holt's nearness, his touch, their conversation, had already turned the key in the lock of her dark closet, and the thought of actually opening the door to that dungeon of pain was frightening. So frightening that the old defenses automatically clicked into place, and the need to run was so strong she could taste the fear.

She was in quicksand, desperate for a handhold.

Moonlight snagged flashes of fear in her eyes like lightning in a stormy sky, and Holt sensed her emotions were equally volatile. He had no idea what had spawned such fear, only that he would do anything to relieve it, anything to make her feel safe.

"So, what do you think of my lake?" he asked softly, deliberately putting space between them, hoping a change of subject would help.

"Y-your lake?" she stammered, struggling for control.

"Just at night."

At her slightly dazed look he chuckled. The sound snapped the bonds of her panic, and Casey thanked her lucky stars for Holt's sensibility. He had offered her a hand, offered to yank her away from the quicksand.

"When I was a kid," he explained. "This whole area was my personal playground as far as I was concerned. And I was a possessive little cuss. Complained constantly about too many people messin' with *my* place. One day I voiced my opinion to an out-of-town customer at the café. The guy said I was a brat, got huffy and left." He grinned, sliding his hands, palms out, into his back pockets. "Gracie was mad as I've ever seen her."

"W-what did she do?"

"Nearly peeled the hide off me, one square inch at a time." The grin softened to a smile. "That night she came into my room and made me a deal."

"A deal?"

"Yeah. She said if I'd quit being so obnoxious in front of the customers, I could claim the lake as mine . . . after dark. She said it was a good thing for me to love this place, but love, any kind of love, dies if you're greedy." He looked straight into Casey's wide eyes. "Love's only worthwhile if you share it."

She almost had the handhold, almost felt solid ground beneath her feet. And lost it. His words slashed into her strength like a sword through silk. In her mind she heard and felt the key make another turn in that rusty lock.

"Y-yes. That s-sounds like something Grace would say."

Her voice was so soft he strained to hear. Moonlight illuminated half her face; the other half appeared a shadowed mask from some haunting masquerade. A tear, small and solitary, clung for dear life to a velvet fringe of black lashes, sparkled for a second, then slid down her cheek.

Holt's thumb ended the drop's shimmering trip over satiny skin.

"Holt, don't," she begged.

"Why not?"

"I . . . it's not you."

"I don't see anyone else here. Every time I touch you I can feel your hesitation. Almost as if you're braced for the punch line in some awful joke."

"Please stop."

"No. Not until you give me a reason."

Casey backed away from his touch. "I don't owe you any explanations." She hung on to what few defenses she had for dear life.

Holt saw her rigid posture, watched the chin lift, the guard come up, and knew he had crossed a well-protected frontier. A moment ago he'd recognized and respected that boundary. Now he felt compelled to test it, if not for his own satisfaction, then because he knew instinctively she had never yielded an inch of personal ground without being pushed to do so.

"No, you don't," he agreed. "But we got off on the wrong foot and I'd like to think tonight is a fresh start."

Her mind leapfrogged to shaky conclusions. He was a normal, healthy male assuming she was a normal, healthy female. He couldn't know how far the assumption was from the truth. He'd exposed her vulnerability, peeled away layers of protective camouflage. *Set him straight. He's too close. Tell him it's a lost cause. Then run like hell.*

"Don't back me into a corner," she said, her voice trembling.

"I'm not trying to back you anywhere. All I meant was—"

"Then why the change of heart?" She swallowed hard and, as usual, flipped her fear into anger. "Two days ago you were ready to run me out of town. Now you're... you're..."

"What?"

"Friendly," she snapped.

"And you think my friendliness is fake?"

"I didn't say that."

"You implied as much."

"Draw whatever conclusions you like. We've got a soft summer night, full moon, and talk of fresh starts. I'm smart enough to anticipate the next logical step."

"Which is?"

"Getting *re-e-e-al* friendly."

She shrugged, trying to appear calm, cool and collected while the exact opposite was the truth. "Look, I've been around. I know how to play the game."

"Oh, you do?" He was beginning to see how well she played the game of keep-away.

"Sure," she said, arms protectively folded across her chest. "I'm only going to be around for a few days. You've probably *had* most of the local ladies. Hey, listen, I don't blame you for trying, after all—"

"It won't wash."

"Of course it won't, because I don't intend—"

"You're not going to run me off that easy."

Casey's head snapped up. "What are you talking about?"

"Your ready-made, handy-dandy defensive shield. The one designed to keep everyone from getting close to you."

"I don't know what you're talking about." The look of determination in his eye sent chills down her spine.

"Oh, yes, you do. And my guess is you've been at it so long, perfected it so well, you didn't figure anybody could tell the sassy, don't-tread-on-me front was just that—a front."

Her precious control rattled against restraints. "What's this, more homespun philosophy?"

"No." The strength of purpose in his voice cut through her sharp reply. The gentleness in his voice cut into her heart. "This is Holt telling Casey that I've got *your* number. That underneath all your bravado there really is a scared little girl, who's just as frightened as the rest of us mortals."

Casey stood very still, afraid even to breathe.

"I understand your need to avoid pain. And I won't back you into any corners."

"Why are you doing this?"

"Because I think you're running from yourself."

"Why should you care?"

Her "whys," ringing with childlike need for assurance, tore at Holt's heart. He longed to give her a simple answer, such as everyone needs someone to care, but that was too pat. She deserved better. He wanted to say he understood her need so well because it was so like his own, but that was too patronizing. They both deserved better. In the end he told her the truth.

"I don't know why," he murmured softly. "But I do care."

Surely, Casey thought, when she was a very small child someone, possibly her parents, probably a nanny, had said they cared. Had actually said the words aloud in her presence. But her memory didn't go that far back. Holt's words were sweet surcease, and for a brief second she believed them. A telltale burning behind her eyes warned that the last shreds of control were perilously close to slipping.

"Holt—"

"You'd like for me to take you home now."

"Yes." His sense of how much tenderness she could handle was uncanny.

Holt knew he had done and said more than he intended. Too much? Maybe. He didn't regret having pushed her to step out from behind her protective shield, but perhaps coaxing was a better approach.

"All right, but don't think I'm giving up. I'm attracted to you, Casey Westbrook, whether you like it or not. Hell," he added almost to himself, "whether *I* like it or not."

Casey didn't remember the ride from the lake to the motel. She did remember allowing Holt to help her into the truck, because as they pulled into the motel parking lot, she still felt the imprint of his fingers, warm and supportive, on her skin. He killed the engine, got out and walked around to open her door. Sliding out of the truck, Casey's shaky legs threatened to fail her.

Terrified he might try to kiss her, she desperately sought some way to shake his hand, thank him and run, all at the same time. *You don't have a thing to worry about,* she assured herself. *Beautiful, sexy women get kissed. Plain Janes don't.*

But he said he was attracted to you.

He doesn't know me.

"Casey."

Startled out of her thoughts, she realized they stood in front of her door.

"I like being with you," he said, forcing her to meet his gaze.

"Y-you do?" Unsure exactly what she expected, his statement caught her off guard.

"Yes. I had a good time. How about you?"

"Y-yes."

"You're a terrific dancer." He lifted a dark, curling strand of hair and rubbed it gently between finger and thumb. "I like the way you wore your hair tonight. Did I mention you look like a wild, beautiful gypsy?"

"N-no." Another first. No one had ever compared her to anything so...romantic.

"After we danced, you lifted all this—" he threaded his fingers through her hair, moving it away "—silkiness from your neck, and I wanted to put my lips against your skin." His thumb brushed one of her golden hoops, and moonlight fairy-danced in a circle along the earring.

His words were a powerful drug, injected straight into Casey's bloodstream, racing for her heart. Against all reason, against all she knew was right, his body felt wonderful next to hers. But she must stop him, must end this temptation before he felt too wonderful.

"Holt—"

"Easy," he whispered. "There's a difference between wanting and doing. And I promised you, no corners."

She relaxed slightly, wanting to believe him, needing to believe.

Gentle hands stroked her hair. "You know where I wanted to kiss you?"

"N-no."

"Here." His fingertip touched the soft skin behind her ear, moving aside the earring, which was warm with her body's heat.

Casey's heart pummeled against her ribs.

"And here...." His finger tracked the line of her jaw. "Here..." across her chin, "and here," and finally skimmed over her lips.

He *was* kissing her, using her own mind instead of his mouth. Her imagination willingly complied, filling in whatever details memory failed to supply. And Casey possessed a very active imagination.

"Gypsy princess." His knuckle skated over smooth skin to her earlobe. "All fire and ice. Sweet and spicy."

Eyes closed, Casey released her hold on sanity. He was too warm, his words were too seductive.

"Open your eyes, Casey."

Slowly she obeyed his command because she was powerless to do otherwise. In the blue velvet and silver-glossed darkness, stars glistened, fireflies winked.

"When I kiss you for real, and I will, soon," he promised, "you won't have to worry about corners or defenses, because you'll want me to kiss you." His slow smile caressed her as intimately as his touch.

"Holt—" His finger against her lips sealed whatever protest she'd intended to make. A second later cool air replaced his touch.

He stepped back, giving her the space he knew she needed. "Have dinner with me tomorrow night."

Regretfully Casey shook her head.

"Why?" he asked calmly, fully expecting her to say no, and fully expecting to talk her into saying yes.

"Because...Holt, I'm not going to be in Crescent Bay for long and I'm not interested in—"

"One-night stands?"

She ducked her head. "Yes." She didn't add that a single night with him would probably be wonderful enough to last her a lifetime. She was simply scared to take a chance.

Gently placing his index finger beneath her chin, he tilted her face toward the moonlight. "Neither am I."

"We, uh, we started out not liking each other very much. Maybe we should have left well enough alone."

"Why? Because it was safer?"

She pulled away. "Maybe."

"Too late. I like you."

"You don't know me," she protested.

He shrugged, reaching out to lift another starlight-silvered curl from its resting place against a soft shoulder. "Educate me. Are you a mystery woman?"

"N-no mystery. I'm just a plain, ordinary photographer. What you see is what you get." That much at least was true. As for the rest ... Well, for reasons she didn't want to examine closely, the rest seemed very wrong at the moment.

"I like what I see very much."

He seemed determined to have her change her mind, and Casey wasn't sure how long she could withstand Holt's persuasive brand of determination. "You don't understand. I'm not—" her mind scrambled frantically for the right word—*beautiful? sexy?* whole? "—like other women," she finished on a rush of breath.

"No argument there. And I still like what I see."

Frustration peeled away more layers of protection. No one but Ramsey had ever succeeded in getting past her initial line of defense. No one but Ramsey had ever taken the time. "But I'm different ... on the inside."

He reached for her hand and was delighted she didn't resist. "Is it so difficult for you to believe you're a beautiful, charming woman? The kind of woman any man would want to have near him?"

The confusion in her eyes was his answer. "Holt—"

"Casey, I want to spend time with you. Talk to you. Tell you jokes and listen to you laugh. Pay you compliments and watch you smile. I want to *be* with you," he said softly, unsure why he was so eager to pursue the very thing he had consistently tried to convince himself to avoid. He was only sure of one thing. He did want Casey.

Oh, God, she felt herself weakening. A soothing balm for a long-standing hurt, his words assuaged the ache she tried so hard to ignore. *Don't give in,* her mind warned. *How can you not?* her heart asked.

"Why?" she whispered.

Holt's heart broke to hear the childlike plea in her voice, a plea he'd bet she wasn't even aware she'd voiced. *Who made you go begging for love, then turned you away? And where are they, so I can wring their worthless necks?*

He wanted to tell her not to give up on love and tenderness, no matter how painful or long the search. Wanted her to trust him to show her the way.

"Because I feel good when I'm with you, and I think you feel good with me. Isn't that enough to start with?"

Enough? It was everything.

Don't, her inner alarm warned.

Just this once. Can't I pretend for a little while?

The risk is too great.

I won't be around long enough to get hurt.

It only takes a heartbeat.

Then it's already too late.

Holt watched the play of emotions cross her face and longed to take her into his arms, until his hands balled into fists, fighting the urge. Desperately he searched his mind for the right word to help her understand, to make her see their potential together. He searched but came up with only one, very ordinary word.

"Please."

His face was darkness and light, cast in shadows and angles as he gazed at her in silent expectation. She looked into midnight-blue eyes and saw hope and an emotion she dared not name.

"Yes," she breathed.

"Yes?" He couldn't believe his ears.

"Yes."

He took a step toward her, then stopped. One touch, and he would kiss her and keep on kissing her. And now was not the time to push. Whatever nameless Everest she had scaled, Holt was certain her fear was never far in the background. Its shadow passed between them with every touch, every tender word. The fact that she had wanted to be with him enough to battle her fear gave him hope.

"Seven-thirty okay with you?" He barely recognized his own creaky, *happy* voice.

"Yes."

"Shall I pick the restaurant?"

"Yes." A small, shy smile tweaked the corner of her mouth.

"Terrific. Wonderful. We can drive to Dallas; it only takes forty-five minutes. What kind of food do you like? Never mind. I'll pick the restaurant." He stopped, inhaling quickly. "If that's okay with you?" Hadn't he just asked her that? He felt like a teenager again.

"Yes, but I'm afraid my wardrobe is limited—"

"Hey, we're not talking black tie," he hurried to assure her. "Just...nice. A nice, relaxing, enjoyable evening, okay?"

"Yes." Her smile grew.

"Fine. Okay."

They stared at each other, grinning for no other reason than that it felt good. They felt good.

Holt's thoughts darted ahead to the following evening, when he would be able to gaze at her to his heart's content over candlelight. He wanted the opportunity to discover firsthand what he suspected—that her lips were a thousand berries sweet. He already knew he was parched for her taste. She filled his senses, mind and body with a spirit-stirring hope.

Casey's thoughts raced ahead to the following evening. To a sweet, brief night of storing memories to last a lifetime. To pretending, if only for a few hours, that love and happiness weren't cruel illusions.

Chapter Eight

You ou should never have agreed to go with him, Casey chided herself, all the while scrubbing her skin to a healthy pink beneath the shower's warm spray in preparation for the outing. *You're asking for trouble.*

She lathered thick masses of curls and massaged her scalp vigorously. *He deserves a perfect woman. What could you possibly offer him?* God knows, Casey Westbrook's name would never be on Holt's list of perfect women, and she tried not to think about the kinds of females who might populate such a list. Tried but failed. Someone tall, blond, beautiful and brainy was undoubtedly the kind of woman Holt deserved to have share his life. Casey didn't need a mirror or tape measure to know that her average, brunette and unlovable self fell far short of the mark.

Irrelevant, Westbrook. If he knew who you really were and why you came to Crescent Bay, it wouldn't matter a tinker's damn if you had Monroe's looks and Einstein's IQ. Casey was asking for trouble, and she knew it. Even if she had been Holt's ideal woman, her profession was the kiss of death as far as he was concerned.

So, why torture yourself? Blow dryer humming, she worked her damp hair free of snarls until it shone, burnt-umber highlights on velvety brown. Why, indeed? thought Casey. Nothing good could possibly come of getting involved with Holt, yet she stood poised on the brink of doing precisely that. Self-inflicted torture, pure and simple, and the only reason for contemplating such madness was equally pure and simple.

He was a magician.

Who else but a worker of magic could put bad dreams to rout and change darkness into light?

Powdered, mascaraed, blushed and incredibly nervous, Casey shivered as she slipped the burgundy-colored silk dress over her head. Cool and soft, the fabric slithered over her hips. Light dancing over the silk, the full skirt billowed like spilled wine around her trim calves. The gossamer creation whispered against nylon stockings as she stepped into high-heeled pumps. Trembling hands wrapped a matching color sash, mingled with cerulean and peacock blue, around her trim waist. The revealing neckline prohibited wearing a bra, and Casey anxiously wondered if Holt would think the absence of a bra two nights in a row was an indication of a "loose" sexual attitude. Maybe she should...

What? Call the whole thing off?

Yes, if you're smart. If she had any sense at all when it came to Holt Shelton, she wouldn't be in a motel room in the middle of Texas, having this ridiculous conversation with herself. But she didn't have much sense or resistance where Holt was concerned. Her head told her the relationship was doomed, that Holt would never accept, or forgive, once he knew the truth. Her heart told her Holt might be the chance of a lifetime.

Trembling fingers withdrew Ramsey's eighteenth-birthday gift to her from a hidden pocket inside her suitcase, and

Casey fastened the small diamond studs in her ears. She had just hooked a matching pendant around her neck when a knock sounded at the door.

A thousand butterflies took flight in the pit of her tummy, soared crazily and kidnapped the remainder of her nerves. She swallowed hard and licked her lips. Twice.

She tried to justify her behavior by telling herself it was too late to back out now. But the justification rang hollow. "Hi," she said, the warmth of her smile belying the cold anxiety eating away her composure as she opened the door.

"You are gorgeous," Holt said. His appreciative gaze swept her from crown to ankle, saying more than mere words, more than she dared hope for, more than she deserved.

"Th-thank you." If the word "gorgeous" applied to anyone, it was Holt. Having already promoted him from good-looking in uniform to attractive in jeans and Western shirt, she felt that pronouncing him merely handsome in a suit and tie was an understatement. Black, elegantly tailored and scrupulously fitted to his powerful frame, the suit was as impressive as the man who wore it.

"Ready?"

Casey was charting a dangerous course for herself and knew it. A course paved with guilt, but at that moment it was the only one she wanted to take.

She nodded and smiled.

He grinned and offered his hand.

As they stepped into the late Texas afternoon, the sun hung low on the horizon, a fat, red-gold sphere resting on velvety purples, mauves and pinks. God was in His heaven, and all was suddenly right with the world.

Moments later the luxurious Lincoln Town Car, substituting for his usual pickup, breezed along Highway 114, headed toward Dallas. At the wheel Holt looked about as relaxed as Casey felt, which put them on an equal footing: nervous and trying not to show it.

"How was your day?" His gaze darted from the road.

"Fine. And yours?" She smoothed a nonexistent wrinkle from silken folds.

"Uneventful, which makes it a terrific day." Not a single worrisome encounter, Holt thought, if you don't count exasperating hours of wondering how to sustain comfortable conversation for an hour and a half with a deliciously desirable woman within arm's reach.

Zipping past the outskirts of Bridgeport, Casey gnawed her bottom lip, wondering how she could possibly make intelligent conversation for eighty miles with a sensual force field between them, positively arcing electricity. Every breath carried the tantalizing fragrance of his cologne; every glance reconfirmed his magnificent and very male presence.

"Beautiful sunset," she said in an effort to distract her wayward thoughts.

"Spectacular," he agreed.

"I've taken some of my best pictures during sunrises and sunsets. They're my favorite times of day."

"Yeah. Mine, too. There's a sense of hope with one and a feeling of peace with the other." Glancing into her eyes, Holt suddenly realized why their unusual color had haunted him since their first meeting. Every day he watched the sun come up, yet lately the dawn had seemed more special, a memory to keep. Cloudless fingers of night had surrendered to the insistent glow of a new day, until finally the sky had grown lighter and lighter and the sun burst into view. The first rays of day gold banished the final traces of night blue, leaving a crystal-clear, fragile blue. The exact shade of Casey's eyes—eyes the color of hope.

"I, uh—" He yanked his gaze back to the road and cleared his throat. "I think you'll enjoy Old Warsaw. The food is excellent, the service and atmosphere are—"

A red and black pickup truck suddenly whipped around from behind the Lincoln, and went flying past at a high speed. The driver, a young cowboy, held a can of beer in one hand, the other was negligently draped over the steering wheel.

"Damn." Holt's own grip tightened momentarily before he reached under the edge of the dash and extracted a mobile phone. Punching in a number, he glanced over at Casey and grinned apologetically. "Sorry, but that kid is hell-bent for trouble." A response on the other end of the line snagged his attention.

"This is Chief Shelton, Crescent Bay Police Department. I'm southbound on 114 with a possible DWI. Texas plates 5544 CL. Vehicle is late-model Chrysler pickup. Looks like a custom job, black over re—"

Simultaneously Holt and Casey glanced up as if to verify the description. Casey's horrified, "Oh, my God!" filled the quiet interior of the car, followed a split second later by the sound of screeching tires and scrunching metal, as the truck smashed into a station wagon, pulling onto the highway from an intersecting road.

Stunned by what she had just witnessed, Casey caught only bits and pieces of information as Holt bit out details of the accident and requested an ambulance. Spitting gravel, the big Lincoln rolled to a stop twenty yards from the accident site. The driver's door of the station wagon was caved inward at a hideous angle. The hood and right fender of the pickup were scrunched like crumpled tinfoil. Smoke curled from the engine.

Sprinting toward the vehicles, suit coat flapping behind, Holt was on the scene before Casey could get out of the car.

"Stay back!" he yelled.

Knowing his warning was to protect her in case of a possible explosion, she clutched the open door in a white-knuckled grip.

As Holt drew even with the pickup, she saw the young cowboy literally slide out of the cab, his wilted body propped against the running board, his head hanging to one side.

Lord, please, Casey prayed as she watched helplessly. *Please don't let anybody die.*

Squatting beside the cowboy, Holt checked his pulse, his eyes and breathing. Evidently satisfied there was either no hope for the injured man or only minimal need for concern, he hurried to the other victim.

Heart-stopping seconds passed, while Holt frantically worked at opening the station wagon's badly crushed door, the hellish scrape of metal against metal cutting through the stillness of approaching dusk. Finally the twisted door creaked free in his hands. As he ripped it wider, Casey saw that the driver was a woman. Her temples were smeared with blood.

The next instant the pitiful sound of a child's whimper turned Casey's skin to gooseflesh.

"Casey!"

The urgency in Holt's voice galvanized her into action, and she raced toward the car. The injured woman's head gently cradled in one hand, his other supporting her shoulders, Holt looked up as Casey skidded to a halt at his side.

"She's not—"

"No," he assured her. "But she's in bad shape."

"The boy?"

"Not a broken or sober bone in his body. He'll live."

The whimper came again.

"On the other side." Holt nodded, hunkered down between the woman and the partially open door.

Casey heard more whimpers strung together by sobs, the heartrending sound wedging her breath in midthroat. Hurriedly Casey circled the car and opened the passenger door.

Still strapped into a safety seat, a dark-haired little girl, green eyes round with fear, gazed back at Casey. About three years old, her slight body trembled as she cried softly. Instantly Casey reached to unbuckle the safety belt.

"Don't move her yet," Holt commanded.

"But we have to do something." Dropping to her knees in the roadside dirt, Casey stroked soft, brown ringlets with one hand while she tried to stem a river of tears with the other.

"Now listen carefully," Holt went on. "Put your fingertips to her throat and check her pulse rate."

"It's all right, baby," Casey crooned to the frightened child and did as Holt instructed. "We're going to take care of you. Don't worry. Everything will be all right."

"Applying light pressure, carefully run your hands over her body," Holt said calmly. "Check for broken bones or swelling." Silent seconds inched by while Casey carried out the examination, his deep voice a rock-solid anchor in a tidal wave of emotions.

"Anything broken?" he asked when she had finished.

"I don't think so."

"She breathing okay?"

Casey nodded. The child's wide, green eyes blinked as if she were suddenly waking. Casey watched as those eyes focused on the face before her, searching for recognition. Finding none, the small, dark head immediately turned toward her mother.

"Momme-e-e-e!" The plaintive cry sliced through Casey's heart as she tried to hold the now struggling child. "Mommy, my mommy."

Holt muttered an oath under his breath, then said, "I was hoping to get her out of here before she saw. It's okay, sweetheart," he said gently to the sobbing girl. "We're going to take good care of you and your mommy." Jerking his chin toward his car, his eyes met Casey's briefly. "Take her, quick."

With trembling fingers Casey unhooked the buckle and lifted the terrified little girl into her arms. Holding the small body against her chest, she hurried back to the big automobile as a siren's wail pierced the air, the fearsome sound rolling toward them through the twilight.

Inside Holt's car, Casey rocked her charge, crooning softly, her heart breaking at each tiny sob. "Everything is going to be fine, you'll see. Soon the doctors will make your mommy all better."

But what if they don't? reason warned. What if her mother dies? *Don't make promises you can't keep. Whatever you do, don't give her hope, only to have it snatched away.*

"Sh-h-h-h, baby, sh-h-h," she said, continuing to rock. "You're such a pretty little girl. I bet you have a pretty name. Can you tell me your name?"

"K-Kerry," finally came a jerky response.

"Kerry. Oh, that's a pretty name. How old are you, Kerry?" Gentle hands continually stroked chocolate-brown curls.

"Th-th-three. A-and a—a half."

"My goodness. Such a big girl." Keeping her voice as smooth and even as possible, Casey went on talking, reassuring, while the ambulance, paramedics and two sheriff's deputies arrived.

Frantically Casey ransacked her brain for a subject to distract Kerry. "Uh, do you like to watch *Sesame Street,* Kerry?" A tear-stained cheeks rubbed a spot on Casey's chest in answer. "Me, too. I love Big Bird." Her words were for Kerry, but her eyes were on Holt as she watched him produce identification for the two officers, occasionally motioning toward Casey while he answered questions.

"M-Mr. Snuffa...lupa...gus."

"What? Oh, yes, him, too."

Working quickly, the paramedics examined Kerry's mother, secured her torso in a cocoonlike upper-body immobilizer, then using a small backboard, removed her from the car and placed her on a stretcher.

All the while Casey asked questions about as many of the *Sesame Street* characters as memory provided, gratefully amazed that her brain could recall enough information to keep Kerry distracted.

She placed her hands over Kerry's ears when the ambulance departed to muffle the siren's wail. Relief oozed from Casey's body when she saw Holt finally shake the deputy's hand. Coat slung over his shoulder, unknotted tie hanging around his neck, head bent, one hand thrust deep into a pants pocket, Casey thought him the most stunning picture of strength and heroism she'd ever seen.

Once inside the quiet of the Lincoln, he heaved a deep sigh, then smiled at their passenger. "How ya doin', sweetheart?"

"She's just fine, aren't you, Kerry?" Over the top of soft curls Casey's gaze met Holt's. *What about her mother?* hers asked.

I don't know, his answered.

"Kerry, huh?" Holt smiled. "Well, Kerry, I just heard your grandmother is on her way to meet you."

"N-nana," sniffed a small voice.

"Yeah. You just rest in Casey's lap, and we'll see Nana in no time," he assured her.

"D-daddy, too?"

Still holding Holt's eyes, Casey kissed the top of Kerry's head.

Reaching around them both, he grasped the seat belt and secured it. His face only inches from Casey's, he covered the slender hand resting on Kerry's narrow back with his, as he said, "Daddy, too."

A tension-filled, exhausting hour later in a Denton hospital, Holt, Casey, Kerry and her family received the happy news that the little girl's mother would recover fully. Several thank-yous, handshakes and many relieved smiles later, they were once again alone, the peaceful interior of the parked luxury car deafeningly quiet after the emergency room's noisy atmosphere.

"What a night," Holt breathed, car keys dangling from a hand draped over the steering wheel. He turned to Casey. "You were fantastic with that little girl."

"Th-thanks. I . . . I . . ." Emotions barely restrained bubbled to the surface, stalling words and cutting the bonds of her control. Tears filled azure eyes and spilled over pale cheeks.

Gently Holt pulled her against him, enfolding her in his arms. He let her cry, crooning to her as she had to the child, rocking her slowly, savoring the sweet feel of her in his arms. "It's okay, baby. You're wound tight. Let it go."

Casey had no idea how long she cried; she knew only that had she wanted to cry herself dry, it would have been safe to do so in Holt's arms. His embrace, soothing voice and gentle caresses shut out pain, healed wounds. When finally Casey sniffed herself back to reality, they were on the road to Crescent Bay, and she was cuddled snugly against Holt's shoulder.

"Better?"

She nodded. Embarrassed by her total lapse of restraint, she started to pull away.

"No, don't . . . please." His eyes left the road only a split second, but long enough for Casey to see that need, not politeness, had fostered the request. Shyly she scooted nearer to him, the welcome heat of his hard, lean body warming her beyond physical necessity.

His arm encircled her shoulder and he drew her closer still. "Thanks," he said, his voice raspy.

They didn't speak. They didn't have to.

An intimacy, born of need and nurtured by the evening's trauma, settled over them, enveloping them in its mellow glow. He would gladly have driven off the edge of the world as long as Casey didn't move an inch from his side.

And Casey would rather have died than lift her head from Holt's broad, sheltering shoulder.

Casey didn't open her eyes again until the car slowed, then closed them again, unwilling to leave her cozy haven. When the motor stopped, she blinked, trying to orient herself to her surroundings. Holt's car. Holt's arm about her. But where were they?

"Are you hungry, Sleeping Beauty?"

"What?" A delicate hand shoved a heavy wave of tangled hair from her face. Holt's suit coat slipped from her shoulders, but she couldn't remember him placing it over her. "Where are we?" Casey asked sleepily.

"My house."

His house was as sprawling as its owner and every bit as naturally charming, Casey thought a few moments later as he snapped on the kitchen light. Even her slightly fuzzy state of mind could appreciate the warm, Southwestern flavor of hand-painted, Mexican tiles and a see-through fireplace that formed a dividing wall between the kitchen's breakfast nook and a small parlor. For one fleeting, hazy moment Casey imagined long, winter evenings snuggled on a love seat in front of the hearth, sharing mugs of coffee and talk of the day's events with—

"How do you feel about omelets?"

"What?" She blinked away the fantasy.

"Omelets. We missed dinner, remember?" He peered into the open refrigerator. "Make that plain scrambled eggs," he amended, closing the door.

"Holt!"

"What?"

"Y-your shirt," Casey exclaimed, rushing to him.

"What about—?" Glancing down, he saw blotches of red on the dress shirt's snowy background.

She reached out to touch his chest. "You must have cut yourself when you helped Kerry's mother...."

"Don't think so." Two buttons sprang free of confining holes.

Casey's breath halved as he stripped shirttails from the waistband of his pants, exposing a bronzed chest. What had begun as anxiety over a possible injury suddenly changed into fear of a totally different kind. Fear, born of the fact that from where she stood his skin looked smooth, gloriously smooth, except for a smattering of golden brown hair. Fear, heightened by the fact that she had an irresistible urge to touch him, to feel the warmth of that bronzed chest beneath her fingers.

Holding wide the unbuttoned shirt, Holt said, "No lacerations. Not even a bruise." Lifting his head from the self-examination, he saw the look in her eyes, and a full breath escaped in a hiss. For one dangerous second he thought about ripping the shirt from his body. Thought about saying, *Touch me, Casey. Touch me, the way we both want you to.*

"Uh—" He swallowed hard. "I, uh, guess I'd better change." *What you better do is get the hell outta here, while you still have an ounce or two of gallantry left in you.*

He turned to leave the kitchen, stopped and swung back to Casey. "Oh, by the way, there's a bathroom right through the parlor, if you want to freshen up. And you might want to take off your..." He pointed to her legs, glad he was across the room, so she couldn't see his hands shake.

Casey's gaze dropped to her trembling legs, their sheer nylon casings displaying a network of webbed tears and snags left by roadside dirt and weeds. When she looked up, he was gone.

By the time he returned, she was bare-legged and barefoot, standing on tiptoe, staring into a cabinet. "I, uh, thought I'd make some coffee, but I can't find—"

"Pantry to your left, but..." he said, feeling his mustache curling into a smile as he rolled the sleeves on a fresh, teal-colored cotton shirt to midforearm. "You'll have to stay out of the master chef's way if you intend to eat before dawn." Raging hormones now under control, he was grateful for a more relaxed atmosphere.

"Master chef, huh?" A dainty hand bridged her hip.

"Highly qualified," he returned in his best lord-of-the-manor imitation.

"I'll bet."

"You doubt my word." He feigned indignation.

"No, no." She raised both hands in mock surrender. "Your word is fine. It's your ability I question."

"Very funny, Westbrook. So, you gonna help, or just stand there looking gorgeous?"

"Help," she said, running a hand over finger-combed tresses, knowing if she didn't, the only thing left to do was recall the tantalizing expanse of his bare chest, her longing to touch, stroke and nuzzle against it.

They ate in the parlor, devouring every morsel of the late-night breakfast, right down to the last sip of coffee.

"Ah-h-h," Holt breathed, patting his middle. He stretched long legs, angling them away from the low serving table between the couch and Casey's chair.

"Does Grace know she has competition?"

"No," he was quick to reply. "And if you breathe a word, she'll have me pinch-hitting next time her cook gets sick."

Casey sealed her lips with an imaginary zipper.

Holt smiled. Interlocking his fingers, he extended his arms toward his knees in a languid stretch, then untangled his fingers to rub the back of his neck.

Instinctively Casey rose from the couch and stood behind him, placing her hands strategically on his shoulders. Nimble fingers began to knead tight muscles.

He sighed. "Hmm. Feels good."

"You were wonderful tonight," she said, her heart aching with pride.

"So were you." His head lolled forward. "Hmm."

"Relax."

"Ahh, oh," he said, reveling in her delicious touch. "Yeah. That's so good."

"Your muscles are protesting, doubling up tiny little fists all across your shoulders."

"Hmm. Hmm, yeah."

"Let yourself respond to the pressure of my touch. Think of the tension as a thick block of ice. First the ice will crack, break up into fragments, then finally melt away, until the river of energy in your body flows free again."

Her voice's husky quality worked magic as skillfully as her fingers.

"Where...ah...in the world...did you...ah, oh...learn to give ahh...massage?" Holt could barely speak, he felt so relaxed.

"My last year in high school I was in a car accident. Thankfully not much damage to my father's Porsche, but I ended up with a cervical fracture."

Very gently, his fingers reached to manacle her wrists. Her fingers stilled. He pulled her around to face him. Blue jeans teased bare legs and wine-red silk drifted over denim. "You broke your neck?"

"It wasn't as bad as it sounds. A small hairline crack of four vertebrae. Therapy was required every day, and my therapists taught me—" She stopped short at the look in his eyes. "What?"

"You must have been in so much pain."

"Yes."

"How long were you in a cast—?"

"Body brace."

"How long?"

"Six weeks, then a neck brace for—"

A string of curses, colorful and succinct, hissed from his lips. "Were you alone?"

Always, she thought, remembering the nights alone with her pain. "Only until I was moved home and a nurse was hired."

Holt looked at her closely, trying to understand her meaning. Surely she hadn't meant she was alone in the car *and* alone in the hospital? Surely her mother and father, *somebody* had been with her? Still holding her hands he asked, "Where were your parents when the accident happened?"

She avoided his gaze. "Europe."

"But they came as soon as they heard."

"I had this really wonderful lady who stayed with me whenever my parents traveled—"

"Casey."

"And they called almost every week."

"Casey."

Finally she met his gaze. "I survived, Holt. Look, I'm good as new." She turned her head from side to side in a mechanical-doll rotation.

Wide hands on either side of her face stopped her in mid-turn. "My God, you went through something like that—the pain, all the procedures—by yourself."

"Please, Holt." Her hands covered his.

"No wonder you could comfort little Kerry the way you did tonight," he said, half to himself. "You *were* Kerry."

"Holt," she begged on a ragged breath.

"I can't stand thinking of you lying in a hospital bed, hurting. Inside and out. Alone. I wish I could have been there."

Tears pooled in her eyes. "You couldn't have done anything."

"Yes, I could." She followed a gentle tug into his arms, not even protesting when he lifted her into his lap. "I could have done this." He kissed teary eyes. "And this." He kissed salty cheeks. "And this." He kissed a trembling mouth. "And I could have held you when you cried."

"Wh-what makes y-you think I c-cried?"

"You're still crying."

Hands cradled her head, his mustache feathered her lips for a heartbeat before his mouth brushed hers ever so gently, ever so sweetly. Holt never intended the kiss to be anything but comforting. He never expected her to kiss him back. But she did, tentatively, then hungrily, the innocence of her kiss achingly seductive. And he thought he would die from the pleasure.

Against Casey's will her hands splayed across his chest, fulfilling her wish. Then her arms slipped around his neck, and she leaned full against him.

The kiss was heaven. The kiss was hell.

Heaven, because a million novas shone inside her, showering a sweet, burning radiance she never knew existed. Hell, because it ended too soon.

"Casey..." he whispered, wanting more of her lips, more of her.

"You were right," she sighed, the sound a breathy imitation of her voice.

"About what?" Holt's voice didn't sound any too substantial, either.

"Me wanting you to kiss me. I did and it was..." Wonderful. Earthshaking. Beautiful beyond imagination. All of the above. How could she express feelings too fragile for words? How could she explain she was perilously close to a yawning, black chasm of emotions, and one slip could send her over the edge?

His warm fingers smoothed a fledgling frown from her brow. "Whatever you wanted it to be." He kissed her temple. "No corners, remember." In the space of a few short days the woman in his arms had become more precious than he ever imagined any woman could be. He stretched out his legs and settled her comfortably against him. Closing his eyes, Holt lovingly stroked sable curls, held the sweet weight of her body and prayed the moment would never end.

If only this moment could last forever, Casey thought, drowsy and content beyond her wildest imagination. Safe.

So safe and protected. A feeling of utter joy washed over her and trickled into her heart, a winding river to her soul.

He sighed and kissed her temple.

She snuggled against a hard, warm chest.

Heartbeat to heartbeat, they fell asleep.

Moonlight brush-stroked silver over Casey's sleeping body hours later as Holt scooped her into his arms and carried her to his bed. Stirring briefly, she nestled deeper into his embrace.

For long moments he stood beside the bed, held her, inhaled the subtle fragrance of her perfume, watched the rise and fall of her breasts, and an overwhelming protectiveness made him reluctant to release her. Finally, careful not to wake her, he laid her gently on the bed, as if she were fragile as moonbeams and starlight. Trembling fingertips caressed the smooth skin of her cheek as he drew the coverlet over her.

Tired but restless, he drew aside the drapery covering a huge bay window. The whispery glide of cloth across glass and Casey's even breathing were the only sounds to disturb the moonlit quiet. Tonight's unexpected turn of events before, during and *after* the roadside drama had him asking himself some tough questions; and if he was honest, the answers scared him to death. Hands thrust deep in his pockets, Holt studied his bare toes as if they might provide an insight into his own feelings, a perspective on the last few hours, but most of all, on the beautiful, perplexing woman in his bed.

He shook his head, unable to unseat the vision of Casey, frightened herself, yet pouring out love and comfort to a terrified child while clinging desperately to slender threads of security. Then quietly, completely, offering him her softness. Dozens of images danced across his mind. Casey, breathtakingly gorgeous in wine-colored silk, looking like a dream. Casey, crooning softly to Kerry, strolling the sterile hospital corridor, hand in hand with the little girl, her soothing voice ever reassuring. Casey, offering him a cup of hot coffee while he recited tedious but necessary accident details to emergency room policemen. Casey, arm in arm with him while they received the news that Kerry's mother would recover. Casey, Casey, Casey....

In the space of a few short, but revealing, hours, Holt had seen many women in Casey, from luscious, desirable female to tender and loving helpmate. She had burst into his life like the warmth of the sun. And if that entrance had been unorthodox and even a little rocky, so what? She was here, and he intended to do his damnedest to keep her. He accepted the fact that there were obstacles. What he didn't accept was the war she waged with her feelings, denying the natural and powerful attraction between them. What or who had forced her to shut herself away from emotions, away from love?

Remembering the personal glimpses she had allowed of herself, he decided on a *who* as the culprit. Her parents? Probably, but he didn't get the feeling they were abusive, at least not physically.

But then, some of the most destructive and far-reaching abuse never left scars visible to the naked eye. He had seen enough troubled humans in his stint as chief of police to know that.

I'm not like other women . . . on the inside.

Perhaps the villain was another man. Unreasonably his hands balled into fists. Had some cruel and thoughtless male in Casey's past caused her so much pain that she couldn't or wouldn't face another relationship? Blind jealousy, white-hot and unexpected, flashed through him, tapping a core-deep and primitive need to shield her from the nameless man, indeed from all who would harm her. *Easy, cowboy. You have no rights here except the ones she grants you. And so far you got zilch.*

Wrong, Holt thought, he had a kiss. And that kiss had revealed far more than he or Casey had ever intended.

He gave his already rumpled hair another raking. He wanted . . . what? To comfort her?

Yes, but more.

To protect her?

Absolutely.

To make love to her?

Ultimately, unquestionably, but it doesn't end there.

Where does it end?

He saw the logical conclusion, but stopped short of yielding to its truth. Only one obstacle prevented him from reaching it. Trust. Five small letters that made the difference between now and happily-ever-after.

The fact that he even considered such a future at this stage of their relationship was crazy.

Is crazy so bad?

The answer came, swift and clear. *No. Sometimes crazy is the only way to live, if you want to live at all.*

But after distilling all the instincts, that one inescapable obstacle remained. Did Casey trust him enough to confront her fears, whatever they were? And did he trust Casey enough to share all that he was, secrets included? Secrets not his alone to share?

This much he did know. Fears or no fears, past or present, he wanted to be with her, wanted to hold her, love her until they were breathless from the sheer joy and power of being together. He promised himself not to let her exit his life before they experienced that power, because if he did, his heart told him, he would lose something precious. Once-in-a-lifetime precious.

The sound of Casey twisting and turning against the sheets drew him out of his thoughts. Closing the drapes, he padded to the edge of the wide bed and watched her moving beneath the covers, an aching tenderness squeezing his heart. *God, she's sweet. Driving-me-crazy sweet.*

It was then he noticed Casey's tossing was too restless, surpassing ordinary sleep movement. She frowned, and Holt realized she must be dreaming. A bad dream?

Gently he lifted the quilted bedspread and slipped in beside her, gathering her slender, light-as-down frame against his. For an instant she resisted, then desperately clung to him, murmuring fitfully. Not a bad dream, he decided, a nightmare. The thought that she should be tormented even in sleep tore at his heart, and the powerful wave of protectiveness he now accepted as normal, washed over him anew.

"Mama, Papa," she mumbled, her frown deepening.

"Shh," Holt whispered. "It's okay, baby." He kissed her forehead, willing his strength to calm her, rid her of the dream.

"...shouldn't listen."

An icy fear crept up Holt's spine, and he held her tighter.

"...all my fault." She clutched and unclutched her fist, wadding the bed covers in a white-knuckled grip. "...Corner's so dark...."

She was in agony in the dream, and he thought fleetingly of waking her, but decided the trauma might be greater if she woke remembering the nightmare. But he couldn't bear to have her relive one more moment of pain and silenced her the only way he knew how. Slowly, gently, taking infinite care not to wake her, he placed his lips on hers and kissed her sweetly. Compassion rather than passion fueled the tender stroking of her parted lips. He kissed her cheeks, her lips again. Holding her to him, he gently rocked her, wanting to absorb her pain.

He had no idea how long he kissed and soothed her. Minutes, hours, days. It didn't matter. All that mattered was that she should feel love, know, even in a dream state, that she was treasured.

Somewhere deep in her dream Casey realized the nightmare was different from the other times. There was a fourth person in the dream. A stranger. No, not a stranger. This person was someone she knew and trusted, someone who would protect her. The stranger who was not a stranger held out his hand to her. And when she took it, he gently pulled her out of the hateful corner and wrapped her in his arms. Strong arms. Wonderful arms.

Instinctively, she conformed her body to the hard-muscled length of her savior's. Her peaceful sigh drifted on the night air.

Chapter Nine

Wherever it was the exquisitely enchanting dream had taken her, Casey never wanted to leave. There was no darkness, only light, beauty and the dulcet melody of a hauntingly beautiful song. She drifted on a dream-soft cloud, padded against reality, surrounded by velvet warmth and tinkling melodies.

Snuggling into the heavenly comfort, the cloud unexpectedly bumped into something substantial enough to puncture her cozy oblivion. Slowly reality oozed in. Reaching to bar the intruder, her hand contacted a furry barrier. Fingertips explored solid warmth, threaded through rough-soft terrain, then coasted on to smoother planes, like moving through a forest into a sunny, flat meadow. Casey's palms slid up, trudged over sandpaper roughness, then retreated. Tangibility verified reality, and reality insisted upon recognition of flesh against flesh.

Flesh?

Casey's sleep-fogged mind struggled to narrow the wide band of her scattered thoughts into a stream of consciousness. Slowly her eyes drifted open. Still muzzy, she blinked, clinging to the last wispy threads of her dream state, curling the hand resting against his throat around his neck, anchoring her to treasured warmth.

"Good morning," Holt murmured, nuzzling the soft skin behind her ear. Drawing her closer, his toes skied the slope of a slender instep, then coasted along the arch. Casey's toes curled in response.

"Holt," she breathed, addicted to the tranquil sound of his voice.

"Hmm," he said, giving her time to wake, to adjust to her surroundings.

"Holt?" Realization crystallized, her hand splayed across his chest, intending to push away. Wide-eyed, she glanced down at the comforter and realized where they were. "We're . . . we didn't . . . last night—"

"We dozed off on the couch. I carried you in here sometime after midnight."

"Here?"

"My room. You were so tired, I didn't have the heart—"

"We're in your bedroom . . . in your *bed*?"

"Yes," he answered, seeing the rising panic in her eyes. "And we're both fully dressed. Well—" he glanced down at delicate fingers against bare tanned chest "—one of us is, anyway."

Casey's gaze immediately followed his, dropping to the trail of brown-gold hair that whorled around his navel, then disappeared into the waistband of his jeans. *If he's dressed, then I must be. . . .* She peeked under the comforter and released a tightly held breath. The red silk dress still covered her. Almost. The hem rode dangerously high on her bare legs, and the bodice was hopelessly scrunched and wrinkled, but she was dressed—correction—covered. Barely.

She looked up, straight into deep, compelling blue eyes. Casey felt as if she had plunged into their hypnotic center, was swirling, drowning in an ocean of fathomless blue. And the water wasn't against-the-shore cool and restful, but volatile as a whirlpool, even hot. Hot, the way vapor rises from a sun-warmed lake on a fall morning. Hot, the way fevered skin feels to a cool touch...hot...skin...touch...

Casey jerked her hand away, and would have scampered from the bed like a terrified kitten, had he not stopped her by tightening his hold on her waist.

"Easy, sweetheart." Gently he drew her back.

Their gazes met and held.

The power required to move her muscles refused to be summoned, and instead of pushing away, she stayed exactly where she was...at ground zero of a deliciously intimate explosion of her senses. She felt tiny detonations along the perimeter of her defenses. His hand on her hip was light, yet detaining in a way a thousand restraints could never be. His warm, exciting breath fanned her cheeks and throat. Lingering traces of his cologne, like the man, were masculine and enticing. His body was hard and powerful. And his eyes...

A woman could get lost in those eyes and never want to find her way out.

Holt decided a man could lose himself in her eyes and willingly forfeit his sanity. She had no idea how delectably, breathtakingly sexy she looked, sleep-tousled hair tumbling about her like a silken river overflowing its banks. Her skin glowed and was exquisitely dewy. He wanted her the way he wanted his next breath. But he wanted her trust more. Recalling the fragmented cries of her nightmare, Holt vowed to make certain in every touch, every kiss that she would feel safe and treasured.

"I'm, uh, I'm not..." Casey stumbled over her words, wondering how she could explain away her awkward and brazen behavior. "I mean, I don't usually—"

"I never thought you did."

"Holt, I—"

"Relax, darlin'." His hand left her hip long enough to brush a strand of brown hair from her shoulder. "I don't want anything you're not willing to give." Ever so lightly his lips touched hers, briefly, softly, undemandingly. "I take that back. I want everything you have to *give*. I told you once before I wasn't interested in *taking* anything from you. Understand?"

She started to nod, then stopped and shook her head.

"Then let me make myself *very* clear. You are a beautiful, desirable woman, and I want you."

Casey's eyes widened.

"I want you naked in my arms, crying out my name as I love your body, and sleeping next to me when the sun comes up. I need you, need your softness. I want you the way I've never wanted a woman before. But the only way we will be together is if you want it, too. What we have...what I think we could have is too important to risk on a roll in the hay. And if you think that scares *you*..." He swallowed hard and felt a tentative grin tickle the corners of his mouth. "Lady, you wouldn't believe what terror it strikes in my heart."

When she didn't answer, he lifted a trembling hand to her cheek. "For God's sake, Casey, say something. Tell me if I've just blown a chance to have you in my arms, in my life. Tell me I'm not the biggest fool of the decade."

Stunned, Casey couldn't believe he had actually spoken those wonderfully sweet, tender words to her. No one had ever said he *needed* her. No one. Her heart filled to capacity with joy and a soul-deep emotion she wanted to name love; but she feared such a label would taint the feeling.

"Casey—"

"No," she whispered at last.

Cold fear swept Holt's body. "No...you don't want me?"

"No. I mean, yes.... I mean—" she took a deep breath "—no, you haven't...you're not a fool—"

"Thank God," Holt groaned. A chuckle followed closely on the heels of his sigh of relief. His hands cupped her face, then slid beneath the heavy waves of hair to caress her neck as his forehead touched hers. "I think you just shaved ten years off my life."

"I—I'm sorry."

"Don't be. I'd give up another ten as long as you don't change your mind."

"Holt?"

"Yes, baby?" He nibbled tiny kisses across her cheek.

"Thank you."

He drew back far enough to look into her eyes. "For what?"

"Last night. For holding me while I—"

"You're very..." Lifting her hand, he kissed the center of her palm. "Very welcome."

Sensual awareness, radiating from the spot where his moist, warm lips touched her skin, trickled into every cell of her body. A part of her wanted Holt to take her in his arms and make love to her, allowing no protests, no time for her to run away from the feelings he stirred. Another part wanted to be sure, had to be sure, her trust wasn't misplaced.

Sensing her hesitation, Holt clamped down on his body's responses, willing his mind, not his hormones, to control the situation. Someone had hurt her, and for the first time in his life Holt seriously contemplated deliberate physical violence. If he knew where to find the bastard, he'd kill him.

"Who did this to you?" he blurted, the primitive need for revenge superseding reason.

"D-did what?"

Holt cursed himself for his insensitivity, yet knew the best way to deal with fear was to confront it head-on. "Who made you distrust..." He started to say love, but changed his mind. "Your own feelings?"

"No—"

"Someone did a number on you, sweetheart," Holt insisted. "I see it in your eyes, feel it when I touch you. And I swear to you, if I could get my hands on them right this moment, I'd make them pay for hurting you. Pay dearly," he whispered.

His voice was low, smooth, sharp-edged steel sheathed in velvet. Watching his blue eyes deepen to indigo, Casey didn't doubt for a moment the truth of his words. And it shocked her. Not that he possessed the strength to carry out his threat, but that he *would*, if she gave him a name.

"Now I'm frightening you, aren't I? Sorry, darlin'." He kissed her temple. "But thinking of you being hurt makes me crazy. You're an innocent and—"

"I'm not...innocent."

Holt went still. *Oh, Lord, I never should have brought up the subject. I don't think I'm ready for this, after all.* Ready or not, Holt knew they had gone beyond the point of ignoring the past.

"You, uh, don't have to be a virgin to be—"

"I'm not that, either."

You asked for it, cowboy. Are you man enough to take it? He swallowed hard. "Doesn't make any difference."

In a soft, fragile voice, she said, "I wish..."

Holt drew her to him, snuggling her head against his shoulder, giving her time to trust the moment, trust him. "What, baby? What do you wish?"

"I—I wish I could turn back time," she murmured, wishing Holt could have been her one and only lover. Wishing she had the courage to ask him to be her lover now, to replace old memories with new. Now, held securely in his arms, for the first time those memories were less painful. For the first time, she felt she could talk about what happened.

"I met...I met Tony my junior year in college," she said, her heart beating fast.

Holt's heart skipped several beats. His body went dead still on the inside, but he stroked her hair, offering what comfort he could.

"He...he didn't know anything about my family, at least he pretended not to."

Holt frowned, wanting to ask what there *was* to know about her family, but instinctively understood she had to tell the story her own way, in her own time.

"My, uh, father has lots of connections with people who make movies, people who provide the money to make movies. My mother was once a top agent. They, uh, know all the right people. Glitzy, glamorous, phony people." Clutching the edge of the blanket, her fingers absently worried the satin binding as she talked.

"I was surprised Tony was interested in me. He was handsome and smart." She inhaled deeply. "And I was so gullible, I didn't realize how smart. He told me he loved me, told me he wanted to marry me. For the first time in my life I felt someone cared about me, really wanted me. We went to my parents' house for Christmas and . . . a-and . . ."

Holt's insides coiled tight as he fought the urge to crush her to him and beg her not to finish, not to relive the pain. Her tears wet his shoulder.

"It didn't take long for me to discover Tony's real interest. He was a hungry, ambitious..." With each adjective her voice became more brittle. "Clever...young filmmaker. He saw a shortcut to the top and took it. Me."

Silence, tangible enough to burden hearts, stretched into the night. Ceaselessly Holt's hand petted her, stroked her, willing tenderness from his soul to hers through his touch.

Finally she gathered the tatters of her courage and pulled back to look into his eyes. "Know what was so crazy about the whole affair?" she said at last.

Holt shook his head, unable to trust so frail an instrument as his voice.

"I didn't really love him any more than he loved me. When we made love, I didn't *feel* warm or cherished, but I pretended. I wanted someone to love me so badly, I was willing to be deaf, dumb and blind to the truth." She lifted her head, and aqua eyes implored understanding. "Once he established contact with my parents, he...he didn't need—"

"Don't. Oh, God, don't." Holt's control shattered along with her voice. He held her to him so tightly that breathing was forgotten. He absorbed her pain, feeling the cuts to her wounded spirit. "Baby, baby." For the second time in twenty-four hours Holt rocked her, only now he clearly understood the depth of the emotions he had witnessed when she held young Kerry.

She had soothed the little girl in her arms—and the little girl inside herself—the way every child needs to be comforted. The way Casey had never been.

There are times in a man's existence when he faces a moment so small the blink of an eye would miss its passing, yet so important it forever changes his life. Somewhere in the last sixty seconds he himself had faced such a moment, and he knew his life would never be the same. He could analyze, theorize and rationalize the moment until hell froze over and still come up with the same truth.

He had fallen unreasonably, hopelessly in love with Casey.

And more than anything else in the world he wanted her to trust him enough to love him back.

Holt had no idea how long he held her, only that eventually tension seeped from her trembling frame and she relaxed. As her body melted against his, Holt's caresses changed. Unintentionally, comforting strokes conveyed sensual messages of need. His need to love. Her need to be loved. Slowly lips that had murmured sweet words of consolation began to whisper honeyed endearments. Words he longed to speak. Words she longed to hear.

"Soft, sweet, sweet woman," he breathed into her hair while he continued to cherish her body with light, sure caresses.

"Holt?"

"Yes, baby."

"I don't . . . I don't have to pretend with you."

Holt held his breath and thought his heart would swell so big that his chest would never be able to contain it. He wanted to love her so badly he could taste it, taste her. But rushing her might scare her so far away he could lose her for good. With a strength of will he never knew he possessed, Holt forced his mind to bypass his body's state of arousal. *Easy does it,* he told himself over and over until his body finally responded. As much as he would like to keep Casey in his bed for the rest of the day, he knew she wasn't prepared to take the next step in their relationship. And he wasn't sure *he* was ready to share the secrets of his past.

Carefully Holt disengaged himself and slipped from the bed, then walked to her side and offered his hand. "Share the sunrise with me, darlin'?" he asked, huskily.

She put her hand into his.

Holt pulled her up and into his arms for a brief kiss. "Then I'll see you home."

Taking her with him to the bay window, he drew the curtain as he had last night, only now the first rays of a new day pushed back the night. Positioning Casey in front, he wrapped his arms securely around her and contentedly rested his chin in her crown of dark curls.

Casey had no concept of time as she stood in Holt's arms, and she had no inclination ever to move from his embrace. As he had so many times before, he defined perimeters and gave her boundaries, so she knew exactly what to expect. He had promised no corners, and his word was as good as gold. But something strange had happened as she listened to him say how much he wanted her. Strange, but wonderful. For the first time, she recognized and acknowledged desire—her own desire. Before, with Tony, she had wanted to please so badly she'd given little, if any, thought to passion other than as a necessary prelude to sex. Now, in the space of a kiss and a few short hours, she had glimpsed the true meaning of words such as *passion* and *desire*. Her passion. Her desire.

She wanted Holt, yearned for him in a way she never had for Tony. Not just a longing to know his body intimately, but a fervent need to know him, all of him. True desire was a fire in the mind as well as the body. And if Casey set aside all her fears, an inescapable truth remained.

She desired Holt.

They watched the sunrise in all its glory and beauty, and with each moment of brightness hope grew, a hope for tomorrow. A hope for love.

As the last patch of night disappeared, Casey turned in strong arms.

"Will you . . . kiss me?"

"Casey—"

"I want you to kiss me. Please, please, Holt—"

His finger on her lips stopped her words. "Don't *ever* beg. Not from me. Never from me. All you ever have to do is ask. I'd give you the world if you asked."

"I'll settle for a kiss," she whispered around a shy smile.

The smile, more than the whispered request, was his undoing. Would he kiss her? Would the world keep turning on its axis? Would night follow day? God, yes, he would kiss her, and heaven help them both.

Lifting her hands, he looped them around his neck as his head lowered, mustache feather-brushing a tentative kiss onto trembling lips. She caught her breath. After a heartbeat's hesitation, he took her mouth fully, demandingly, coaxing her lips to part for the gentle intrusion of his tongue.

Casey's heart beat a wild rhythm as Holt leaned into the kiss. Her breasts flattened against hard, warm flesh, and she felt them bloom into fullness with a sweet ache. She wanted to ask him to touch her the same way she had asked for the kiss, but her courage had limits.

"I need . . . you're so . . ." His lips moved over hers again, deepening the kiss. Sweet heaven, she felt so good in his arms! He wanted to touch her, wanted to stroke her breasts until he heard her breath catch, as it had the instant before he kissed her. Slowly, carefully, his hand slid down her back, then up her side to press lightly against the swell of her breast. She moaned, and Holt almost lost what was left of his mind. But instinct warned him. Regardless of the fact that she wanted him and her body was ripe for loving, her mind wasn't. Easy does it, Holt reminded himself. He wanted much more from the woman in his arms than slow kisses and quick touches.

"Casey, Casey," he breathed, ending the kiss. Loving hands stroked her cheeks as his forehead came to rest on hers. "We have to stop."

"But I don't want—"

"Neither do I, but when we make love . . ." He tilted her head up to look into her eyes. "You do *know* I want to make love to you?"

"Then I don't understand—"

"Sweet, sweet woman." He kissed her temples, her cheeks. "Will you trust me when I say the time isn't right? I think you've got emotions left over from the accident and protecting Kerry. Your feelings and my kisses are all mixed up together and that's not surprising. But I'm greedy where you're concerned. I don't want anything to stand between us giving each other pleasure. I want it to be special. Now do you understand?"

She nodded, disappointed and relieved at the same time. He knew her better than she knew herself.

"There's no hurry." He gave her one last tender kiss, then wrapped her securely in his arms. "Let's just let nature take its course."

A short time later Casey wondered if nature had any better idea of where their relationship was going than she did. Nature hadn't been a breath away from physically and emotionally committing herself to a man she had known scarcely more than a week. And nature, whatever her course, could hardly control a situation already spiraling *out* of control.

As the big Lincoln rolled into the motel parking lot, Casey worriedly fingered the hem of a shirt Holt had loaned her to ward off the morning's dampness. "I'll wash this and return it to you as soon as—"

"No hurry."

Then why did she feel as if she were being flung headfirst and at an incredibly high speed, spinning toward a moment that would forever alter her life? And why was the need to run as far and as fast as she could from such an alteration almost palatable? Casey felt her earlier courage slipping slowly away like so much sand on an ever-changing beach.

Holt cut the engine, got out, walked around and opened her door. As if he could read her mind, he locked his fingers with hers, refusing to release her hand until they were at her door.

"Casey." He turned her to face him. "I know you're running from a past that made you stop believing in love or tenderness. But I'm not going to let you convince yourself this morning was a mistake." He kissed her mouth softly. "Nothing has been more right in my life for such a long time that I'd almost given up on myself until you came along."

Running his hands, knuckles against fabric, up the front of her borrowed shirt, lightly brushing her breasts, he gently gathered fistfuls of yoke and collar, drawing her to him. This time his kiss was possessive, staking a claim on territory he considered private and wholly his. His tongue mated with hers, demanding she acknowledge his primeval right— the right of a man powerfully attracted to a woman—and her own right to possess, as well.

She yielded to him, feeling slightly disoriented when his mouth finally left hers. Disoriented and aroused.

Moments later, inside her motel room, Casey's first tear hit the carpet beneath her feet before the sound of his truck's engine faded in the distance. Bittersweet tears tinged with profound guilt. She was in too deep with Holt.

Glancing at her photographic equipment scattered across the dresser, she tried to focus on the tools of her trade, tried through her tears to make out their familiar shapes. She couldn't. And with that admission her control teetered on the brink of collapse. Casey held tightly to one solid truth. She had to finish the job she came to do, then get the hell out of Holt Shelton's life.

The first two hours of her shift were filled by the usual, manic breakfast rush, and Casey welcomed break time. Grace was clipping handwritten lunch special inserts into menus, and April was setting tables with clean silverware and condiments by the time Casey poured herself a much-needed cup of coffee.

Grace stopped her work and looked at Casey. "Somethin' eatin' you, honey?"

For Grace's benefit she put on her best smile. "Do I look like anything is wrong?"

"Frankly, yes. You went through the entire breakfast rush with a frown on your pretty face. Wanna talk about it, or would you rather I just minded my own business?"

The smile warmed to genuine. "I appreciate your concern, but—"

"Butt out." The silver-blue head nodded. "Well, if you change your mind..."

Casey would have liked nothing better than to tell Grace the truth. All the truth. But she couldn't. Deep in her heart she knew the best thing for Holt, Grace, April and everybody else, including herself, was to get what she came for, then get out of their lives for good. And tonight she would do precisely that.

"Can I help?" Casey took the stool next to Grace.

"Sure. These old fingers of mine ain't quite as fast as they used to be. Here—" She shoved a pen and a stack of paper at Casey. "You can write, and I'll clip."

The older woman eyed Casey as she copied the lunch information from the original sheet of paper to the top page of the clean stack. "Reckon I ought to get somebody to type these things, but I never get around to it. Just seems simpler to write 'em out by hand. Besides, folks round here don't like changes, even little ones."

Always appreciative of stability, Casey had come to realize its value even more since arriving in Crescent Bay. "I can understand how they feel. Change isn't always for the best."

"Neither is stayin' put."

"But you've stayed in one place your whole life."

"Good heavens, no. I was born on a farm in Oklahoma. Then my folks went West to pick fruit, when that part of the country turned into one big dust bowl in the early to mid-thirties."

Casey had assumed Grace had been born and raised in Crescent Bay. "Then how did you end up in a café in Texas?"

Grace chuckled. "Oh, Lordy, that's a story so long and twisted, we could be here all day with the tellin'. You don't wanna hear all that," she said with a dismissive wave of her hand.

"You have to admit from picking fruit in California to running a restaurant in Texas is a big jump, geographically and economically." Casey was truly interested in what kind of life experiences had helped form this unique woman, whom she had come to admire. Besides, it took her mind off Holt.

"Honey, you don't know the half of it. My folks was dirt-poor all their lives and never been more than fifty miles from home. They just didn't figure life could get any tougher than a dried-up, useless farm. All they really did was trade one bad spot for another."

"From what I've read, lots of families during the thirties found themselves in the same place."

"You can say that again. But we made out all right, I guess. Then Mama took sick, so I quit school to help out and wound up working in one of them mansions. When she passed on, Daddy kinda kept to himself. Couple of years went by, and he just laid down and died, too."

"I'm sorry," Casey whispered.

"Oh, well," Grace sighed. "That was a long time ago."

"What about Holt's mother?"

A faraway look drifted into Grace's eyes, and she shook her head sadly. "Pretty as a movie star and wild as a March hare. And trouble from the minute she came into this world."

"You were a lot older, weren't you?"

"Yeah." Grace studied Casey's face. "Has Holt mentioned his mama?"

"Just that she left and that she, uh, never—"

"Married his father." At Casey's nod she added, "Yeah. Broke my heart, and I don't care what any psychology book says. Broke Holt's, too. She died a few years later."

"Yes. He was about nine, I think he said."

"Yeah." Grace grinned, the earlier sadness gone. "And cute, Lordy, he was cute. But he got his mama's stubborn streak, that's for sure. Only thank heaven, he got some common sense along with it."

Casey propped her elbow on the counter and rested her chin in her palm. "Courtesy of his aunt, no doubt."

"Honey, if I'd had any common sense, I'd probably never have wound up slingin' hash in the first place. Lord knows, spending the rest of my life behind this counter was the last thing on my mind when I rolled into Crescent Bay.''

''Why did you stay?''

''Broke. Couldn't go no farther.''

Casey frowned. ''I don't understand. If you didn't have any money, how did you manage to buy the café?'' When she realized what an outrageously personal question she had asked, Casey was embarrassed. ''I'm sorry. That's none of my business.''

''It don't bother me,'' Grace said. ''Truth of the matter is, after a few weeks here the folks and the café felt like home, and I'd been looking for a place to settle. Took me two years to earn enough money to buy half of the business.''

''Waiting tables?'' Casey decided Grace must have hidden financial talents to pull off such a savings plan.

''Nope. I had one of the best-paying jobs in the county.'' Grace clipped the last plastic holder to the last menu and slapped it closed. ''Workin' for Norah Tanner.''

Chapter Ten

Casey's eyes widened and her chin popped out of her palm. If her arm had not been resting on the counter, she probably would have lost her balance and fallen off the stool.

"Y-you mean *the* Norah Tanner?"

"Didn't know there was but one," Grace said nonchalantly.

Stunned by Grace's statement, Casey's mind reeled with a million questions. "Grace," she said, wide-eyed. "I—I may be out of line, but I'm curious—"

"Did I ever see her?"

Casey nodded.

"Some. But my days on the estate were a lo-o-ong time ago."

Casey couldn't believe her ears. She was actually talking to someone who had *seen* Norah Tanner! "I never dreamed—"

"Yeah, well, I don't broadcast it," Grace said calmly. "Those weren't the best years of my life, but they sure as hell weren't the worst. Only reason I took the job in the first place, besides the money, was because they weren't picky about me having Holt with me. We lived in a room hardly big enough to cuss a cat, but it came with the job."

"So that's how you saved to invest in the café."

"Yep. The owner wanted to retire, so soon as I got enough money, we worked out a partnership. Five years later I bought him out. Holt and I lived upstairs. He worked after school and summers to help me hold things together. I tell you, Casey, I couldn't be any prouder of that boy if he was my very own son."

"He's someone to be proud of," Casey agreed.

"Yeah, he's a pistol, ain't he? Worked his butt off for that ranch, too. Reckon if he didn't learn nothin' else from his ol' auntie, he learned hard work pays off."

"Grace," Casey said softly, placing her hand on the other woman's. "Do you have any idea how fortunate you are?"

"Depends on your definition of fortunate, honey. I got a good life and lots of friends. I figure that makes me real fortunate."

"Of course, but you've also actually seen one of the living legends of the twentieth century."

"She's just a miserable old woman, Casey."

Casey's excitement wilted like cut flowers out of water. "Miserable?"

"Like I said, my days out there are long past, but even then I always thought she was kinda pitiful. Just think about how lonely she must be now that she's old. How would you like to live your entire life without any family or friends around? Even a golden cage is still a cage."

How well Casey knew the truth of Grace's words. "But she doesn't have to live the way she does."

"Oh, I don't know," Grace sighed as she poured herself a glass of iced tea. "There was so much gossip when she first came. I figure she wanted to hide out for a while, then it sorta became a habit. Maybe she's been livin' like that for so long, she don't know how to live any other way."

"You mean, her exile is self-imposed?"

"Somethin' like that." Grace's gaze scanned Casey's. "You sure a little bit of reporter didn't get mixed up with the photographer in you?"

"I—I don't think so, why?" Casey's heartbeat accelerated. Had she asked too many questions?

Grace shrugged. "Understandable that you'd be curious. At least your curiosity is honest, not like those jackasses who come sneakin' around here, lookin' to sell information to those sleazy tabloids."

Casey didn't respond. What could she say? No, her picture would be a *tasteful* invasion of Norah Tanner's privacy? A rose by any other name is still a rose, Casey reminded herself, guilt cutting deeper inroads each day she had to live a lie. Grace had trusted her enough to share part of her past. Casey wanted desperately to do the same, but she couldn't. "I, uh . . . I've always been a fan of hers," she said lamely.

"Yeah, well, I reckon lots of folks sorta think of her as one of them, uh, whaddya call 'em, cult figures."

"I always thought of her as a beautiful heroine out of a tragic novel," Casey said honestly. "As a little girl I remember watching her films. She filled the screen with beauty, grace and a..." Casey struggled for the right word, her voice filled with awe and respect, ". . . life force." She glanced away, slightly embarrassed at her display of sentimentality.

"You really *are* a fan."

"There are thousands, maybe even millions, who feel the same way. Norah Tanner is a legend."

"Yeah," Grace whispered, clearly drawn into the moment almost as if they were delivering a eulogy. "She was great."

Silence stretched between them, until finally Grace looked at Casey and frowned.

"Ain't we a pair," she chuckled. "Sitting around here talkin' about her as if she's dead and buried, and the woman's probably laughin' in her beer."

"Champagne," Casey amended. "Probably from crystal goblets."

"Beats the hell outta iced tea in tumblers." Grace raised her frosty glass in salute. They both laughed.

"Wanna let me in on the joke?" April asked, exiting the kitchen.

"Ah, I think we're just kinda punchy from pourin' too much coffee and waitin' on too many yahoos."

"Amen to that," April agreed. "But I don't think you're gonna have the last laugh."

"Why?" Casey asked, wiping laughter-induced tears from her eyes.

"'Cause." April pointed toward the door. "The first of the lunch crowd just walked in."

Casey's "Ohmigod," and Grace's "Holy Moses" were quickly drowned by the raucous arrival of hungry "yahoos."

By the end of the frantic lunch hour, Casey realized she had been waiting, hoping for Holt to come in. When he didn't, she was disappointed.

"I need a favor."

Casey glanced up from cleaning the counter to find Grace on the other side, holding take-out containers of food. "Would you mind walkin' Holt's lunch up to the office?"

"Lunch? Uh, no, sure, that'll be fine," Casey said, wondering if Grace was clairvoyant.

She longed to see Holt, but the more she saw of him, the more she wanted him, and the more she knew she shouldn't—a dangerous dichotomy. She argued with her better judgment every step of the short two blocks to the police station. How would he act after their night together? How would she act after their morning together?

She was undeniably attracted to Holt in a way and at a depth she'd never dreamed possible—over her head *impossible*. Probable or not, the feelings were too strong for her to deny; though, God knows, she had tried from the minute Holt left her at her motel.

She should have asked April to take her place.

Then why didn't you?

April was busy, and Jody Lee showed up for a late lunch, just as Grace made the request.

How convenient.

This is a simple errand, not a rendezvous. What could possibly happen in a police station?

Remember what happened the last time you were there?

Holt had touched her. Accidentally, but nonetheless he had touched her. One swift, heart-stopping, upward stroke along the curve of her breast. Recalling that moment brought fresh memories of a sunrise kiss, her breast pressed against Holt's chest, while his tongue did wonderfully wicked things to her mouth....

Casey swallowed hard, suddenly aware that her grip was almost crushing the plastic cartons in her hands. His one quick and innocent touch had turned her world topsy-turvy, and it was still spinning wildly, more so every time they were together. She definitely shouldn't have agreed to deliver lunch. And she told herself she didn't want to see Holt. *Liar.*

At the entrance to the station Casey paused, took several deep breaths and pushed open the door.

Holt, standing in front of a file cabinet with his back to her, offered Casey a brief opportunity to admire his magnificent build, a pastime she decided could be addictive. She took advantage of the moment.

The khaki uniform fitted him better than anything other than a woman's hand had a right to. He was absolutely gorgeous. A waist narrow enough for a woman to encompass it in an embrace, shoulders broad enough to shelter oceans of tears, arms powerful enough to make a woman feel totally protected—all announced to any who cared to look, here was the ultimate shape of man. And the holstered pistol strapped across trim hips emphasized his masculinity the same way.

The moment he saw her Holt immediately set aside the file in his hand and came toward her. "Hi."

"I, uh, brought your lunch." With both hands she extended the cartons. The inside of her mouth had gone desert dry, and her chest felt too small to contain her drumming heart.

"Thanks." A single, hot sweep of his gaze devoured her. As he took the containers, fingertips brushed fingertips, and Casey could not deny the surge of electricity at the contact.

"Well..." Nervous, Casey folded her hands behind her back. She rocked on her heels for a second, uncomfortable and unsure how to make a graceful exit. "Guess I better get back." She turned to leave.

"And just where the hell do you think you're going, lady?"

She spun to face him.

"You're not leaving this station until I get a smile and a kiss." The irresistible grin she liked so much crooked a corner of his mustache. "But not necessarily in that order."

If his charm could be bottled, Casey thought, watching him walk toward her, he would be independently wealthy overnight. *And if you could resist, you wouldn't be caught between want and shouldn't.* Her resistance melted faster than ice cream at a Fourth of July picnic. Without hesitation he kissed her, tasted her, sipped the warm, moist nectar of her mouth.

"Holt!" she gasped. "Someone might see—"

"We're completely alone." His teeth nipped a spot on her lower lip. "I was hoping Gracie would send you. I didn't

dare ask, or she would have hounded me for every detail.''
His tongue investigated a corner of her mouth, then
skimmed along a full upper lip. "God, you taste good. I
thought I'd dreamed how sweet, soft and delicious you
tasted. No dream was ever this good." Abandoning playful
strokes, his tongue slipped into her mouth, and they both
sighed with satisfaction.

Some distant and still rational part of her mind theorized
it must be a sin for anyone to kiss the way Holt did. Anything that felt this good *had* to be sinful. Wonderfully sinful. A thrill, high voltage and hot, ricocheted through
Casey's body, leaving her breathless in its wake and weak in
Holt's arms. If she'd had any doubts about his reaction to
their time in his bed, they disappeared the instant his mouth
touched hers.

"Now," he said, reluctantly ending the kiss. "I'll take my
smile."

Smile? Casey wasn't sure she had any strength left to
smile. Knees weak, arms trembling, she might not have
enough brainpower left to will her lips ever to move again.
Except possibly for another of Holt's kisses. Despite fears
to the contrary, she managed a tiny smile.

"Yeah," he said, returning the smile. "Now do me another favor?"

"What?"

"Have dinner with me tonight."

Her smile faded. "I—I don't think I should."

Holt watched uncertainty creep into her expression and
knew he shouldn't pressure her, but couldn't stop. "I told
you before, Casey. When it comes to something I want, I
don't give up easily. And I..." He caressed her cheek.
"Want..." His thumb grazed her lips. "You."

Another kiss silenced whatever protests she might have
intended, but when he lifted his lips from hers, the uncertainty was still evident in her eyes and Holt relented.

"Because I'm in a generous mood, and because I promised no corners, I'm going to let you push me around. Once. But . . ." He gave her one last, quick kiss and another sexy grin. "Don't let it go to your head. I'm going to ask you again tomorrow, and the day after, and the day after that, until I wear you down."

Tomorrow. Tomorrow she might be gone. If she had the courage to do what she knew was right. To leave without what she came for. To leave before she hurt Holt.

"Hey," Holt said, his fingertip tapping the end of her nose. "Where did you go?"

"Nowhere." *Yet*. She sought and found her bravest smile. "But if I don't get back to the café, Grace is going to send a posse out looking for me."

"Shall I put you in protective custody?"

"Sounds kinky."

"Just your average public servant."

"Tough job, but somebody's got to do it, right?"

He grinned. "Yeah."

"And speaking of jobs..." Regretfully she wiggled from his embrace. "I need to get back to mine."

"Okay, darlin'. But remember I won't be far away."

Holt's words echoing in her head, Casey almost ran the distance back to work. When she walked through the café's door Grace, hands on hips, was verbally tearing a customer limb from limb. Stopping beside April, a puzzled Casey asked, "What on earth is going on? Some guy try to walk his check?"

April's head whipped around. "Some guy repeated a bit of gossip about a friend of Grace's, and she took him on."

"Which friend?"

"You."

"M-me!"

"Seems Ollie Waterman and his wife passed the motel on the way to church yesterday morning, and just couldn't wait to tell everybody about seeing you and Holt, standing outside your room—''

"Oh, my God," Casey whispered.

"Yeah, well, with Grace Malone in your corner, I'm not sure you even need to bother Him."

"I've got to explain," Casey insisted, but April's hand on her shoulder stopped her.

"I wouldn't step in the line of fire, if I were you. She's on a roll."

Indeed Grace was rolling right over poor Ollie, who sat openmouthed as she lambasted him. Casey couldn't make out exact words, but facial expressions surpassed mere verbiage. From the man's shocked look, he was flabbergasted. And from the fire in Grace's eyes she was rip-roaring mad.

A few seconds later Casey watched a frowning Grace snatch the check from Ollie's hand, tear it into shreds and walk away.

"That old fool ought to have his mouth washed out with soap," Grace snapped as she approached the counter. "If he thinks he can come in here and bad-mouth people I care about, it'll be a cold day in hell before he ever sets foot inside my restaurant again. Why, I'll throw his worthless carcass out in the street, I'll—!"

"Grace."

"What?" Breathing hard, she glanced up at Casey.

"I'm sorry. You must be upset to have Holt's name—"

"Holt?" An expletive Casey would never have suspected Grace knew, much less used, hissed from coral-tinted lips. "Holt's a big boy. A damned big boy. He can take care of himself. It's you I'm concerned about."

Oblivious to the stunned expression on Casey's face, Grace ranted on. "Well, I don't mind tellin' you I set him straight. Swappin' tall tales and fish stories is one thing, but gossip is somethin' else. I hate it worse than sin. Won't have it in my place. And *certainly* not about people close to me."

"M-me? You were worried about me?" Casey breathed, still stunned to be the reason for Grace's defensive tirade.

"Why, of course. You and Holt aren't the kind of people to go sneakin' around at sunup."

"Grace," Casey said, hating to be the one to paint a less-than-perfect picture of her nephew. "We *were* standing outside my room shortly after sunrise."

The silver head snapped around. "Well, if you were, there musta been a damned good reason. And even if there *wasn't*, it's nobody's business but yours," Grace finished with a "so-there" huff.

Casey couldn't decide whether to laugh or cry at the unsolicited and clearly biased refutation.

"What Ollie saw looked incriminating, but it wasn't. On our way to dinner, we stopped to help an accident victim, and by the time Holt talked to the police and we finally left the hospital in Denton, we were both exhausted. Since we missed our dinner reservations, Holt fixed a late supper and we...fell asleep." She neglected to add she'd slept in his bed, deciding a pared-down version of the truth might be better. "I spent the night *at* Holt's, not *with* him."

"See. I knew you had a good reason."

A rush of tenderness coursed through Casey, bringing an overwhelming desire to throw her arms around Grace's neck and hug tightly. At the same time she wanted to cry and announce she wasn't worth such unconditional support.

"Thanks," Casey said, conscious that her voice was husky with emotion.

"For what?"

"For trusting me. Defending me."

"Good Lord, what kind of person would I be, if I didn't take up for kin and friends?" A wrinkled hand patted Casey's arm. "You'd do the same for me."

A painful fullness swamped Casey's heart. No one had ever stepped forward to champion her as Grace had. Casey was more grateful than she could ever express with mere words. Tears stung her eyes as she simply nodded agreement.

Surrounded by suffocating guilt, Casey merely survived the rest of the day. By the end of her shift she was more than glad to take her tiny conscience back to the motel.

Alone in her room Casey tried not to think about what she had to do. And if she were successful, what then?

Then you never see this place or these people again.

These people?

Holt.

But I don't want to think about Holt.

Yeah. And while you're at it, don't think about the pain of never knowing if this could have been the chance of a lifetime.

"Stop!" The sound of her voice shattered the quiet of the small room, shattered her feeble attempts to hang on to her control. She had to take the damned picture, end the assignment, before she wound up crying over a broken dream she'd had no business having in the first place.

It was just past ten o'clock when Casey quietly closed the door to her Volkswagen, parked at the end of the dirt and gravel road leading to the Tanner property. From where she stood she could just make out the spot where she'd first encountered Holt.

Instead of heading toward the mansion, she carefully situated herself on a nearby outcropping of rock along the hillside. Night sounds filled the darkness. Doubts filled her mind.

So what are you waiting for? reason asked.

I'm going, don't rush me.

Sure. Don't let a little thing like conscience bother you.

It's my job. And I owe Ramsey.

So let Ramsey take the damn picture.

I'm a professional—

You're a fool. Worse, you're a self-deluded Peeping Tom.

Her own words echoed through her mind, an endless, hollow wail. Not once since Ramsey had placed her first, inexpensive, camera in her palm or she had sold her first photo had Casey ever thought of herself as a Peeping Tom.

Until now.

From the rock beneath, leftover heat from the Texas sun seeped through the seat of her jeans. She hardly felt the warmth. Wind from the lake, cool with the scent of wildflowers blew across her cheeks. She barely smelled the fragrance. The night, with its ever-present chorus of crickets, birds and nocturnal creatures, cloaked her in silver and black velvet. But all Casey's senses were focused on her own soul stripped bare in the moonlight.

She didn't like the picture.

From the moment Ramsey had suggested the assignment to photograph Norah Tanner, Casey had pushed her misgivings to the back of her mind, because she wanted to make Ramsey proud of her and she'd wanted to be proud of herself. With her camera she was going to make the world see Norah as *she* had always had—ageless, glorious and innocent—a star of the greatest magnitude, who had personified the dreams of millions of people.

The end might be beautiful, but it didn't justify the means. Nor could it ever justify the ripple effect her action would have. Before she came to Texas, the people in Crescent Bay had been faceless, formless and without a role in her grand scheme. Now those faces had names, and the smiles belonged to people she knew and cared about.

And then there was Holt.

As quickly and mysteriously as waving a magic wand, he had changed her life. In an incredibly short time, he had become more to her than she'd ever thought possible. Because of Holt she'd made the first, tentative overtures toward new feelings and emotions she hadn't dared explore and old ones she'd thought never to experience again.

He had turned the key in the rusty lock on her emotions and opened the door.

He lit up the dark corners of her life.

Suddenly Casey knew. Self-deception simply no longer worked. She had done the most unreasonably insane, *wrong* thing, done what she had sworn never to do again—she had fallen in love.

She loved Holt.

Casey had no idea how long she sat there, numb in the cold light of her startling realization, before she climbed into the car and returned to her motel. Back in her room, without removing her clothes or washing her face, she fell backward onto the bed. Blindly staring at the ceiling, it was a long, long time before she realized her shirt collar, hair and pillow were wet from an endless stream of tears. She cried herself to sleep.

Dawn was an insistent, angry spear of light, intruding on Casey's state of blissful escape. Rolling over, she groaned into a still-damp pillow. The events of the night before broke in an icy wave of reality just as the phone began to ring.

"Hello."

"Casey?"

"Ramsey?" she asked, her voice scratchy from crying.

"What the hell is going on? You sound like rusty pipes on a cold morning in Jersey."

"Think I'm coming down with a sore throat," she lied.

"Oh. Well, for God's sake, gargle or something."

"I thought I asked you not to call," Casey snapped, unreasonably irritated by Ramsey's call.

"Take it easy, cookie. Don't bite my head off."

"Sorry, H.A., I'm a little grumpy this morning."

"A little?"

Casey rubbed the last cobwebs of sleep from her puffy eyes. "Okay, a lot, and I apologize."

"What's wrong?"

"Nothing."

Casey could hear him switch the phone to his other ear, and guessed he was probably reaching for a cigarette. She gave him time to light up, knowing it would improve his disposition and afford her an opportunity to think how to tell him about last night's decision.

"Come on, cookie. Give."

"You're a distrustful soul."

"What makes you think I've got a soul?"

"Point taken." Casey's exhaled full breath died as a weary sigh. "I'm sorry, Ramsey. I *am* a smart-mouthed brat."

"Knock it off. I may call you names, but nobody else can and that includes you. Now, you wanna tell me what's got you tied in knots? And don't bother denying it, I can hear it in your voice."

How could she tell Ramsey what she didn't know herself? How could she explain feeling trapped in an emotional logjam, being carried away on a fast-moving current, rudderless and out of control?

"A lot has changed since I left L.A."

"Such as?"

"Such as, I'm more unsure than ever about doing this piece at all." Casey was backpedaling, and she knew it.

"We've covered this ground. So, what's the problem?"

"Something called invasion of privacy."

"I see. You've never stubbed your toe on that particular occupational hazard before. Why now?"

"I never considered myself a Peeping Tom until now."

"Sounds like a severe attack of killer conscience, probably caused by too much time in Dogpatch."

A long, heavy silence stretched out between employer and employee, friend and friend. Finally Ramsey sighed and said, "You're backing out on me, aren't you, cookie?"

Casey chewed her bottom lip for several seconds before answering. "Yes."

"Has your decision got anything to do with the long arm of the law?"

In their previous conversations Casey had purposefully kept any mention of Holt to a minimum and always as casual as possible. Maybe Ramsey had a crystal ball. "Why do you ask?"

"Because whenever you speak his name, your voice changes. Sorta wistful. Which accounts for the sudden attack of Peeping Tomitis, right?" Another long silence. "I trust you know what you're doing."

"I do." Another lie, but she needed confidence, even if she had to manufacture it herself.

"So, I take it you're not hopping the next flight home?"

"N-not for a few more days." *Trust me again, Ramsey, and please don't ask questions I would only sound like a world-class fool trying to answer.*

Another sigh, from Ramsey's end. "Don't get in over your head, cookie."

"Too late."

"You know, don't you, that if this is real, then I'm happy as a cat in cream? And if it's not . . ."

He didn't need to finish the sentence. Casey had completed and repeated similar thoughts to herself a thousand times since Holt's first kiss.

"Just do me a favor, will ya?" Ramsey said, his tone of voice clearly indicating that he was reconciled but not overly pleased.

"What?"

"Take care of yourself."

When Casey hung up the phone, she couldn't help feeling Ramsey was as frightened for her as she was for herself. As she rolled from the bed and headed for a shower, she desperately hoped she wasn't in too deep where Holt was concerned, because in the fast-moving current of emotions she wasn't sure she could swim against the tide. In fact, since a certain chief of police had entered her life, she had been doing well to merely tread water.

Thoughts of Holt swirled around in Casey's head all morning and through lunch, so when she looked up and found the man himself seated on the other side of the diner's counter, she thought for a moment she must be daydreaming.

"Hello, darlin'."

No daydream could sound so sexy or look so breath-stealingly handsome. Had to be real, Casey decided, tempted to reach out and touch him to be sure.

"Hello."

"I came to pay my debt."

"Your—?"

"I owe you a dinner, and I'm ready to pay up." He reached across the counter and took her hand. "Have dinner with me. This time we'll go casual. Nothing fancy. And I promise not to allow anything to interfere with a simple, relaxing evening. Please."

Why couldn't she follow the same advice ad campaigns offered to people hooked on dangerous substances—Just Say No? For as surely as any junkie, she was addicted to Holt, to his deeply soothing voice, those blue eyes peering into her soul, and his touch... most of all his touch. She could lie to herself from now until doomsday, but in truth, she craved his touch, longed for it as the desert longs for rain, as flowers yearn for sunshine. And like the petals of a new, unfolding blossom leaning into light, her body swayed toward Holt.

"Yes," she heard a voice respond, unrecognizable as her own.

Holt smiled, and suddenly it didn't matter whose voice had spoken.

It was her answer, and it was the right one.

Chapter Eleven

Casey watched him as he drove. One of Grace's phrases, "handsome as sin," popped into her mind, and she decided it must surely be sinful for anyone to be so absolutely, wonderfully handsome. She couldn't help but admire the way Holt's rust-colored Western shirt fitted his broad shoulders. As usual, the sleeves were rolled to midforearm in a manner Casey thought incredibly sexy. She watched the way his hands rested, fingers negligently wrapped around the steering wheel, yet never doubted for a moment his complete control. Just as he was in complete control of his life, sure of himself, his world and his place in it. How marvelous to know such self-confidence, Casey thought, particularly since her own short supply dwindled to nothing as they rode toward Holt's ranch. Why hadn't she the courage to walk away from this man? No, not walk—run. Every time they were together, she grew more and more dependent on the way he made her feel. He made her feel good. Cherished. Protected. Lov—

"Here we are."

Casey yanked herself out of her thoughts, to discover they were parked in the driveway beside Holt's house. Recollections of her previous visit were shadowy night images, but even in the dark and as tired as she had been, the one word Casey associated with Holt's home was *warm*.

His house was a modern version of a Spanish hacienda, complete with red-clay-tiled roof, white-bricked exterior and black, wrought-iron trim. The lawn, lush, green and beautifully kept, swept from an arcade along the front of the two-story building. Even a darkening sky and the threat of a summer storm failed to deter her photographer's eye from a rapid judging of angles, light and shadow, and the mental snapping of a hundred different shots. The architecture, like the owner, was solid, substantial and made a statement for grace, power and simplicity.

"Your view of my home was a bit limited on your first visit. Come inside, and I'll give you the grand tour." As usual, he held out his hand, and, as usual, she took it.

As Holt showed her his home, Casey realized he was showing her bits and pieces of the man he had worked so hard to become. The house had been designed and built to eliminate wasted space and with an eye toward openness and maximizing light, modern in every sense, yet cozy and warm, using rich earth tones splashed with navy, hunter green, rust and peach. Traditional furnishings, sprinkled with antique accent pieces, evoked a feeling of solid strength tempered with ageless beauty.

"It's ... absolutely beautiful," she said as they ended the tour in the kitchen.

"Thanks. I tried to talk Grace into living out here, but she wouldn't have it. Said she was too old to live with anyone, and I was too young to give up my privacy."

"But I'll bet she still cooks for you."

"Occasionally. But I have a housekeeper who cleans and does most of the cooking."

"Except for scrambled eggs," she added, remembering his tenderness.

"Yeah," he grinned, remembering her vulnerability. "Except for scrambled eggs."

"You must be very...happy here." Casey couldn't keep the longing from her voice, any more than she could keep from staring into his eyes.

I could be, Holt thought, never realizing until that very moment why he hadn't been completely happy in his house. Without someone to share it with, it was just a place to sleep and eat, not to *live* in.

"Well, as far as I can see," Casey said, "you've got a perfect life."

"Almost," he said, his voice husky. She was dressed in the same, softly sexy, peasant blouse and full skirt she'd worn the night of the dance. A slight movement of her head swung dark hair and offered a glimpse of a golden earring. The metal caught the light and sparkled, recalling a vivid memory of lifting the warm circlet aside in order to place his lips against her skin. Soft, dewy skin, his memory added.

He cleared his throat. "I, uh, I'm afraid I'm going to have to break a promise."

"A promise?" she asked, inhaling deeply, drawing the fragrance of his after-shave into her lungs. She licked her lips, fully expecting to taste him on her skin.

At the unintentionally seductive gesture Holt's whole body clenched, and he knew he'd made a major error in judgment, inviting her to his house for a cozy dinner. How could he be in the same room with Casey and not want to take her into his arms and pleasure her? Pleasure them both.

"Yeah. I promised you no interruptions, but one of my mares decided to be very uncooperative, picking tonight to foal. I'll have to check her progress during the evening." *Thank God. At least it will give me a few moments to cool my jets and prevent me from drooling over her like a sex-starved animal.*

"I don't mind," she said, smiling sweetly one second, and killing his hopes in the next. "Could I . . . would you mind if I went with you?"

"Fine. No, that's fine." He stepped back. "We, uh… Are you hungry?"

"Starved."

"Good." Running his palms flat against the legs of his jeans, Holt wondered how in the hell he would survive an entire evening of wanting her.

The expected interruption came while they were eating their salads. Holt's foreman, John, a wiry cowboy with a weathered face and a toothy grin, announced that they should "git to the barn, pronto."

Inside the barn, at the end of a row of stalls was a penned area at least three times the size of the other stalls. As they approached the pen, Holt held Casey's hand and bent his head to hers.

"Lady Gray's not snooty about watchers, but it'd be better if you stand very still and speak softly, so we don't upset her. Mares can get downright stubborn sometimes if they feel they've drawn a crowd."

"I don't blame them," Casey whispered.

Holt squeezed her hand as they lightly stepped up to the foaling stall. The soon-to-be-mother, a chestnut-brown mare with a white blaze on her forehead, stood amid clean straw, her swollen belly tight with the anticipation of birth. At Casey and Holt's arrival, the horse turned her head, looked at them for a second, then gave a short whinny, as if granting permission for them to stay.

"How's she doin', John?" Holt inquired softly.

"Right as rain. Gonna be a fine young 'un." The foreman lovingly stroked the animal's neck and forehead as she fidgeted.

"Is she in pain?" Casey asked.

"Not really," Holt said close to her. "She's just like every other mother, anxious to see her baby."

As Casey watched, the mare went down onto her fore-legs, then rolled to her side, breathing hard. A contraction pulled at her huge, distended abdomen. In a matter of min-utes the front hooves and nose of the newborn made their appearance in the world. The actual birthing process was over almost before Casey realized it. One minute the mare was laboring and the next the foal was born.

"It's a filly," John said proudly. "Pretty little thing, ain't she?" The latest addition to Holt's stock blinked big, brown eyes at its new world. Identical coloring and a white-blazed forehead, still wet from the birthing, undeniably stamped the baby as Lady Gray's.

"A real beauty," Holt agreed, flashing his own proud smile.

Casey noticed mother and baby were both lying quietly. "Are they all right?" she whispered worriedly.

"Yes. In a minute they'll be talking up a storm—"

Before he could complete his sentence, Lady Gray began to lick the foal, inspecting the little body very much the same way a human mother counts fingers and toes. Then she whinnied to her offspring, and the baby answered with a series of squeaky nickers. Astonished, Casey realized the two were communicating. Muzzle to muzzle, mother and child engaged in an age-old interaction. Casey felt privi-leged, yet somewhat embarrassed, as if she was eavesdrop-ping on a private conversation never meant for human ears.

Her fingers itched to hold a camera, to capture this won-drous miracle of birth and bonding. Witnessing the begin-ning of the life cycle, Casey was awed and suitably humbled. She had never seen anything more life affirming.

Tenderly the horse nuzzled her baby, "talking" softly. Through nature's implementation of God's marvelous plan, she seemed to be saying, "This is life, little one. Go ahead. Don't be afraid." As the baby struggled to face the world on wobbly legs, Casey felt hot tears trickle down her cheeks.

Totally unaware of her actions, much less their motivation, she moved closer to Holt, slipping her arm around his waist.

Encircling her shoulders with his arm, Holt drew her snugly against his side and said softly, "The foal will start to nurse in a few minutes—" He looked down into Casey's face and words died; indeed, speaking was impossible. Joy, so stunningly powerful that it was breathtaking, shone in her eyes. Her creamy skin was translucent with a soft glow, almost ethereal in the muted light around the foaling stall.

And tears glistened like crystal raindrops on her pale cheeks.

Holt had never seen anything more incredibly, utterly beautiful in his whole life. He wanted to wrap himself in her beauty. Wanted to love her until all the joy and wonder he saw on her face infused her soul and his. He wanted to be in her, with her, *for* her so badly that the wanting was a soul-deep ache. Oblivious to his foreman's discreet disappearance, Holt's trembling hand collected a new tear, slowly transferring it from her skin to his lips.

He tasted her. Tasted her salty-sweet innocence and fragile beauty of spirit, imbibing it into his body, heart and soul. The realization that she had gone through most of her life without knowing how precious and unique she was filled Holt with a primitive rage, tempered only by the knowledge that love was the ultimate healer. He offered a silent prayer that his love would be enough.

Casey raised blurry eyes to Holt's, and her heart threatened to stop beating. His already moist fingertip skimmed his lower lip, barely avoiding the mustache, then returned for another crystalline drop.

This time he painted her lips with the tear.

The feather-light touch set off a riot of sensation so startlingly sensual and arousing Casey closed her eyes, dizzy with tremors of excitement. Turbulent emotions rocked her, and she clung to the only security in her reeling world. She held on to Holt. Slowly she opened her eyes and looked at him, hopelessly caught in the whirlpool of deep blue.

He was going to die if he didn't kiss her. If he couldn't feel her mouth under his right now, this very instant, he would perish on the spot.

With a certainty born of need, Casey knew his kiss and only his kiss could prevent her world from spinning off into space, could stop her from being whipped away into some vast blackness.

He inched his mouth downward, ever so slowly, brushing her trembling lips ever so lightly. Her lips parted, offering honeyed temptation and gentle welcome, seeking, tasting his mouth.

Oblivious to rumblings of the impending storm, to their surrounding, indeed to anything but the touch, taste and heat of each other, the kiss went from wanting to needing in the time it took for his tongue to sweep across hers.

She was lost. Lost to this man, this kiss. Lost to her own desire. She wanted Holt to kiss her, wanted it desperately the moment she looked into his eyes, need shimmering through her body in a flashing bolt of heat. If she could have found her voice, she would have begged him to kiss her.

Hot…sweet…wet. She tastes good. So good. Hot, clear through. He was hot, clear through. Hot and thick, and he wanted Casey so badly it hurt to breathe. But not here. She deserved a bed fit for a queen and satin sheets. He couldn't give her either, but he could give himself, wanted to give himself.

The realization shot through Holt, breaching the last barrier of his defenses, dissolving the last of his doubts. If ever the question of his trusting Casey had been an issue, it no longer was.

He trusted her. With his heart. His love. His soul.

Thunder rumbled across the heavens, and lightning streaked the night sky. Shades of gray, white and black thrown through the barn's open door competed with light and shadows.

"Wh-what's that?" Casey asked breathlessly, dizzy from the kiss, feeling her lips begin to swell from his tender torment.

"We're in a storm," Holt said, not even considering taking shelter from the sensual hurricane that was whipping their emotions with a force powerful enough to blow away the world. This was one storm he intended to ride out, one storm he hoped would wash away both their pasts and carry them toward a future. Together. He kissed her cheek, avoiding her mouth only because he knew if he took her lips again, now, he might not be able to stop.

Slow and easy, cowboy. Holt knew her body longed for his, and he knew what tremendous courage it must have taken for her to risk giving herself to him. Such trust made him weak with tenderness and made him want the night to be perfect for her.

"We, uh . . . we'll have to make a run for it."

Reluctantly Casey slipped out of his embrace. He held her hand as they headed toward the barn's entrance, headed toward an inevitable fate. They paused at the door, their bodies outlined by flashes of lightning as they looked into each other eyes.

Windblown fringes of the driving rain wet her face as Holt's hand settled on the side of her neck. Darkly velvet hair danced across his wrist, silken fingers reaching to hold him to her. Casey's hand found his waist, absorbing the warmth, power and energy rushing through his body.

Lips parted, her face lifted to his, Holt had no choice but to kiss her. No choice but to indemnify her for a loss she admitted only in nightmares, realizing fully his own commitment in doing so. The realization gave him the strength to tamp his passion for the sake of a deeper desire.

He lowered his head.

She rose on tiptoe, met him halfway.

The kiss was a preamble, a promise of things to come. Of the night to come. His tongue traced the seam of her lips, tenderly slipped inside and filled her with warmth and moisture. Holt's warmth. Holt's moisture. And she longed for him to fill her woman's body the same way, yet at the same time feared that fulfillment.

The kiss deepened.

He remembered holding her while she cried and while she slept, remembered waking up next to her and thinking how right she felt in his bed, in his life.

She remembered waking up next to him. Remembered him telling her he wanted her naked, lying beside him at sunrise, wanted her as he had no other woman.

And God help her, she wanted him as she had no other man.

"Ready?" he whispered hoarsely, ending the kiss with a series of tiny kisses at the corner of her mouth, as if he couldn't bear to withdraw from her sweetness all at once.

Ready. One word, yet it asked a question she both wanted and feared to answer. Her head knew he referred to racing for cover from the storm, but her heart recognized the deeper significance in his words. And she couldn't help but wonder if they were merely dashing for temporary shelter from the tempest of their mutual attraction, or sprinting toward a future together. Was she ready to rush into love? Gazing into Holt's eyes, Casey knew she wasn't rushing into anything. She was born for this man, this moment. He was her destiny. A magician, a banisher of dreams, who had wrapped himself around her heart, a bandage covering her wounded spirit and soul.

And he drew her gently from the dark corners.

Air thick with more than one variety of storm-tossed turbulence, Holt waited for her answer. Prayed for her answer.

"Ready." The wild, hungry wind almost snatched the single word away.

Holt heard it. And his heart nearly burst with joy. He gave her hand a gentle squeeze and pulled her with him into the rainy night, into the maelstrom.

Breathless and dripping wet, they dashed onto the covered patio at the back of the ranch house just as the sky opened up, its renewed angry grumbling accompanied by fresh torrents of rain. Sheets of water poured off the patio's overhang, curtaining them from the rest of the world.

"Whew! Made it just in time." Holt said, stomping rain from his boots. He scoured his face with his hands and raked tributaries of water from his hair, then knuckled moisture from his mustache.

Casey tried to wring the river of water from the sodden mass of her hair, but finally gave up. It was too heavy, too wet to do anything but cling wherever it fell. Her clothes were worse. They were a second skin plastered to her body, particularly the blouse. Hopelessly trying to pluck the saturated garment from her breasts, she glanced up, straight into the starved-for-softness hunger in Holt's eyes.

"We're going to catch...our..." His hot, heavy gaze devoured her.

Light from inside the house danced over her body, glittered on soft, glowing wet skin. She was his Venus wet from the sea, a sleek she-cat, damp from the rain forest. Rain-darkened tendrils of hair fell across her neck and shoulders, cascaded over her breasts like silken fingers attempting to shield her from his burning gaze. The wet fabric clung to her, molded her as he longed to. He could see the delicate outline of her breasts, not too round, not too small. He saw the silhouette of her nipples, hard from the chilling rain. He saw... not enough. Not nearly enough.

Casey felt as if he could see right through the fabric to her skin, felt his eyes caress her, stroke her. A white-hot tingle kindled at the hardened peak of her nipple, curling around and through her flesh, left her aching for the feel of Holt's hand—his mouth. If the blouse vanished, would he touch what his smoldering gaze so hotly caressed? Would she want him to? *Yes. Oh, yes, a thousand times, yes.* She envisioned his mustache grazing against her breasts. Skimming her tummy. Stroking...

He burned to touch her. *Easy,* he reminded himself, knowing her vulnerability.

"Casey, I..." He swallowed hard, trying to quench his desire. Trying and failing. "We, uh...we better go inside."

She was neither brave nor experienced, but she knew he would never touch her unless he was positive she wanted to be touched.

"Kiss me first."

"Casey, listen—"

"Please."

His fingertip against her lips silenced her, then moved away, so quickly she might have imagined it.

"I told you, never beg." His hands reached to stroke her cheek, then stopped. "Sweetheart, if I kiss you, I'll touch you. And if I touch you..." He swallowed around the lump in his throat. "I'm not sure any power on earth could stop me from making love to you."

Without looking away she said, "I understand."

"Do you? Do you understand what's happening here? You're a fire in my blood. I didn't know it was possible for a man to want a woman as badly as I want you. But not just your body, though God knows..." He closed his eyes briefly, struggling for the strength and presence of mind not to slip the few flimsy restraints on his control. "I can think of nothing more wonderful at this moment than being buried so deep inside you I don't know where I stop and you begin, but...I want more. I want *you*. Everything you are. And I want you to want me."

His words made her bold, summoned courage from an unknown well deep within herself. This was Holt. This was right, her heart assured her.

Translucent blue eyes stared unwaveringly back at him. "Kiss me, Holt."

His heartbeat faltered, then started again with a lurch. Blood pumped through his veins like a runaway train, drummed loudly in his ears. At first he thought he'd wanted to hear the words so badly he had imagined them. Then he thought he had merely misunderstood. Then he thought . . . oh, hell, he thought he was going crazy.

When he didn't answer immediately, Casey's courage sagged but didn't vanish. She waited, half afraid he wouldn't respond, half afraid he would, completely certain she loved him enough to conquer both fears. Still holding his gaze with hers, Casey's trembling hand sought the elasticized edge of the blouse. . . .

And slowly pushed downward.

In a heartbeat his hand covered hers, halting her motion. His eyes asked, *Are you sure?*

Hers answered, *Yes. More sure than I've been about anything in my life.*

Holt's body was so hard and thick he couldn't breathe. Both hands rested on her bare shoulders. Slowly, ever so slowly, giving her time to change her mind, time to say no, he moved the wet material down her upper arms—the neckline glided to the top of her breasts. Down to her elbows—the ruffle stopped, precariously captured by pouting nipples. With his heartbeat hammering through every cell in his body, he rested his palms ever so lightly against her sweet fullness and pushed the snagged garment down . . . down. . . . His hands fell away and breath stoppered his throat.

She was perfection.

Raindrops glistened on the column of her throat, tiny crystals infused with light sprinkling miniature rainbows on her skin. Her breasts rose and fell in a tantalizing rhythm that quickened as he watched.

"You're so . . . incredible. All soft and pink, the color of dawn. God, you take my breath away, you're so perfect." He *had* to touch her or die. Trembling with excitement and anticipation, his hand sculpted her sweet fullness.

The raging storm had nothing on this moment. Contact was incandescent, shimmering through his body, hot, fast, sizzling.

Every inch of Casey's skin was static with scorching sensations, yet she felt weightless, anchored to earth only by the fiery feel of Holt's hands holding her breasts.

The pads of his thumbs petted aching crests, and Casey gasped for air. "Kiss me. I need you to kiss me," she whispered, her voice urgent with passion.

This time he gave no arguments, no explanations. He gladly granted her wish, his tongue taking blistering possession of her mouth.

"I w-want to touch you," she whispered as his tongue left the soft wetness of her mouth long enough to trace a path to her ear.

"Then touch me. Whatever you want. All you want."

The metal snaps of his Western shirt made a muted, popping sound as they gave way to insistent fingers. Shaky hands pulled and tugged the wet fabric, peeling the material away from his body until his chest was as bare as hers. She looked into Holt's eyes, surprised at the depth of arousal reflected in their blue-black pools. Tentatively her hands touched his warm, damp chest. For long seconds her slender hands remained still, then she began to caress the softly curling hairs and hard-muscled beauty. When her flesh grazed his stiff, male nipple, a harsh gasp hissed between his lips.

"You're killing me by degrees, darlin'." His hands caressed her smooth back and carefully eased her closer, closer.

"Am I?"

"Don't you know what it does to a man when a woman wants him?"

"No," she said, honestly.

"Makes him crazy and hard with desire."

"Are you crazy and . . . ?"

"Yes, and yes." He coaxed her the last few inches, bringing them chest to chest, warmth to warmth, desire to desire. She melted against him, and Holt thought he would surely lose his mind.

He groaned.

She breathed a tattered sigh.

Then he kissed her. Hot and deep, making the kiss hotter and deeper with each thrust of his tongue. The heat rose from rain-slick bodies like vapor from a fiery volcano. They sweltered in its seductive steam until Holt knew he must have all of her against all of him, no barriers, only flesh to flesh.

Carefully he reached behind her and hooked a finger into the handle of the sliding glass door, giving it a shove. Slipping one arm beneath her thighs while keeping the other across her back, he swept her into his arms, crossed the threshold and kicked the open, glass panel shut with a whack. As they reached the top of the second-floor landing, the lights flickered momentarily. Then the entire house was plunged into darkness.

Casey gasped.

"Don't worry, sweetheart," Holt said, his husky voice inches from her ear. "I've got all the electricity we need right here in my arms."

A brief kiss later, he skillfully navigated the way into his bathroom, where he set her on a plush, oval rug. A skylight in the center of the ceiling framed a lightning-streaked sky, offering flashes of illumination. Outside the storm raged. Thunder and lightning split the night sky. Inside, the only sounds of importance were the whispered preliminaries in their ultimate game of seduction.

Wet fabric gliding over skin. A gentle plop sounded as her blouse landed in the nearby bathtub, followed closely by a second, then a third as her skirt and his shirt joined the pile. Leather-soled sandals kicked free, tripping over the rug's edge to skid across the tile floor. Boots thudded on plush pile, then scooted the way of her sandals. The snap of jeans. A zipper's rasp. Denim tugged over powerful hair-roughened legs. Nylon sliding down slender, smooth legs.

As Holt whipped a towel from a rack and rubbed dry her rain-dampened body, Casey knew a fleeting moment of doubt. What if she had closed herself off from love and tenderness for so long that she couldn't be the woman Holt needed? The only intimacy she had known had been based on fraud. What if she didn't . . . couldn't please Holt?

As if he could read her mind and wanted to banish such thoughts, Holt made one more deliberate sweep of her body with the towel. But this time, instead of rubbing, he brushed with maddening, feather-light strokes, transforming mere terry cloth into an erotic instrument of arousal as it flicked across sensitive breasts, fanned over tightened buttocks and swept down her thighs. While lightning filled the sky, their breaths, his hard, hers quick, swirled around the movements, choreographing the scene into a sensual pantomime in black and white.

Holt's unique method of distraction worked. All thoughts of the past were whisked away as the towel sailed onto the tiled floor.

Guiding her to his bed, he deftly flipped back coverlet and sheet in one quick motion. Lightning danced again outside the bedroom windows, casting her body in ivory relief as he gazed into her wide eyes.

"Are you frightened?" Worshipfully he brushed a strand of damp hair from her cheek.

"A—a little," she whispered, more than slightly surprised and delighted her fear hadn't compelled her to run, as it always had before.

"So am I. A little."

"Y-you, scared?"

"Because I've never been with a woman as beautiful as you, as sweet as you."

"You th-think I'm ... pretty?"

Holt understood the motive behind her question and only hoped he could convince her of the truth.

He smiled, gently. "Yes, I think you're *pretty*. I think you're the loveliest, most exquisitely perfect woman God ever created."

"Holt?"

"Yes, baby."

"It's been a long time. What if—?"

Sliding his fingers through the hair at her temples, he held her, his eyes burning into hers.

"There's no right or wrong, baby, just you and me. Whatever we want, whatever we feel is right."

"I—I'm not sure I know what I want. Before it was just—"

"There is no before. Only now."

"Only now," she agreed, loving him more than she thought it possible to love anyone. Whether from relief or pleasure he didn't know, but her sigh drifted about him and his heart skipped a couple of beats.

On a low groan Holt fitted his mouth to hers. His tongue stroked and demanded.

He eased her onto the bed. Stretching along her length, he captured her lips, molding their bodies, allowing her to feel his hardness, to know how much he wanted her.

"Ah, sweet heaven. Holding you is like stepping into a flame, being consumed with your sweet fire," he said, taking her mouth in a slow, savoring kiss.

If she was flame, he was fuel. His touch, his words stoked the fire into an inferno. She fitted her body to his, seeking more of him, more of the heat.

Holt felt the hunger in Casey, the hunger she barely recognized as hers, the hunger he longed to satisfy. He cautioned himself to go slowly, all the time wondering how he could possibly accomplish such a feat when she arched against him, as she had the instant his tongue touched hers.

"We'll play it anyway you want, sweet woman. Tell me what you want. If you want slow and easy, I'll drive us both to the brink of madness with patience. If you want hot and deep, we'll just get to the madness quicker."

She couldn't think, couldn't breathe. Their combined heat was suffocating. "Yes. Both. All."

Good intentions warred with primitive instincts for possession of his willpower. Tenderness fought need. And lost. A soft chuckle rumbled from his chest, he lowered his head and captured a nipple between his teeth. "That's how it is with me. I want all of you. All at once."

She gasped as his tongue replaced his teeth and he drew her into his mouth, suckling her. The flame he had ignited deep within Casey blazed higher, threatening to reduce her to ashes. His lips moved to the valley between her breasts, leaving her nipples wet and wanting. Slowly he licked a path between those soft mounds of flesh, slipping ever downward. Detouring around her navel, his wickedly seductive tongue made a game of discovering the most sensitive spot on her tummy. He found it. Kissed it. Teased it. Casey's stomach muscles tightened involuntarily, and a breath-stealing thrill speared her body and centered between her thighs.

Retracing the path to her passion-flushed breasts, his lips took her mouth as his hand found the hot, moist center of her heat. She moaned into his mouth and strained against his hand.

"That's it. Purr for me, kitten," he whispered, stringing a line of love bites from her kiss-swollen lips to her ear. "Sweet kitten. You're so *soft*. I need your softness, need to sink into it, lose myself in it. I need your softness as much as I need your fire.''

Casey wanted to tell him how loved she felt when she was with him, but couldn't. She could only feel as their hot, sweat-slick, eager bodies hungered for satisfaction. As their souls yearned for the fulfillment only they could give each other. As he moved over her, gently parting her legs, the first touch of his maleness against her moistness sent a shock wave of sensations exploding through her like chain lightning—swift, hot and electric. Eyes closed, she arched her hips into his.

''Open your eyes.''

Slowly, hazy with desire, she opened her eyes.

''I want to love you the way you were meant to be loved. Completely, forever.'' He sealed her lips with a bone-melting kiss. Staring into aqua pools he lifted his hand, positioning it over the one of hers resting beside her head. ''Take my hand.''

As she laced her fingers with his he entered her.

Her soft cry filled the room, and he filled her, his strength a sweet completion she'd never dreamed of. Instinctively she moved against him.

''Yes, yes. That's it, baby.'' He let her take as much of him as she wanted.

Casey's hips rotated slowly in response to a primitive demand she could no more deny than she could deny her next breath. She tried to tell him she wanted all he could give her. All of his love. All of his body. Tried to tell him she loved him, but the words disintegrated with the beginning of tiny eruptions deep within her body. Small explosions that grew and grew until a conflagration swept over her, carrying her higher and higher, swirling, flinging her up and into a fathomless, wonderful oblivion she'd never imagined.

Body sweat-sheened, restraint barely held, Holt felt the explosions and gloried in her release as she came apart in his arms.

Thunder ripped the night. Lightning seared the sky in celebration.

"Yes. My beautiful...." He kissed her mouth. His tongue skated over her neck, her collarbone, then back up the column of her throat and into her waiting mouth.

Casey cried out his name as her body went wild with a renewed blaze of white-hot bursts of rapture. Holt's control snapped, and he poured himself into her as they climaxed as one.

The storm rent the night, moving across the land, leaving in its wake fresh-washed earth and the promise of a rainbow with the sunshine. A new day, a new beginning.

Chapter Twelve

Dawn, pink, shiny and new, peeked around the edges of the bedroom's draped windows like an anxious child on Christmas morning, its warmth bathing the lovers in the softness of sunrise.

Wide-awake and feeling more contented than she could ever remember, Casey had spent the last half hour watching Holt sleep. And during that time she had reached several extremely profound conclusions. Namely, that Holt Shelton was the tenderest, sweetest, handsomest, most sensitive—and enough other praiseworthy adjectives to stretch from New York to San Francisco—man in the entire world. "Wonderful" did not adequately describe the man lying beside her.

Quite simply, he was the most perfect man on earth, and wonder of wonders, miracle of miracles . . . he wanted her.

The other startling discovery Casey made was that she was a sensual woman, a creature both giving and seeking pleasure. Before, the only vent for her passion had been through her photographs. On a detached, spiritual plane, light and color had substituted for a more substantial kind of feeling. And had been a poor substitute, at that.

Studying Holt's face, Casey wondered what absolutely, positively right thing she had done in her life to warrant such joy. Her gaze wandered over the lean frame outlined beneath the sheet. His shoulder, the same shoulder that had absorbed her tears and sheltered her from the storm. So broad, so powerful. His arms, the same arms that had carried her, held her. So warm, so strong. His hands, the same hands that had stroked her, caressed her, given her so much pleasure. So big, yet so gentle. His hips, the same hips...
Recalling exactly the delicious capability of Holt's hips brought a flush to her already sleep-warm skin. She wanted to touch him so badly her fingers actually throbbed with the need.

Last night had been beyond any hope, any dream. Holt had loved her, loved her body more sweetly, perfectly than she'd ever thought possible. Not only had he introduced her to an unbelievably breathtaking level of erotic awareness, he had also filled her empty soul with light and beauty. And Casey had reveled in every gloriously sensual moment.

Her gaze roamed again over the body partially draped by the sheet. Over long, powerful legs, trim hips, a broad chest, and right into beloved, sapphire eyes.

Neither spoke, content simply to look at each other.

Her mouth is swollen from my kisses.

His hair is mussed from my fingers.

I remember drinking every soft sound, every sweet, sexy, cry from her mouth.

I remember tunneling my fingers through his hair, loving the way its coarse thickness caressed my skin.

She's so beautiful.

He's so beautiful.

Unable to withstand the force of her need to touch him, Casey simply gave in and stroked a whisker-stubbled cheek. "I ... I've never felt like this before."

Holt's hands trembled as he pulled her against him and nestled her head snugly into the crook of his shoulder. He stroked her hair. "And how do you feel?"

"Wonderful, marvelous ... complete."

Knowing how difficult it must have been for her to admit her feelings to herself, much less to him, made the treasured words all the more precious. He felt a smile hike the corner of his mustache. "Yeah?"

Against his shoulder he felt her lips curl into a smile. "Very yeah," Casey said, subtly, naturally, fitting her body sweetly to his. She lightly kissed his bare skin. He tasted of sleep, faint, lingering traces of his after-shave and some indefinable flavor that could only be labeled Holt. Her Holt.

"Me, too."

"Last night was the most special night of my life. Thank you, Holt."

"You're welcome, but I don't want your appreciation. I want ..." *Your love,* he wanted to say, but didn't. "... you to be happy. I want to make you happy." *For the rest of our lives.*

Casey drew away to look into his eyes. "You do. Very happy. So happy, I wish we could stay right here, locked away from the rest of the world...." Tilting her head, she glanced heavenward and sighed. "Forever."

Dark, tangled waves of hair tumbled down her bare back. Taking advantage of the delicately exposed column of her throat, he placed a string of kisses from the base of her neck to her ear. "Don't see any flaws in your plan."

The soft, tinkling notes of her laughter danced through the room. "I'm afraid wishing ... ahh ... is all we can do." Holt's tongue investigated the rim of her ear. "I have to go-o-o, oh-h-h ..." He nibbled her earlobe, lightly nipping her flesh. "... to work."

"What a mundane thing to say while you're in your lover's arms."

Lover. My lover. The word scampered through Casey's mind, and snuggled in a corner of her heart. *Holt and I are lovers.* Once more her heart threatened to exceed her body's capacity to house it. "My boss might not...ah, that feels...not accept making, ooh...love, oh...to her nephew as a suitable excuse for being late."

"Are you going to be late?" He cupped the fullness of one ripe breast, his thumb feathering a taut crest.

"I...think...so." Casey's body coiled tight with need. A need she had never even recognized until one handsome and very persistent cowboy entered her life. Make that deliciously persistent, Casey thought, as Holt's hands treasured her breasts.

"I know so," he said, filling her waiting mouth with his tongue as he lovingly pulled at the pebble-hard peak. "God, your mouth is sweet and soft...wet and warm. Just like your body. I love the way you fit me. Tight, hot. Perfect." His wide hands sailed over her rib cage to the spot where her waist dipped to smooth, trim hips. "Your body was made for mine."

Every caress, every touch, every embrace from Holt was a gift from heaven. Casey gloried in his hands on her body.

"Yes." A harsh breath hissed from her lips as his hand coasted over her tummy, down her thighs, caressing, parting. He touched her in the most elemental, most intimate way, the essentially primeval way man had touched woman since the beginning of time. He stroked her. Petted her. Drove her to the edge of the sweet abyss until she ached with the brand of hot, slick madness only he could create, only he could cure. She cried out his name, softly.

Outside dawn paint-brushed the coming day with more light, more color. Pale pink deepened to coral fringed with amethyst as it flowed through the window and tiptoed across the carpet.

"My beautiful, sweet woman." He brushed his mustache over the peak of her breast and thrilled to watch it pearl into hardness. "You like that?"

"Y-yes, yes."

His tongue duplicated the path of his mustache, laving tender flesh. "And that?"

A husky moan was her answer.

"You were made to be loved. Made for me to love."

"I want you . . . inside me," she whispered on a ragged breath.

"Not yet, darlin'. Not yet. First I want to see you come apart in my hands. I want to watch your face, and I want you to watch mine as your warm honey melts over me." His voice caressed her every bit as sensually as his touch. The edge of madness came closer with each word, each touch.

Dawn inched closer, coral and amethyst giving way to vermilion, magenta and violet.

"Open your eyes, darlin'. Look into my eyes and know how precious you are."

Eyelids lazy with the wine of pleasure opened, and Casey saw herself reflected in sapphire pools darkened with desire and a soul-deep longing.

Casey threaded eager fingers into his golden-brown hair and pulled his head down to hers for a kiss. "I want you," she murmured against his lips. "I . . . want . . ." He entered her slowly, igniting the fuse to the longed-for explosion that would hurl her over the edge and into the abyss. ". . . you."

"I'm yours. Now. Forever." He rocked against her. Higher. Harder. Taking them both to the stars and beyond. As they tumbled into the sweet, glorious heat, twisting willingly in its flame, the sunrise spilled across the bed, filling the room in a golden blaze, raining topaz fire over their love-sated bodies.

Casey was late to work. Hurriedly tying an apron around her waist, she almost jumped out of her skin at the sound of

Grace's voice directly behind her. "Lazybones this morning, huh?"

"What?"

"Overslept?"

"Oh, yeah. Sorry, I—"

"No sweat, honey. Happens to all of us. Besides, if a few extra minutes sleep could make my skin all soft and glowin' like yours, I'd sack in every day."

"Uh, thanks." Casey wondered if Grace would be so understanding and complimentary if she knew the real reason for her tardiness. Her hand automatically went to her cheek, as if to verify Grace's observation. Did she look different today? She certainly felt different: happy and content in a way she'd never experienced in her life.

And all because she loved Holt Shelton.

Warmth from such happiness could do more than make skin glow and faces light up. It could keep a cold loneliness at bay. It could light up dark corners for a lifetime.

A lifetime? Did she want a lifetime with Holt? The answer emblazoned itself on her heart and mind in bold print. *Yes.*

Joy flooded Casey's heart, but just as quickly reality dammed the waves of elation. Before she could contemplate spending the rest of her life with Holt, she had to tell him the truth about herself and why she had come to Crescent Bay in the first place. Casey knew what she must do, but she also knew the risk involved in telling him. What if he turned away from her?

The thought was too painful, too all-the-way-to-the-bone-hurtful to consider.

The fact that she had effectively resigned from the assignment eased Casey's conscience only slightly. She had to tell Holt. And soon. But not yet, her heart pleaded. Not until she had wrapped herself in this marvelous happiness for a while. It was so warm, and she had been cold for such a very long time.

Satisfied with her self-indulgent stay of execution, Casey worked through the morning, literally with a song in her heart and a smile on her lips. When the lunch rush wound down, the already-glorious day took on added shine.

"Hi."

At the sound of Holt's familiar voice, Casey swung around from making a fresh pot of coffee, stringing a trail of grounds from serving station to counter. "Hi," she replied, more than slightly breathless.

She smiled.

He smiled.

"How are you?" She was exquisite, delicious. His.

"Fine. And you?" He was marvelous, sexy. Hers.

"Fine. Great, in fact."

"Wonderful," Casey whispered. His firebrand gaze touched her everywhere, and she marveled at her shamelessness.

"Yeah, me, too." Her skin, flushed to a deep rose, only stirred Holt's desire to touch her.

Casey was more than fine, now that he was here. She had spent anxious moments wondering if any awkwardness would arise when they saw each other again. Casey had never felt less awkward in her life. Instead, she felt supremely comfortable. This was right. This was good.

She wished they were alone so she could tell him how handsome he looked, how much she wanted him, though only a few hours ago they had loved each other with a breathless wonder. Forcing herself to remember where they were, Casey tried to steady her voice as she asked, "How's Lady Gray?"

"Doing beautifully," Holt said, his gaze never leaving Casey's face.

"And the baby?"

"Goin' strong."

"That's nice." A long silence followed while they simply looked at each other. Finally Casey said, "Now that we've established we're both fine, mother and baby are fine, what should we talk about, the weather?''

"Last night's storm?" With three words he destroyed her good intentions and left a dizzying onslaught of erotic memories and sensations. Holt toweling her dry. Holt caressing her thighs and hips. Holt kissing her breasts....

"N-no, I don't think—"

"Will I see you tonight?"

His deep voice poured over her like the rain had poured over her skin last night, and her body responded in ways that would have shocked her yesterday. Today she reveled in her own sexuality. His words' double meaning tweaked an untapped coquettishness, still another facet of her sensuality that Holt had unveiled. "If you want to."

Did he want to? Did the stars want to shine? Memories of the sunrise painting her skin gold, filling the bedroom with brilliance, even as he filled her woman's body with his man's heat, washed over him.

He smiled again, the delicious, sexy little smile barely lifting the corner of his mustache and elevating her temperature several degrees. An erratic heartbeat thrummed in her ears.

"Oh, I definitely want to. Anything special you'd like to do?" Holt was delighted she felt comfortable enough with their relationship to tease. And he had several ideas about how they could spend their time together, all of which were very special.

"Can't think of anything in particular. You?"

"Hmm, possibly." His gaze rested on her breasts.

A soft, involuntary gasp escaped Casey's lips as her nipples tightened against the sheer fabric of her bra.

Holt heard the familiar sound, saw the melting look in her eyes, and had to stop himself from leaping over the counter and wrapping her in his arms right then and there. Instead he cleared his throat.

Casey glanced around to see if anyone else had taken note of her reaction, relieved they hadn't. "I'll, uh, leave the plans up to you. My shift ends at five."

"How long will it take you to change?"

"Not long."

"Shall I pick you up at five-thirty?"

"Five-fifteen."

They looked into each other's eyes and laughed a slightly naughty and very private laugh.

Holt didn't stay for lunch, and Casey decided his reasons had more to do with whetting an appetite than losing one. Mildly relieved, she admitted she was unsure how well her show of decorum would have withstood long minutes of watching Holt perform a task as simple and yet as sensual as putting food into his mouth. A shiver chased a memory of strong, white teeth nipping at the aching fullness of her breasts.

"Casey?"

She snapped out of her daydreams to find a distraught April beside her. "What?"

"Will you wait on the guy in the second booth?" She nodded toward a fortyish-looking man wearing a starched, Western shirt and an immaculate Stetson.

"Sure, but you usually—"

"It's Emmett Thomas, Jody's daddy. I hate to wait on him. Every time he comes in, he stares daggers at me."

"Why?"

The young waitress ducked her head, avoiding Casey's eyes. "Cause he knows Jody and I are...cause he thinks I'm trash and not nearly good enough for Jody." Gnawing her bottom lip, April heaved a sigh. "Reckon he's right."

"No, he's not," Casey insisted. "And you shouldn't let him intimidate you."

"Whaddya mean?"

"Don't let him undermine your self-confidence. April, you're a lovely, intelligent young woman. Any man, including Jody Lee, could count himself lucky to have you."

When April didn't respond, Casey followed a hunch and asked, "You think standing up to Emmett Thomas will only make matters worse for Jody, don't you?"

"Yes."

"What does Jody say?"

April's doe-soft eyes met Casey's. "That h-he's gonna keep on lovin' me, no matter what his daddy thinks. Jody takes up for me all the time."

Casey smiled. "A girl doesn't find a hero very often, April. Isn't it about time you showed Jody *he's* worth fighting for?"

"I s-suppose so."

"Maybe you could start by showing Mr. Thomas you're not afraid of him."

"B-but how can I—?"

"You're a good waitress, April. Just do your job. Give Jody's dad the same sweet smile and excellent service you offer to every other customer who walks through the door, and you'll be just fine."

"Just like that?" she asked incredulously.

"Just like that," Casey assured her.

April looked across the room at Jody's father, then back at Casey. "Jody *is* the best thing that ever happened to me."

"Then don't run away from this, April."

"I reckon I been running from myself for so long, I don't know any other way."

"Is that how you want to spend the rest of your life?"

The big, brown eyes blinked away a tear. She stared at Casey for long seconds, then finally said, "No. I wanna spend the rest of my life with Jody." With that, April picked up her order pad, squared her thin shoulders and walked toward the second booth.

"You've done somethin' I haven't been able to do in almost a year," Grace said, standing behind Casey. Both women's attention was riveted on the young waitress who bravely confronted her adversary.

"I hope I haven't sent her into the lion's den."

"You haven't. Emmett's ornery, but deep down he loves that boy of his. That's one thing he and April have in common, and it's as good a place as any to start." Grace sighed, picked up a rag and began wiping the counter. "Lord o' mercy, I'm glad I'm past all that foolishness."

April appeared to be holding her own, and Casey breathed a sigh of relief. "Foolishness?" she asked, turning her attention to the older woman.

"Yeah, you know, all that ragin' hormone stuff you young people seem to feel you can't live without."

"Are you trying to tell me your hormones have never taken a wild swing or two?"

A wrinkled hand bridged an ample hip, and Grace laughed. "Oh, yeah. A few times."

"Was there ever a love of your life?"

"Yeah. I reckon you could call him that. Gawd, but he was a handsome devil. And a smooth talker? Like molasses on a summer day," she said, answering her own question. "Lord, but that man could sell ice cubes to Eskimos."

"What happened?"

The cleaning motion stopped, and Grace stared into space, or perhaps back in time. Then she blinked, refocusing on Casey and today. "Just woke up one mornin' and he wasn't there anymore." Her voice was soft, wistful. Regretful.

"I'm sorry. I didn't mean to make you remember something you would rather forget."

"Ah, hell, honey. Don't give it another thought. That was so many years ago, it ain't hardly worth rememberin'. That kinda lovin' is best when you're young and full of passion . . . like you and Holt."

Casey was taken aback. Had Holt confided in his aunt? "How did—?"

"I got eyes, honey. And it don't take a genius to figure out what's goin' on, when the two of you strike sparks off each other like two pieces of flint. Just bein' in the same room with you is enough to make a body wanna crank up the air conditioner."

Grace chuckled. Casey blushed.

"Now, I've gone and made you think I don't approve." She placed a hand on Casey's arm, quickly adding, "And nothin' could be further from the truth." The teasing light went out of Grace's warm, brown eyes. "He needs a woman like you, Casey. Somebody real and honest. Somebody he can trust."

Grace's words yanked Casey's mental stay of execution right out from under her feet. *Somebody real. Somebody he can trust.* But she wasn't real, she was a fraud. And if Holt knew the truth, she would be the last person on earth he would deem trustworthy.

Suddenly the truth was a living, breathing demon clawing to be free, and Casey had an overwhelming urge to tell Grace everything, to unburden herself. But at whose expense? She might be free of the lies, but Holt would be faced with the knowledge that she was a fake and a phony. Once the "truth" was revealed, he might even regret loving her at all. She couldn't take the chance.

Run. Run and hide, her fears demanded, knowing full well that sooner or later she would have to face reality. She couldn't hide forever.

No, just until I share a few more dawns.

Holt arrived at her motel room at five-fifteen, on the dot. Casey's heart nearly shot out of her body when she opened the door and saw how breath-stealingly gorgeous he looked.

"Ready, darlin'?" He held out his hand.

Gazing into his handsome face, she again sensed the same need to purge herself as she had with Grace earlier in the day. But the need came in a poor second to the driving desire to be held in Holt's arms, to be a part of him.

"Ready," she replied, placing her hand in his.

During the following week Casey never regretted her decision. Each moment spent with Holt was savored, treasured, enjoyed to its fullest. They rode horseback across Holt's land, exhilarated as the wind whipped their hair and clothes.

And they made love.

They double-dated with Jody and April, behaving like teenagers. And they made love.

They watched a video about a child of one world befriending an abandoned creature from another world and shared tears.

And they made love.

They talked, joked and played, shouted for joy and whispered quietly. They talked about the future and avoided the past.

And always, always, they made sweet, hot love.

Sometimes their coming together was raw, swift and deep. Holt would scarcely glide into her welcoming, silky heat before they both slipped over the edge of the world. Other times their lovemaking would be torturously slow, maddeningly erotic to the point that one earth-shattering climax shuddered into another, and another, leaving their bodies glistening with sweat, sated beyond their wildest dreams.

They learned each other's likes and dislikes and became acquainted with habits, good and bad.

Holt discovered she didn't really function on all eight cylinders until after her morning shower.

Casey determined that his occasional insistence on oatmeal for breakfast qualified him as sadistic.

He uncovered her secret penchant for Disney movies, and marveled at her unique and expressive love affair with photography.

She acquainted herself with his often risqué sense of humor and understood his need to be part of the land, not just a landowner.

And through it all Casey *sensed* Holt was holding something back, perhaps a secret. Not a dark brooding kind of secret, but something that deeply troubled him. On several occasions she had the feeling he was a heartbeat away from confiding in her, then stopped himself. Most of the time Casey denied thoughts of secrecy on any level because of her own subterfuge, deciding that the inevitable functioned on its own timetable, and all she had was now, today. She continued to fool herself—right up to the moment Ramsey called, as she was preparing to join Holt at his ranch house.

"Hello, cookie. You've been out of touch."

"I know," Casey sighed. The inevitable was knocking at her door.

"Still enjoying the rustic life?" The sarcasm in his voice rankled.

"Yes."

"Still convinced you can't do the Tanner pictures?"

"Yes."

There was a long silence before Ramsey said, "I sure hate to hear that, gorgeous, because if you don't do it, someone else will have to."

His attitude grated on her nerves like fingernails across a blackboard. "Listen, Ramsey, if you're trying to bully me—"

"On the level, cookie." The tone of his voice was just that—on the level. Casey had heard the tone too many times to mistake it. "Say, don't they have newspapers out there in the boonies?"

"Of course they do," she said defensively. "What does that have to do with this assignment?"

"I told you the major studios are going all out for this Hollywood's Golden Anniversary thing. Well, they decided to do a Tanner/Garbo/Dietrich film festival and release all of their work in home video packages. The marketing scope of the project would blow your mind."

And blow Crescent Bay to hell, Casey thought, recalling Grace's description of the chaos during the last resurgence of Norah's films. The picture forming in Casey's mind was not a pretty one. "If what you say is true—"

"Not *if*, sweetie. It's a fait accompli. Made all the trade papers and most of the major city papers."

"It won't change a thing, H.A."

"I'm not above bribery."

"Are you talking about me?"

"Tanner."

Casey almost laughed. "It's been tried before. Besides, you don't have that much money."

"Then how about an employee? A maid, or butler, maybe."

"Ramsey, have you been living in a cave for the last thirty years? All of those avenues have been tried."

"But *not* in a long time," he said confidently. "Maybe she's mellowed in her old age."

"Then why hasn't she come forward with her own offer?"

"Listen, cookie. Eighteen or eighty, actresses are all alike in one respect. They *love* drama. Ten years have passed since anyone I know has actually approached her staff with a legitimate and *generous* offer. The magazine didn't even get to first base before the door was slammed in our corporate face. Maybe she's just waiting for the right moment. And believe you me, the moment couldn't get any righter. Not in her lifetime."

"I don't think she gives a damn about the money."

"You're probably right, but I still say, as I have from the very first, she can be got. We just need to find the right key."

"Well, I don't have it," Casey said flatly.

Ramsey's sigh was deep and long. "Look at it this way. She was invisible for twenty years after she left Hollywood. Since then a number of vague, long-distance, out-of-focus shots have surfaced. None of them worth much. I'm not asking for an eight-by-ten glossy, suitable for framing, just something good enough to beat the competition. Whaddya think?"

No response.

Another endless silence, then Ramsey's quiet, "If you refuse, I'll have to put another shooter on the assignment and right away. That's how big this thing has gotten. I don't have a choice, Casey. It's do-or-die time."

Casey was dying inside by creeping, tearing inches. She felt as if someone had sliced open her heart. Her first thought was to protect Holt, Grace, then all the others she had come to care for, not the least of whom was Norah Tanner herself. Without realizing it, Casey had become part of Crescent Bay. But more importantly, she was now deeply involved in what Crescent Bay represented—hard work, clean living, honest loving.

She had been closer to H. A. Ramsey than she had to her own father. He had been her friend, teacher, mentor and guardian angel. But he was wrong.

As wrong as she had been when she accepted the assignment. Because no matter what fancy words or professional trappings were applied, what she and Ramsey were doing was nothing less than invading privacy. Ramsey had preached from the public-has-a-right-to-know pulpit, and Casey had been a willing disciple. Until now. Now she saw clearly the difference between the true meaning of words such as *morality, virtue, ethics* and the interpretations of her fellow journalists. And the difference was vast. Daylight and dark. Right and wrong. And somehow she had to make Ramsey understand. Somehow she had to stop him.

"Cookie?"

She didn't reply.

"Cookie," he repeated, this time more urgently.

"You're probably not going to understand this, H.A., but I've come to terms with some not-so-simple truths."

"What the hell are you talking about?"

"I'm talking about honest self-evaluation, Ramsey. You should try it sometime. You might be surprised what you find."

"Yeah, yeah. And I'd probably find a press where my heart should be, and printer's ink flowing through my veins instead of blood, right?"

"No. But somewhere down the line the stories became more important than the people in them."

After a prolonged silence he cleared his throat and said, "Listen, cookie, I don't know what the hell is going on in that smart little head of yours, but we are still in the business of writing and photographing the news. Now, I'm going to ask you one more—one last—time. Are you going to complete this assignment?"

Casey's heart and self-respect dictated the only answer she could give. "Send your shooter, Ramsey, but tell him he'll have to get around me first."

"Casey, do you know what you're doing? Jesus, cookie, you've lost all perspective on reality since you left L.A. What the hell has happened to you?"

"A miracle," she said quietly.

"A what?"

"Love happened to me, H.A. I fell in love."

"Oh, God, that cop."

"Yes."

"Babe, that life isn't for you. C'mon home."

"I am home."

"Oh, and I suppose you're going to give up your career and can vegetables and diaper babies."

"I can base my career from any city—"

"That's crap, and you know it."

"Then I'll open a studio and take photographs of prize-winning vegetables and babies. You don't seem to understand, Ramsey. With Holt, with these people, I've found a peace I've never had, never thought I would have, and I won't walk away from it. But even without Holt I couldn't go ahead with the assignment, because it's wrong. We've been wrong, Ramsey."

"Wrong?"

"Maybe self-deluded is a more comfortable concept for you. Whatever label you choose, we have no right to invade Norah Tanner's privacy."

After several seconds he asked, "We're not going to be able to work around this, are we, cookie?"

"No."

"Okay," he said on a sigh. Casey thought his voice sounded much older than his fifty-two years. "But answer me this. In your search for self-truths, how did you handle facing lover-boy when he finds out who you are? And he *will* find out, you know. You're living a lie, babe, and sooner or later lies will catch up with you.

"You know I have to send someone, cookie. I've got no choice," he said finally.

"Neither do I."

Then Casey hung up on her lifelong friend, snatched up the bag once used to carry cameras and now containing a new, but scarcely worn silk nightgown, and blindly turned her back upon reality.

At that moment the only thing real, solid, worthwhile in her life was Holt—his arms holding her, his lips kissing her, his love protecting her.

Chapter Thirteen

Holt was standing outside talking with John, his foreman, when Casey wheeled her Volkswagen into the driveway and screeched to a halt. The minute she got out of her car, he knew something was wrong.

Casey walked directly to him, rose on tiptoe and regardless of John's shocked expression, kissed Holt on the mouth.

"I missed you," she said, her husky voice raking over him like a cat's softly serrated tongue.

"Uh, we can finish later, Holt." John tactfully retreated.

"Thanks," Holt said, without taking his eyes from Casey's face. "What's wrong?" he asked, soon as the foreman was out of earshot.

"Can't a girl kiss her guy without something being wrong?"

"Hey, I'm not complain—"

"Then shut up and kiss me."

Holt's eyes widened, then narrowed dangerously. "We aim to please, ma'am."

Her kiss was a challenge, demanding he wipe every thought from her mind except thoughts of his mouth, his tongue, his searing, all-consuming touch. Holt met the challenge and triumphed.

"Sweet hell, lady," he rasped, reluctantly dragging his lips from hers. "We're gonna need the fire department if you keep that up."

"I thought you weren't complaining," Casey breathed against his mouth.

"Darlin', what I'm doin' is hanging on by a thin thread, until I can get you out of your clothes and into bed."

"Then why are we standing here talking?"

"You got me."

"Exactly."

"Maybe I *should* put the fire department on standby."

"You won't have time."

An hour later, neither could remember getting from the driveway to the bedroom. Neither could remember anything but the way they made sweet, wild love.

Holt watched as Casey dozed somewhere in the netherworld between sleeping and waking. She sighed. Her breasts enticingly rose and fell, and he smiled.

She was some woman. His woman. Sweet and soft as a rose petal one minute and smoldering hot the next. Tonight she'd blazed.

Holt frowned. She was in a strange mood, one he'd never seen before. In their time together he had witnessed her happy, thoughtful, even sad, but never... He searched for a description of her humor and was surprised when the word *desperate* came to mind. Holt started to reject the idea, then changed his mind. There *was* a desperation about her, a burning need over and above physical desire.

Tonight he'd found her startlingly bold, initiating their lovemaking with a passion that literally took his breath away. Then afterward she had clung to him, almost in despair. Yet when he had questioned her, she'd dismissed his concern and held him tighter. Now, gazing down at her peaceful, angelic face, she looked anything but desperate. Holt shook his head. Maybe *his* was the strange mood.

All day he'd felt the razor-sharp edge of his conscience, as it insisted he needed to share vital pieces of his past with Casey. She had to know his history before they could plan any kind of a future together.

And he *did* want to spend his tomorrows with Casey. All of them. *Till death us do part.* Similar thoughts had darted in and out of his mind throughout the day and undoubtedly accounted for the prodding conscience. Tell her, a small voice counseled. She, of all people, will understand a longing for love and the need to protect it.

But will she understand why I've deceived her?

Love understands, his heart replied. And Casey loved him, of that he was certain. But did she love him enough?

You're gutless, cowboy. Just tell her and get it over with.

Casey stirred, opened her eyes and gave a lazy-cat stretch. She glanced at the window. "It's still light out."

"Uh-huh."

A faint blush tinted her cheeks. "I was shameless, wasn't I?"

"You were wild, fantastic, wonderful."

"I never acted like that in my entire life."

"Well, speaking as the recipient of your first genuine attempt at seduction, I can honestly say you've got a real flair for it. You were sultry and inventive. In fact . . ." His eyebrows wiggled up and down a second before his head lowered and his tongue teased her parted lips. "I wouldn't have been surprised to see you whip out your camera and start flashing away." He nibbled his way from her mouth to her throat. "No pun intended," he said against her pulse beat.

The word "camera" was a reminder of things Casey wanted to forget. Parts of Ramsey's conversation inched forward and she shoved them to the far corners of her mind. *Tell him. Tell him now,* reason screamed. *I'll lose him. And if I lose him, I'll die,* love responded. Surely not, some intermediary assured her. After all, she was no longer an outsider. She belonged in Crescent Bay with Holt. Surely her love and loyalty would count for something when she told him. Surely?

"Hello? Anybody home?" Holt snapped his fingers scant inches from her face.

"What?" she asked, coming out of her haze of thoughts.

"I said, how about feeding the body, now that we've fed the soul?" He brushed a wisp of hair from her cheek. "Besides, we need to talk."

Talk?

As she tied the sash to Holt's mammoth bathrobe around her waist, grabbing handfuls of cloth to keep it from dragging the floor, her anxiety grew. What did he want to *talk* about? Casey told herself she was probably projecting her own shaky conscience onto the situation. She was, as Grace might say, "making a mountain out of a molehill." Then why did she feel as if she were standing at the edge of a cliff, about to be pushed over?

As they had on the evening of their first date, they prepared a late-night breakfast, featuring Holt's infamous scrambled eggs. By the time the meal was ready to be eaten, Casey was in an advanced state of inner turmoil. Agitation had been building ever since Ramsey's call, and she had fought it with every ounce of her strength, knowing if she allowed it even a tiny foothold on her precarious sanity, she was lost.

Barefoot and bare-chested, his lean legs encased in worn jeans, Holt carried the tray laden with their food and followed Casey into the den. He poured coffee, buttered a slice of toast and handed it to her. If he noticed her hand tremble, he didn't comment.

"You eat and I'll talk," Holt said at last.

"About what?"

"You and me. The past and how it will affect our future."

At his somber tone of voice a sense of dread clutched at Casey's heart. What could he possibly have to say that was so... serious? Her nerves tightened.

Rising from the couch, Holt walked to the empty fireplace and rested his hands on the mantel. Head down, he seemed to be gathering his thoughts, then he dropped his hands and turned to face her.

"The first time I laid eyes on you, I knew you were gonna change my life." He grinned sheepishly. "For a minute or two, I also thought you were another one of those low-life reporters or photographers, only interested in making a buck at Norah Tanner's expense. Thank God, I wasn't fool enough to get hung up on that first impression."

His blue eyes darkened. "You were such a little spitfire. I think I fell for you right then and there."

"I—I think you called me a smart ass," Casey said inanely.

He laughed. "Yeah, I did, didn't I?"

Casey's mind, like her emotion, was fragmented. Propelled by supreme nervousness, one part spun off crazily into space, trying to protect her in some unbalanced way. The other part struggled valiantly to concentrate on and comprehend Holt's words, intuitively understanding their importance.

What was he leading up to?

Can't think... gotta run.

He's talking about honesty and loyalty.

Keep running....

And how sometimes secrets are necessary.

Can't stop... dark corners.

He's talking about love, trust and . . .

"Am I making any sense, Casey?"

She blinked. Focusing on his beloved face, she nodded, but only because some fringe of reason she couldn't understand told her it was the right response.

"I want to share a thousand dawns with you and make love in a million sunsets. I want to see your face the first thing every morning, see our children born and watch them grow up strong, healthy and happy. I want to love you until we're very old and, God willing, die in each other's arms."

Holt crossed to where she sat on the sofa. "Casey, there are things from my past I've never trusted anyone enough to tell. But I want you to know now. I trust you."

Trust. Love. The words swirled inside Casey's head, entwining the opposing thought paths, drawing them together like the strings of a pouch, collecting, merging, channeling the paths into a single road leading to one inexorable truth.

She couldn't pretend anymore.

Since the first time Holt had kissed her, touched her, she had been living a wonderful dream. A princess in a fairy tale, pretending she had at long last found her Prince Charming and they would live happily ever after. No matter how much lip service she herself paid to the contrary, she had blindly refused to face reality.

She pretended, when deep in her heart of hearts she had always known it was too good to last.

Sweet heaven, what had she done to Holt, to herself? He was talking about babies and trust, and she couldn't let him go on. She wasn't worthy of his trust or his love. Having run toward love all her life, it was ironic that when she finally found her heart's dream, the only choice was to run away from love.

"It's important for you to understand—"

"It doesn't matter," Casey said suddenly.

"It does matter. I want you to know everything—"

"No." Tears pooled in Casey's eyes. "Please don't say any more."

Holt saw the tears, noticed her rigid posture and knew she hadn't been listening to him, but instead had been warring with some inner demon of her own. In his anxiety, his need to unburden himself, he'd been too caught up in his own attack of nerves to notice. Instantly contrite, he said, "Casey, what is it? What's *wrong*?"

"Everything."

He reached for her. "Baby, talk to me. What in the hell is wrong?"

She drew away. "Us."

Confused, Holt tried to get her to look at him. She refused. "What do you mean, us?"

"We're wrong. And we have been from the first." Her voice was feather-light, belying the stone-hard pronouncement.

Stunned, Holt couldn't believe his own ears. She loved him, he knew she did. They had shared too much, come too close....

Come too close.... The phrase echoed in his mind.

Unaccustomed as she was to intimacy and loving, Holt decided he had gone too fast. This was brand-new to her, and he was talking about commitments. He had pushed her too far, too quickly. No wonder she had put the brakes on. Knowing her history of putting up barriers against possible pain, it made all the sense in the world that she should bolt like a frightened mare when he started talking about children and growing old together.

Holt sighed, relieved and convinced that he had discovered the reason for Casey's rejection, yet frightened over her inability to move past her fear. "Darlin', listen to me," he said gently. "I . . . I'm sorry. I never meant to scare you or back you into a corner—"

"I have to go," she begged.

Holt recognized the defense mechanism. He recognized it, understood, but still found it difficult to contain his anger at her refusal. Somehow he had to make her see she had nothing to fear from their love. My God, didn't she know he would cut out his heart before hurting her?

"Let me go, Holt. Please."

Holt heard the strength in her voice and knew that any moment she would be into full-blown denial and he might never get through to her.

"No." Frustrated, he raked his fingers through his hair.

Casey bolted from the sofa. He caught her before she got three feet.

Yanking her around to face him, Holt said angrily, "I'm not going to let you throw away the best thing that ever happened to either one of us. Casey, oh, God, don't do this. I love you."

The words she had waited a lifetime to hear sliced across her heart. "Don't love me. I'm not . . . right for you."

"This is crazy! Of course you're right for me. We're right for each other. Casey, don't . . . do . . . this." He tunneled all ten fingers through her hair, holding her head between his powerful hands. "I . . . love . . . you."

"I don't believe in love."

Her words snapped the bands of control on his anger. He *wouldn't* let her turn her back on their love. If she wouldn't listen to reason, he would *make* her respond to him. The only surefire way he knew how.

"Then believe in this." His tongue plunged into her mouth. Hot. Hard. Deep. "Believe in the fire that burns like a melting sun when I touch you." He kissed her again. Harder. Deeper. "I don't give a damn what you call it. Believe in the way we make each other come alive, wanting the heat, needing the heat." His mouth took hers in an endless, savage kiss.

The kiss was a fire-out-of-control inferno. Casey whimpered, her body going boneless beneath the bruising kiss that bordered on violence. He ravaged her mouth. Over and over until there were no thoughts, no beliefs, nothing but the raging, roaring, furnace torching their minds, incinerating their bodies.

On some elemental level, the last civilized fragments of Holt's reason prevented brutality, reminding him this was Casey, the most precious of gifts. He gentled the kiss, but it was too late to tamp the flame.

Casey's body was disintegrating. In a matter of seconds she would be nothing more than a pile of ashes, and she couldn't have cared less. She was dying from a beautiful, consuming flame and did so willingly. Mindless with the need to be part of him, possibly for the last time, her own fingers untied the robe's sash. Her own hands yanked and pulled until she was free, naked and reaching for him again.

Holt was ahead of her. Free of his jeans, he met her more than halfway, pulling her with him onto the couch. One swift, sure stroke and he was inside her, sheathed in her fire.

Casey gasped at the wildly erotic combination of pleasure and pain.

Holt groaned and held his breath. For seconds he remained still. Desire shimmered through him, expanded, consumed.

"Ahh." He threw back his head, unable to resist the demands of his body. "I need ... so hot ... so ..."

"... good ... love ..."

"... you ... don't leave ..."

"... never ..."

They burned down the night in a blazing mutual orgasm, the fire showering sparks on love-slick bodies.

Sometime later, drained and exhausted they finally moved back upstairs and tumbled into bed.

They didn't make love again. This time they cuddled like two homeless kittens.

At three in the morning Casey was still awake. Beside her, Holt slept peacefully. While her body remained absolutely still for fear of waking him, her mind whirled with a feverish energy, searching for answers to her confusing questions and feelings. She had made a holy mess of things, and now she wasn't sure they could ever be put right.

Her earlier denial had been an act of total selfishness on her part, and there was no way for Casey to pretend otherwise. *Selfish, selfish, selfish. Now look what you've done.*

Self-pity washed over her, dragging her even further toward despair. *Stop feeling sorry for yourself and figure out what you're going to do!* What could she do?

Ramsey would send his damned photographer, come hell or high water. He was her friend, but he was also an editor who knew the value of a good story. In his business, circulation was the name of the game, and Ramsey played it as well as, if not better than most. Nothing personal, strictly business. But it was *very* personal to Casey.

So... She forced her frantic mind to settle into some pretext of rational thought patterns. *Now what?* Now she put some distance between herself and the problem to get some perspective.

Carefully she slipped out of bed, stealthily gathered her clothes and went downstairs. She dressed quickly, then scribbled a note to Holt, sliding the slip of paper beneath his car keys, so he would be sure to find it.

She drove around the lake, unconsciously winding up at the spot where she and Holt had taken that first moonlit walk. There was no moon tonight, only a blanket of darkness. Suitable, Casey thought, to her mood.

She knew Ramsey's photographer *could* get the picture, but the likelihood was neither simple nor probable. If she hadn't been able to get a shot of Tanner, how easy could it be for someone else? Of course, Casey had to admit, she hadn't tried very hard.

But others before her had and failed, so why should she worry that Ramsey's next shooter would be any better? *Because there's always some hungry opportunist, willing to do whatever it takes to get a sensational exclusive. Big bucks draw big egos.* And Casey knew there were plenty in her profession ready, willing and able to supply tabloids with all the sneak-and-click shots they wanted.

Casey's major concern was how such a photograph would affect the sleepy little community she had adopted. Grace had mentioned that the entire town had been thrown into an upsetting whirlwind of activity when the last Tanner film festival took place. The event Ramsey had described would undoubtedly be grandiose. And there was nothing grand about the depressing feelings Casey couldn't shake. After an hour of searching for a way out of her dilemma, she was no closer to a solution than when she'd slipped out of Holt's arms. Well, almost.

There was always the coward's way out.

Sunrise was a whispered promise at the edge of the night when Casey finally parked her car in front of her motel room. Noticing the light shining from the café's kitchen windows, she headed that way. Usually Grace arrived before her employees, at around four or five in the morning, to make preparations for the day.

Casey stuck her head in the kitchen door. "Can a girl get a cup of coffee in this establishment?"

Grace looked up from measuring the ingredients for homemade biscuits. "If you can't, I better close the doors."

"Speaking of doors," Casey said stepping inside and turning the lock. "Don't you think you should lock this one when you're here by yourself?"

"What for?"

Casey shrugged. "Against intruders."

"Well, I reckon where you come from, intruders are a way of life. Not around here. Besides, everybody within fifty miles probably knows I'm in here every mornin' before the crack of dawn. You'd be surprised the number of folks that stop by."

"I suppose."

Grace eyed Casey's slightly disheveled appearance, apparently doing some supposing of her own. "Yeah. Some just visit while I work. Others got things on their mind and want a sympathetic ear."

"And do you provide that sympathetic ear?"

"Honey, I learned a long time ago, there's not a trouble in this world that don't get lighter with the sharin' of it." She held out a fresh cup of coffee, and Casey accepted. "So why don't we cut to the chase and talk about what's botherin' you?"

Casey's gaze darted once again to Grace's face. "I don't think my problem can be solved before the breakfast rush."

"Try me."

The gentle understanding she had come to depend upon sparked in Grace's eyes, but Casey wondered if that understanding would last after she told her story. Practically since the first moment she'd met the sage proprietress of Moon Lake Café, Casey had felt a kinship, a unique "connection" she had experienced with very few people in her life. Call it seeking the maternal bond she'd never experienced or simply the desperate need to have another human offer solace, but whatever name Casey chose, the end result was the same—she trusted Grace completely.

Casey's gaze dropped to her cup. "You won't like what I've got to say."

"I don't like a lot of things, but that don't keep me from understandin'."

Please, God, let that be true, Casey prayed. She could tell Grace and lose a friend. Or gain an ally. A risk. But then everything Casey had done since coming to Crescent Bay had been a risk. Risking jail, risking discovery...risking love, happiness...pain.

Casey took a deep breath, gathering all her strength. "I, uh...I'm in love with your nephew."

Grace smiled. "Now tell me somethin' I don't know."

Casey's head snapped up. They had been so careful since that first morning, when they had been seen in front of her doorway at sunup. As much as she had thrilled to have Grace come to her defense, Casey had decided the wisest course was to keep her relationship with Holt low-key. They'd made no secret of the fact that they dated, but she hadn't realized her emotional state was so obvious.

"I didn't think anybody noticed."

"Doubt many folks paid any attention, but it was there if you cared to look. I couldn't be more pleased."

"It's not that easy," Casey said, absently fingering the rim of her cup.

"Love never is, honey. And Lord knows, Holt's not an easy man to love. But I bet he's hell on wheels when he loves a woman back."

In spite of herself, Casey smiled. "And then some."

"So what's the problem? You're both free and over twenty-one. Reasonably sane and obviously healthy. Wait a minute." Grace held up a flour-dusted hand. "That boy hasn't been leadin' you on without sayin' his true feelin's, has he?"

"No. It's not Holt, Grace. It's me. I . . . Oh, damn." She gnawed on her bottom lip. "There's just no easy way to do this."

"Straight out is usually the best. That way you get it over with quicker."

A quick end was precisely what would happen. An end to loving Holt—no, she could sooner stop breathing than stop loving him—certainly an end to their future, an end to her treasured relationship with Grace. All of that and much more swayed back and forth on the fine line between dreams and reality, hope and despair.

Clutching the coffee cup like a lifeline, Casey swallowed hard. "I am exactly what Holt thought I was, the first day I came to town. I came here to take a picture of Norah Tanner for the magazine I work for."

"I see."

At the calm response, Casey looked the other woman in the eye. "Y-you don't seem—"

"Surprised?" Grace asked. "Hell, Casey, nothin' much surprises me anymore where people are concerned. So why haven't you taken your picture?"

Casey, however, was surprised. "How do you know I haven't?"

"Because you would have been long gone if you had." There was no censure in the green depths, no frown worked into the already wrinkled brow. "And that leads me to believe you don't intend to. Am I right?"

Casey nodded.

"I take it you haven't told Holt."

"No."

"Well . . ." Grace sighed. "He's probably gonna be bent outta shape. But I'm bettin' he loves you enough to forgive and forget."

"I wish it were that simple. I refused to go through with the assignment. In fact, I quit the magazine."

"Then there's nothing to worry about," Grace said, calmly continuing to prepare her dough.

"Grace, you don't understand. My boss will send someone else."

"Let him. He probably won't have any better luck than anyone else has."

"This time I don't think luck will enter into it," Casey said, hoping she could make Grace understand the seriousness of the situation. "MGM has decided to release all of Tanner's movies in a video package, coinciding with a knockdown, star-studded, Hollywood blowout of a film festival. Tanner, Garbo and Dietrich. Big bucks are in the offing. This time perseverance, not luck, will be the key, and enough money can buy a great deal of perseverance."

Grace spat out several very colorful expletives. "All hell is gonna break loose around here. That deal two years ago was a circus. Wish to heaven there was something we could do to prevent it from happenin' again.''

"We can't do anything about the festival," Casey said regretfully.

"Hellfire." Angrily, Grace wiped her hands on her apron. "Must be somethin' we can do."

"There is. I have to tell Holt. Maybe he can take some official action to keep reporters and photographers away."

"Ah, hell, honey. Anybody can get *onto* the estate if they want to. Now, gettin' close enough to get a picture is a horse of a different color," Grace added.

"With a high-powered, one-eighty-millimeter lens you don't have to be close."

"Well, even with one of those whatchamacallits you can't look through brick."

Casey's sleepless night finally caught up with her, making rational thought process a muddle, but one thought stayed clear. "The best thing to do is for me to tell Holt and hope—"

"I'm not so sure about that."

"But you just said—"

"That was before I knew about the festival and all that other garbage." At the stricken look in Casey's eyes, Grace rushed to add, "Oh, I don't think he'll throw in the towel where you're concerned, but I can pretty well predict how he's gonna react when the town goes haywire. But I'm also dead-level certain about what will happen when all the media jerks show up here. These people get downright hostile when you disturb their routine. I'm tellin' you, Casey, it won't be pretty, and I'm afraid you're gonna get caught in the backwash."

"But I *have* to tell Holt," Casey said, determined to end the deception once and for all.

Hands on hips, Grace studied the floor for a few seconds before saying, "I agree, but how is the important thing. And *when*."

"When?"

"Yeah. Will you hold off till tomorrow, and let me have a chance to think?"

"Grace, I appreciate you're trying to—"

"Casey," she interrupted. "I *do* want to help you. And Holt. But I want to help the people in this town, too. We all like things the way they are, 'cause they're good, clean and honest. And I'd do battle with the devil himself to keep 'em that way."

"So would I, Grace," Casey whispered fervently. "Crescent Bay has changed me, changed the way I look at reality."

Grace smiled, came to her and put an arm around her shoulder and for the first time Casey felt less hopeless. At the compassionate gesture, Casey's heart filled with renewed hope, and her cold, starved-for-tenderness soul was blanketed in loving warmth.

"Let me tell you somethin', honey. The only reality worth hangin' on to in this world is love," Grace said, her head close to Casey's, as if they were sharing a secret no one else in the world could know.

"Not necessarily man-to-woman love. Though, Lord knows, there ain't a thing wrong with that kind. But what I'm talkin' about is just plain ol' *love*, love. Like lovin' the way the sun looks when it sets, and lovin' the sweet smile on a baby's face asleep in its mama's arms. Or the way a body feels deep down inside, when they've done what was good and right. And lovin' the Lord, just 'cause He made it all possible. That's what reality is. Anythin' else ain't worth the power to blow it to hell."

"That's a beautiful philosophy," Casey said, her voice rough with emotion. "I only hope I get a chance to apply it in my own life," she whispered.

"You will." Grace patted her cheek, leaving behind a smear of flour. "But first we got to figure out how to overcome a few obstacles."

A few obstacles? From where Casey sat, "a few obstacles" constituted the understatement of the decade.

"How much time do we have?" Grace asked.

"Almost none."

"Damn." Grace scratched her nose, leaving a dot of flour behind. After long seconds of contemplation she looked at Casey. "If *you* got the first picture, maybe those other media-mongers would stay home. I *might* be able to get you into the Tanner house and—"

"No," Casey insisted. "Grace, I'm not dragging you into—"

"You ain't draggin' me anywhere, I'm movin' under my own steam. And if what I have in mind works, we'll all come out smelling like a rose. If it doesn't..." She shrugged. "We're no worse off than we are now."

I could be, Casey thought. *I could lose Holt.*

Chapter Fourteen

Casey dragged herself through the day, surviving on nervous energy and sheer determination. She longed to see Holt, yet was relieved he had elected to stay away from the diner. She loved him and wanted to literally ride off into the sunset with him, but as time constricted to a narrow band, she was caught in the ultimate squeeze play.

"You look awful," April commented toward the end of the lunch rush. "You're not sick are ya?"

"I don't think so," Casey said. *Unless you count sick at heart.*

"Well, all the same, you ought to ask Grace to let you knock off early."

"But that will leave you shorthanded."

"I'll live," April insisted. "Wednesdays we don't get more than a handful before closin' on account of 'most everybody goes to church. Besides, I owe you one."

"One what?" Casey asked, massaging knotted muscles across her shoulders and neck.

"Favor. I, uh . . ." Nervously April glanced away. "Well, uh, I'm not much on askin' for help or thankin' once I get it. But I want to thank you for helpin' me stand up to Jody's daddy. You were right. Sooner or later, I had to stop runnin' long enough to let the good stuff catch up to me."

Casey smiled. "I'm so glad, April. You deserve 'good stuff.' "

"Know what?" She grinned shyly. "Wasn't as bad as I thought it was gonna be. Mr. Thomas ain't exactly welcomed me with open arms, but least he knows I'm no coward, and he for sure knows how much I love Jody. I reckon that's a beginnin'."

"Yes," Casey solemnly agreed. "That's definitely a beginning."

In an unexpected display of affection, April gave Casey a hug that lacked nothing in sincerity, despite its brevity.

As Casey watched her young friend hurry away, she wished she were half as brave as April. Maybe then she would be able to face Holt without falling apart.

"Think I've got a solution," Grace said a short time later as Casey carried a pot of coffee into Grace's upstairs apartment.

"And I've reached a decision," Casey replied, placing the coffee on a warming pad lying on the kitchen counter. If she could show one tenth of April's courage, maybe her luck would be as good. "I'm going to tell Holt the truth and take my chances. I'm sick to death of all the lies."

"Wish you'd hear me out before you go barrelin' over to Holt's to spill your story," Grace said as she poured two cups of coffee. "What could it hurt to listen?"

When Casey nodded her reluctant agreement, Grace forged ahead. "There's no question that your boss—"

"Ex-boss," Casey corrected.

"Was or is, we can figure he ain't gonna back off an inch, right? I mean, he sounds like a real hard-nose."

"Actually, he's the only friend I had until I came here. But he's also one of the best editors in the business. To

Ramsey, a good story is what life's all about. Besides, he doesn't feel about Norah as I do. His theory is once an actress, always an actress. Ramsey thinks she's just waiting for the right time to make a *grand entrance* back into the world. But I don't agree.''

"Me neither.'' Grace sipped her coffee for a moment, then said, "You remember the chauffeur that was in the café one day a while back?''

"Yes.''

"Well, him and his wife are the only servants left. They don't hardly more than keep up appearances, 'cause most of the estate you can see is a fake.''

"What?'' Even though Casey had only seen the property through a telephoto lens and only part of the house was visible behind the stone wall, she had assumed that Tanner employed a full staff to help keep the house and grounds in shape.

"Well, maybe fake is too strong a word,'' Grace amended. "More like just for show.'' At Casey's perplexed expression, Grace said, "The whole front part of that house is empty. Oh, it's got furniture, lights and all that, but nobody *lives* in those rooms. It's just for looks. The whole damn house, except for Tanner's suite, a kitchen, parlor and Jake and Dora's room is shut down.''

"Who?''

"Jake and Dora Clark. He's the chauffeur, gardener and handyman, and his wife Dora is the cook and maid. There's only three people livin' on that great big ol' place. Jake, Dora and Tanner.''

"But why?''

Grace shrugged. "Guess she figured, why bother? Nobody ever comes to visit.''

As soon as Casey voiced the question, the obvious answer popped into her head. "Or maybe she can't afford a staff any larger than two. Maybe the money finally ran out, and she's broke.''

"Nope. She's still loaded.''

"Maybe she's in such poor health—"

"Nope. Over seventy and fit as a fiddle."

Suddenly Casey realized that Grace was giving answers far more informative than a casual observer would know. "Grace—"

Grace held up her hand to interrupt. "Now, before you ask how I know so damned much, I better tell you I've been doin' a little story-tellin' of my own. When I told you I hadn't seen Tanner in years, it was a bit shy of the whole truth."

Surprised at the admission, Casey stared at the other woman.

"Maybe I better explain," Grace said hesitantly. "I met Jake and Dora when I worked out there, and we got to be real close friends. I go out there to visit about once a month, and a couple a times, when Dora was ailin', I've done the cookin' in her stead. And, well, sometimes...once in a while I see her, uh, Norah, I mean. Anyway, what all this is leadin' up to is, I think I can get you inside the house." Before Casey could find her voice to raise her first question, Grace added, "But there's two conditions for my help."

"Wh-what?" Stunned, Casey still couldn't believe her own ears.

"First, you got to be sure your picture won't show every wrinkle, ache and pain."

"I thought you said she wasn't sick."

"She's not. Just old."

"You mean a good shot, but not a close-up."

"That's right." At Casey's nod, Grace continued. "Second, I'd like to see the picture before you send it to this Ramsey fella."

"Of course, but—"

"Not that I don't trust your judgment, but I think it'd be better if you had a second opinion." She looked Casey directly in the eye. "I want to help you, and I'd do damned near anything for Holt's happiness, but I can't hurt good people into the bargain."

Casey reached out and took her hand. "If I thought for one minute that will happen, trust me, Grace, I would burn the negatives myself."

"Honey, I started trustin' you the day you walked into the café. No reason to stop now."

Trust. It always came down to that one word, Casey thought. Her trusting Holt, Grace trusting her. "Thank you, Grace."

"Might want to hold on to your thanks till after this is all over. You got everything you need to take the picture tonight, soon as it gets dark?"

"Y-yes," Casey answered, still shocked by the rapid turn of events.

"You go on and get a nap. I don't want you keelin' over on me tonight. And Casey?"

"Yes."

"Don't worry. Everything will work out fine. I promise."

Three hours later, the ringing of the phone woke her.

"Are you okay?" Holt said the minute Casey answered.

"Holt—"

"Casey—"

"I'm sorry," they said in unison.

"I didn't call or see you all day, because I thought you might need a breather."

"Thanks," she whispered.

"My intentions were good, but I couldn't hold out another instant. I had to hear your voice and know you're okay."

"I'm fine."

"Really fine, or are you just saying that, so I'll stop pestering you?"

"Really fine, and I like for you to pester me."

A river of silence flowed between them, each fighting the current of need to stay what was in their hearts. Holt was the first to go under.

"You scared the hell out of me, leaving like that. Don't you *ever* disappear again. I aged ten years when I opened my eyes, expecting to find you, and found an empty space instead."

"I shouldn't have gone without waking you. I'm sorry."

"And I'm sorry if I pressured you—"

"You didn't."

"Casey?"

"Yes."

"I love you."

Oh, God, don't be sweet to me. I can't bear the thought of losing your sweetness.

When she didn't answer, he said, "We're still playing by your rules, darlin'. Any way you want it. Any way you want me. No more dark corners, I promise—"

"Always. Forever."

"What?"

"That's how I want you."

"That's how you've got me, sweet woman. Always. Forever."

They smiled into their respective phones and slipped into a comfortable silence.

"So, I caught you napping," Holt said finally.

"Hmm," she answered on the tail end of a yawn. "How did you know?"

"Your voice. And it sounds so sexy. Wish I was there beside you."

"Then we probably wouldn't be napping."

"You got that right," he growled.

"Hmm-m-m-m."

"Hungry?" His velvety voice sent shivers scampering down her spine and implied appetites for things other than food. Her heart somersaulted into an erratic beat.

"Yes." One softly sexy word implied she too recognized certain hungers.

"How about a sunset picnic at my place?"

"Sounds delicious."

"So do you. Be ready in an hour."

Two hours later Casey sat on a quilt spread beneath a gargantuan pecan tree, gazing at the late-afternoon sky spectacularly streaked with gold. She decided Texas must have a monopoly on breathtaking sunsets. And this one was world-class, top-of-the-line. Holt had gone to check on their grazing horses while she repacked the last of the fried chicken, potato salad and fruit. Casey glanced up in time to watch him walking back to join her.

Some men were born to wear denim the way the day was born to wear sunshine. Watching Holt saunter toward her, Casey's mind snapped a thousand mental photographs: boots, dusty and molded to his feet as if they were a part of him. Those wonderful jeans that gave new meaning to the word *fitted* and sent her pulse off the Richter scale. The blue work shirt stretched across broad shoulders, sleeves rolled past his elbows, banding powerful arms. The V of the shirt exposed tanned skin, a dusting of golden-brown hair and the sweat of a virile man. And Holt's face—the strong jawline, the mustache she adored, and stunning eyes. Head to foot he was man enough for a lifetime and beyond.

"You having a good time?"

"Wonderful." *As long as it lasts.* Casey consciously stayed thoughts of what the night might bring. "I honestly don't know how you stand to leave this place, even to do your job."

He joined her on the quilt, stretching his long frame alongside hers. "Some mornings it's damned hard. And lately it's been worse."

"Why?"

"Not only do I have to go off and be the long arm of the law." He wrapped the aforementioned arm around her shoulders and drew her against him. "But to do it, I have to leave a bed occupied by the most beautiful woman in the world."

"In the world? Don't you think that's an exaggeration, even for a Texan?"

"No, ma'am. Exaggeratin' would be if I said, the universe."

"Oh, well that's diff— Ah-h-h, oh, Holt, what are you doing?"

"The best I can, ma'am." Two buttons of her blouse were already free of their buttonholes.

"Holt...we're out here in the middle of nowhere." She tried to stop him, but he effectively brushed her hands aside.

"With any luck, in about ten seconds we're gonna be in the middle of each other. And, baby, that's *somewhere*." He whisked the blouse from her shoulders.

"But we can't—"

"We sure as hell can." Discarded, her bra landed at the quilt's edge in a pale blue, crumpled heap.

"What if someone saw—?"

"We're too far from the house." His mouth took immediate and total possession of one dusky nipple.

"Ohh...ah, the road...someone..."

"Private. Gate's closed." Snaps on two pairs of jeans, first hers, then his, gave way. She lifted her hips accommodatingly, and the air was filled with the whoosh of denim moving over bare legs.

Holt's shirt quickly joined the pile on the far side of the quilt. His index finger teased the lace-trimmed edge of silky panties, tugging them down over slender hipbones and a smooth, flat tummy. When he placed his palm against that warm, taut surface and began rubbing leisurely circles, he heard Casey draw in a sharp breath.

"Your skin's so soft...smooth...like warm silk." His lips kissed a path from one hipbone to the other. "And you taste so good."

Casey arched her back off the quilt, rising high enough to place small, wet kisses over his chest and throat. "So...do you."

Her tongue danced across his throat and over his chin to tease his mustache. Holt groaned, holding her to him while her busy, wicked tongue stroked him closer and closer to the exquisite fire they created together. Until he couldn't stand it a moment longer.

"I can't think for wanting you," he groaned, turning her face up for a savage kiss. "I want you now so bad I can't breathe."

"Then have me," she whispered into his mouth, her voice rife with need and a vaguely familiar desperation.

Driven by her need, his need, their desperation, Holt nudged her thighs apart and giving one long, smooth, hot stroke, glided into the folds of her melting sweetness. She closed around him like a hot, velvet fist. He moved inside her, hard, hot power.

Day rushed toward night in a last blaze of color, and they rushed toward climax, one mind, body, and spirit. Then while the sun collapsed in the waiting arms of its night lover, Holt and Casey held each other, sharing contented sighs, soft kisses and whispered endearments.

"Don't go back to California," Holt said after a prolonged silence filled with nothing more than the rustle of leaves in a summer breeze. "Stay with me." He ached to say, "marry me," but after last night he didn't want to pressure her.

From her favorite place, snuggled against his chest, Casey first thought she'd heard him wrong. But when he repeated the words a second time, she couldn't ignore the thrill soaring through her. Or the fear.

"Can I assume by your silence that I've taken you by surprise?"

She drew back far enough to look into his eyes. "Completely." He had just granted her most supreme wish, and she could not accept. Not until she was able to look him in the eye with the truth. *Oh, God, Holt. Please don't do this. Not now.*

"I love you, Casey. I want to spent the rest of my life with you. I know I told you earlier I wouldn't pressure you. But I'm not asking for us to go get a license tomorrow. I just want to know you belong to me."

A tear crowded the corner of one eye. "I do belong to you, Holt, and nothing will ever change that."

He frowned. "Then why do I get the feeling there's an unspoken 'but' at the end of your sentence?"

"I—I don't think this is a good time to talk about... It's too soon to be making plans," she stammered, trying to keep her voice from breaking, trying not to let him see *she* was breaking apart into tiny pieces.

"And when would be a good time?"

"I...don't know." She glanced away.

"Casey, look at me."

When she refused, strong fingers cupped her chin, forced her head up, forced her eyes to meet his. "You remember the night we witnessed the accident and you comforted little Kerry?"

"Yes."

"You had a dream that night and talked in your sleep."

Casey's eyes widened.

"Know what you said?"

When she failed to answer, he pressed on. "You mumbled phrases about your mother not smiling at you, about your parents saying bad things to each other. You seemed to assume it was your fault. You apologized for not being pretty or...lovable."

On Holt's lips the words sounded far less harsh than they always had inside her head, but the words still stung with remembered pain. Tears trickled down her cheeks.

"I think I understand why you're so afraid to trust what you feel," Holt said softly. "Your parents didn't have the good sense to treasure you for the wonderful child you were or the woman you've become. It's impossible for me to make up for all the pain they caused, but I can sure as hell make certain you've got someone to turn to when you hurt, now and for the rest of your life."

He hugged her closer. "Healing old wounds isn't easy. But baby, you can't let your past determine *our* future. I know you have ties to California and a career you enjoy. But you've told me yourself all you need to do your job is a camera, a decent film lab and the U.S. mail. Stay with me, Casey. Be happy with me. I promise you'll never regret it.''

The trickle of tears became a river. What could she say to such honest eloquence? Casey's heart felt as if it were being ripped to shreds. Trembling hands stroked his cheek. "I'm happy with you, and I want to stay with you more than I've ever wanted anything in my life. But there's something I have to—"

"You're going back to California."

The disappointment in his voice sliced into her resolve. "Y-yes."

"When?"

"Soon."

"You're sure you *have* to do this?"

"Yes." Right now she wasn't sure of anything except the incredible pain she saw reflected in his eyes. "But—"

He smiled that crooked smile she adored. "I've trusted you with my heart. What's a little time?"

Their lips met in a kiss lavish with unspoken promises.

Casey was greatly relieved Holt was content to end the kiss—and the evening—early. He seemed to sense her need to be apart from him. At her motel room he didn't prolong the goodbyes but kissed her tenderly, wished her sweet dreams until tomorrow. As Casey watched the taillights of his truck disappear into the night, she wondered if her dreams would indeed be sweet after tonight. She prayed so, because the bad dreams she'd known all her life would pale in comparison to the nightmares she would surely suffer if she lost Holt.

"Thought you might have changed your mind," Grace said, when she opened her door to Casey at nine thirty-five. "Scared?"

"Terrified," Casey admitted.

"Well, don't be, honey. This is going to work out, you'll see."

"I hope so, Grace, because if it doesn't, we don't have a Plan B." Casey remembered a similar statement she had made the first day she arrived in Crescent Bay and thought how different her "plans" were now. Her whole life had changed in the space of the last two weeks.

And might very well change again in the space of the next hour . . . for the worse.

"Now, don't forget how we planned it. The room you're gonna be in is big enough to house a barn dance for the whole town, but you should be able to see her soon as she walks in. She has tea in the parlor and listens to classical music every night and always sits in one chair. It's way-the-hell across the room, but even with that highfalutin lens of yours, you better get your picture soon as she comes in the parlor, just in case. Oh, and one more thing . . ."

Nervously Casey licked dry lips. "Yes?"

"If anything goes wrong, you skedaddle and leave the explainin' to me."

"But, Grace—"

"This is my idea. I'll do the talkin' if we get caught, and that's all there is to it, you hear?"

"I hear," Casey repeated, knowing full well she had no intention of abandoning her friend if trouble did arise.

A short time later Casey's rented Volkswagen made the turn onto the road leading to the Tanner estate. From the main approach Grace had described, the grand old house appeared to be in total darkness. Then just as they reached the main gate, Grace indicated that Casey should take a side road, which took them around the estate, toward the back. Casey could see light glowing from two rooms facing the lake. After parking a quarter of a mile from the house, they walked the rest of the way.

By the time Grace led Casey through a gate and across the garden to a side door, one thing was painfully clear. The imposing entrance to the once great estate was a total facade. From a distance the building was a splendid reminder of a woman and a time when glamour, beauty and prestige were the measures of success. Appearances were everything. But up close the house was an aging structure badly in need of repairs. The garden had all but gone to seed except for a small section of roses and what looked like a vegetable patch. The lawn was hardly more than a regularly mowed crop of impossible-to-kill Texas weeds. The trim begged for a paint job. The pool was empty, the tiles cracked and discolored.

Casey was stunned. She felt as if, after admiring an alluring flower from afar, up close the fragrance didn't match the blossom's soft petals and beautiful color. In some inexplicable way she felt cheated. And sad. Now she understood the pity she had seen in Grace's eyes when she spoke of the house and its owner. Had Norah, like her once-magnificent home, slid into a state of neglect?

"Wait here," Grace whispered, then she slipped inside. She reappeared in minutes and motioned Casey to enter, leading the way through a kitchen, along a hallway and into what Casey assumed was the parlor. Heavy, faded drapes covered the windows, and judging from the floor-to-ceiling bookshelves along two walls, the room had served not only as a sitting room, but a library, as well.

Once inside the dark, dusty room, Grace pointed to an intricately carved, antique, Oriental prayer screen, situated in a dimly lighted corner. "Stay out of sight, close to the bookcase. There's enough space for you to see her without being seen . . . if you're careful. Now go . . . go." She waved her hands, shooing Casey into position.

Behind the screen, Casey checked lighting, setting and focus, while nervously pondering the situation. Why hadn't she asked where Grace would be while this little caper unfolded? If something did go wrong, how would they reconnect and get out of the house? Why hadn't she insisted Grace stay with her? Why had she thought this incredibly wild scheme would work in the first place?

Time inchwormed by.

Finally Casey's heart shot into her throat at a noise in the hallway.

Nervous perspiration covered her entire body, her hands shook and her heart threatened to hammer itself out of her body. Casey experienced a dizzying mixture of anticipation and naked fear.

At the first glimpse of a colorful flash of material, she recognized the Arabic style of garment Norah Tanner had made famous over fifty years ago. The flowing folds of the garment swirled into Casey's line of vision, and her heart went wild.

But before she could make out facial features, much less focus her camera, the woman stopped as if someone had called out, her gray, pageboy hairdo swinging as she turned toward the caller. The low rumbling of a male voice carried into the room, but Casey was unable to recognize the words or the voice. And with her back fully to the camera, Tanner's body partially blocked the view of the newcomer. But when the man stepped into the room, Casey had no difficulty in identifying him.

Holt!

And he was furious. A scowling anger etched his face. His body language was defiant and hostile.

Casey had assumed that Grace had taken into consideration the nightly check of the estate grounds performed by Holt or his deputy. *Oh, Holt, why, tonight of all nights, did you have to be the one?* And what if he accidentally saw Grace?

As that thought reared its ugly head, Casey realized that although Tanner's soft voice still made her words indistinguishable, it was clear from her gestures and head movements that she wanted Holt to leave. Hands on hips, his mouth thinned in annoyance, it was just as clear that Holt had no intention of going anywhere.

As inconceivable as the idea sounded, from Holt's expression and body language, Casey could tell he was . . . *arguing* with Norah Tanner. But why?

The only logical explanation was that Holt had stumbled onto their outrageous venture. *Oh, God. What have I done?* Grace Malone was a clever woman, but Casey doubted even Grace could wiggle her way out of this twisted predicament. Casey's hands started to tremble. Then the tremble blossomed into a full-blown shake. Her hands shook so violently that the camera tapped against the wooden screen.

Holt's head snapped up, and his gaze quickly scanned the room.

No! Casey's mind screamed, even as his sapphire-blue gaze zeroed in on the screen. On the only barrier between her and discovery. Between her and everything.

Casey was only dimly aware of Norah Tanner's hand, outstretched to warn Holt away, before the scene unreeled into a slow-motion tableau, a nightmare video played at the wrong speed.

Staring through the viewfinder, Casey froze as Holt moved toward her hiding place.

Norah turned. And there, framed in the Nikon's viewfinder, was the face of a woman who had seen the hard knocks of life and triumphed. The face of a woman who has suffered and survived—the face of Grace Malone.

Chapter Fifteen

In one swift, angry motion, Holt yanked the screen aside, exposing the intruder.

Casey!

Recognition was quickly followed by another and much more stunning realization. *Casey with a camera.* While his eyes confirmed his worst fears, his heart cried out in denial. He felt as if an invisible fist had landed a lethal blow to his gut.

Casey's gaze shifted to the other two players in the freakish scenario, finally centering on the costumed Grace Malone, the woman who had trusted and befriended her. The woman who had been willing to lie for her.

"Casey, I..." Grace took a step toward her, and the camera slipped from Casey's grasp, stuck the edge of the Oriental rug beneath her feet, then clattered over the polished, hardwood floor. The sound filled the room, bouncing off the walls like a ricocheting bullet.

Holt watched the camera come to a stop, and some logical part of his brain pondered the resiliency of high-tech plastic. He couldn't take his eyes off the small, black, rectangular... *thing*. It seemed phenomenal that an object so ordinarily fracturable had the power to destroy his life. But it had, if the suspicions marching across his mind to an obvious, but hateful, conclusion were confirmed.

"What the hell is going on here?" Holt demanded, his hands knotted into fists. Although his eyes never left Casey's face, he couldn't look directly into her eyes for fear of what he might see. Or not see.

"Holt, calm down," Grace cautioned. "If you'll just listen—"

"Calm down!" He whirled to face her. "I knew the minute I saw the lights burning this late that something was wrong, but I had no idea—"

"It's not what you think."

"You know what I think? I think you've lost your mind. You have any idea how crazy—" he waved his arm in Casey's general direction "—this is? My God, what have you told her?"

"I know how crazy it *looks*, Holt, but—"

He turned slowly, purposefully toward Casey. "It looks as though we've both been played for fools, Gracie."

Grace moved close enough to put her hand on his arm. "Holt, until you hear the explanation, don't say something you might regret. Don't—"

"Don't what, Grace? Don't drag all the secrets out of the dark corners? Isn't this the time to get all the secrets out in the open?"

He glared at Casey, his voice icy shards of pain slicing at her heart. "Time to uncover all the lies... and liars."

"Holt!" Grace said sharply. "There are circumstances you know nothing about. Casey's had a bad shock—"

"Casey's had a shock!" he bellowed, glancing at Grace. "Oh, that's rich. And just what the hell do you think *I* had, when I walked in here and found the two of you together—

found her..." Without looking at Casey, he pointed an accusing finger in her direction. "...hiding behind that screen...with a camera?"

"It...it's all my fault," Casey whispered, finally recovering her voice. "She did...it for me."

Holt's head snapped around. "You're damned right it's your fault. If you hadn't sweet-talked your way into Grace's affections, she would never, *ever* have let you come within a mile of this house."

"Casey and I—"

"No," Casey cut her off quickly. "No, Grace. I have to be the one to answer him."

Holt's eyes were hard, dark, piercing as he watched her. He was no longer the Holt she loved and had made love with only hours earlier. His face was set, contempt etched in every line.

"Start talking."

Casey's heart fractured, breaking into a million tiny pieces, exactly the way her world was breaking apart, crumbling before her eyes. "I—I...y-you were right about me from the very first. I c-came here for one reason and one reason only. To get a picture of Norah Tanner."

A pain sharper, deeper, hotter than anything Holt had ever experienced pierced his soul. The sensation was so violent, he entertained a fleeting thought that if he looked, he might just be bleeding. Until the moment he actually heard the words from her own lips, he had prayed, oh, how he had prayed that he was wrong.

"But I...I couldn't."

"What stopped you?" The contemptuous sneer in his voice told her to save her breath, but her heart refused to give up without at least trying to make him understand.

"I fell in love."

Holt's gaze moved over her face, skimmed down her body, then back up. When his eyes again met Casey's, the heart she had thought merely shattered disintegrated at the look of raw torment in his eyes.

Betrayal.

He thought she had betrayed him. And in a way he was right. No matter how good her intentions, she had violated his trust, and in whatever fragments were left of her heart, Casey knew if he couldn't trust her, he couldn't love her. She had lost him.

"How convenient."

"Holt," Grace begged, "please try to understand—"

"Let her finish," Holt insisted. "I want to know what makes a person accept…" He almost said love, but stopped himself. *Oh, God, but I love her, and it's killing me.* "Friendship, then turn traitor. Did they offer you a lot of money, Casey?" he asked, lashing out, wanting to hurt as badly as he had been hurt. "How much? What's the going rate for a Judas these days?"

"That's enough, Holt! You're hurt and upset, but I won't let you talk to Casey this way. Can't you see she's hurting, too?"

"What I see is a stranger. A woman who used me and you."

"You're wrong," Grace insisted.

"No. I was wrong to believe, wrong to trust." His gaze drilled Casey's. "You did a good job on me, lady." When Grace opened her mouth to protest, he cut her off with a curt, "Stay out of this, Grace."

Casey had no defense against his rage and pain. Instead, she told herself, perhaps the only way left to demonstrate her love was to allow him to spill his anger, vent his wrath upon her. He stalked across the floor, jerked up the camera, crossed back to Casey and shoved the Nikon into her hands. "This is what you came for, isn't it?"

When she didn't answer, he leaned toward her, so close she could feel his breath on her face. "Well, isn't it!"

"Y-yes."

"Tell me something," he continued as if she hadn't answered, his deadly soft voice sending frissons of fear over her body. "Were you plotting how to use me to your best advantage that first night while we danced? While I held your soft body against mine and swayed to the music? Or did you think of it the first time we kissed? Or maybe..." His eyes narrowed to stone-cold slits. "Maybe it was when I slid into your very warm and willing body—"

"Holt!" Grace gasped.

"Get...out." His steel-edged command sliced through the tension with a deadly finality.

The room grew dark, and for one fleeting moment Casey thought she was going to faint. So much pain and bitterness. So much resentment in his voice. Casey fought the blackness, the cold, empty numbness that seeped into her and threatened never to leave.

The dark corners of her nightmares loomed larger, more lonely and threatening than ever before. This time there would be no rescuer, no one to comfort her in the night.

Casey snapped open the camera's film compartment. In one fluid motion she removed the film with one hand, tucked the Nikon beneath her arm and with her other hand yanked the narrow band of celluloid, imprinted with only one image, and stretched it toward the only source of light in the room.

The exposed strip of film fluttered to the floor as a single tear slid down her cheek. Then Casey did the only thing left for her to do.

She took her battered and bruised spirit and fled.

Casey saw nothing out the window of her Los Angeles apartment but another day, empty and lonely. Exactly like the rest of her days promised to be for the remainder of her life.

She had lost all sense of time. How long had it been since she left the rented Volkswagen in a parking lot at Dallas-Ft. Worth Airport? Two days? Two years? What difference did it make?

Curled up on one end of her overstuffed couch, staring at the television screen with unseeing eyes, she nursed a cup of coffee and reminded herself she had already had too many. But then, what did it matter if she consumed huge amounts of sleep-robbing caffeine? She couldn't sleep, anyway.

The male and female hosts of a popular morning show conversed, laughed and entertained their audience. Casey barely noticed. She'd only turned on the set hoping to find some comfort in the sound of human voices. It hadn't worked.

The phone rang, but she made no move to answer it. Casey knew the caller would be Ramsey. He'd left a string of messages on her answering machine, none of which she had returned.

Sure enough, her prerecorded message ended and Ramsey's voice boomed over the speaker. "Listen, cookie, I know you're there. I called Texas and some kid at the café told me you quit. So, don't pull this fade-into-the-woodwork act. Answer the damn phone!" When he received no response to his frustrated demand, Ramsey tried pleading. "Please, Casey. Something god-awful must have happened for you to run off, then stay locked up in that sterile, cracker-box apartment. Please, just talk to me. We can work it out." His deep sigh traveled through the machine and filled the room. "Dammit, if you won't talk to me, at least come and get this Hound of the Baskervilles of yours." A short pause was followed by, "For God's sake, call me back, or I'm coming over there, and you'll have to—" The sound of the beep ended the message in midsentence.

Some still-functioning part of Casey's brain told her she should remove Sugar from Ramsey's bad influence, and warned her she would have to leave before Ramsey showed up, but the message never quite reached her legs. It didn't matter. Nothing mattered, she thought, watching sun paint the sky of a brand-new day with a prism of breathtaking color. *The color of hope.*

She didn't feel hopeful. Hope, like wishing, didn't make dreams come true. A pain, so sharp it almost took her breath away, pierced her soul. She kept telling herself that she should try to rejoin the human race, that if she looked long enough, she would find a reason to embrace life again.

Won't work, you know. You're in bad shape.

In fact, she was in the worst shape of her life. How would she ever be able to look at a sunrise or sunset without wishing she were sharing it with Holt?

Leave me alone, she demanded of herself.

Precisely where you are.

The phone rang, and Casey prepared herself for another well-meaning temper tantrum from Ramsey. She was surprised he wasn't pounding on her door to pick her brain for any information he could use in a story. While a part of her knew she was being unfair, another part recognized she was probably right.

The answering machine clicked on.

"Casey, this is Grace—"

Casey was across the floor in two seconds, snatching up the telephone. "Grace? Grace, is that you?"

"Yeah, honey, it's me."

At the sound of the belovedly familiar voice, Casey started to cry. "H-how...are you?"

"I'm fine."

When Casey didn't speak after long moments, Grace said softly, "Casey? You still there?"

"Yes."

"You're one tough lady to track down. I been trying to reach you ever since you...for two days. Finally got that no-good varmint ex-boss of yours to give me your unlisted number."

"How did you accomplish that?"

"I threatened to nail his worthless hide to the nearest barn door if he didn't come across."

Casey had to smile at the mental image Grace's statement created.

"So...how are you?" Grace asked after another lengthy pause.

"Fine."

"Yeah? Well, you sound like somethin' the cat dragged in, and we both know why, so let's stop beatin' around the bush."

"All right," Casey said at last. "I'm—"

"Miserable," Grace finished. "So's Holt. Both of you hardheaded as a couple of army mules."

"Grace, I appreciate what you're trying to do, but—"

"Mind my own business, right? Okay, okay," she said on a sigh. "I promised myself I wouldn't interfere, but it's damned hard." Grace fell silent, then added, "Listen, honey, I really didn't call to make you feel worse. I just wanted to make sure you were all right and to tell you I'm sending something along to you. A keepsake, you might say."

"I can't accept a gift."

"Yes, you can," Grace insisted.

"It isn't necessary."

"Damned sure is. Now you listen here, Casey Westbrook. You're as dear to me as my own kin, and if I wanna give you somethin' special, I'm gonna do it whether you say so or not."

"Yes, ma'am," Casey said meekly, her heart a few pounds lighter. Still, what were pounds compared to tons of hurting without hope?

"I want you to keep in touch," Grace said, softly, but no less forcefully.

"Yes, ma'am."

"Promise?"

"Promise."

"We all miss ya, honey." Grace's voice cracked.

Casey knew the "we" didn't include Holt. "I—I miss you, too." Until this moment Casey had thought she didn't have any tears left in her. She was wrong. The wonderful woman at the other end of the line was dearer to her than she could ever express in mere words.

There was a sniffle from the other end of the line. "Oh, hell," Grace said. "Told myself I wouldn't cry. Now look at me, I'm blubberin' all over the place. Better get off this phone before I flood the place. Take care, darlin'."

They said their goodbyes.

Then Casey was once again alone with only her thoughts for company. Solitude closed in like the jaws of an invisible vise, finally, reluctantly driving her into the kitchen for a fresh cup of coffee. It tasted bitter, and she set the steaming cup aside. She should get up and do *something*, she told herself. She couldn't spend the rest of her life hiding out in her apartment. Sooner or later she *had* to face reality.

Not yet.

Always before in times of crisis, she had been able to accept what life dished out. She had learned to be adaptable. Less pain that way. Fewer scars. Not this time. She didn't feel flexible, just flat, empty. And alone.

In an effort to help shake her blues, she walked to the stereo system and turned on the radio. The notes of an acid rock tune blasted into the room, and Casey turned the station selector, skimming over the wavelengths until . . .

Patsy Cline's sultry voice drifted from the speakers, crowding every corner of the room with achingly lonely lyrics about sweet dreams of a lover. Dreams that couldn't come true.

The room blurred, and fat, wet drops plopped onto the sleeve of her oversize sweater. Holt had taken away her nightmares, replacing them with sweet dreams—dreams that would *never* come true.

The song's plaintive words went on, talking about forgetting the lover and starting life anew.

Forget Holt? Casey would sooner forget to breathe.

A knock sounded at the door, and Casey groaned out loud. She decided to ignore the intrusion on her misery. The knocking persisted. It was undoubtedly Ramsey trying to ruin his knuckles, and he wouldn't stop until she answered.

"Go away, Ramsey," she said, opening the door. "I don't want . . . to see . . ."

Across the threshold stood the man she most wanted to see in all the world, in all the universe, in all the galaxy, looking incredibly, wonderfully handsome. For a moment Casey thought she had actually conjured him up out of her imagination.

Her eyes were puffy and moist, probably from recent tears, her bottom lip was slightly swollen where she had chewed the tender flesh. The sight made his insides knot. And Holt thought she was the most beautiful woman ever created, and he prayed to God he hadn't driven her away forever.

She wanted to touch him, just to be sure. Her fingers itched with the need to verify his warm, wonderful presence. For one heart-in-the-throat moment she entertained the idea that he had come because of her, then her heart sank. He was probably only delivering Grace's gift.

"May I come in?"

"Y-yes. Yes, of course." Numb, Casey moved back, and he stepped inside. "Grace just called," she said inanely. As he walked past, she caught a whiff of his cologne. He smelled like Texas and sunrises.

"Did she?" Holt turned to face her, and they stood staring at each other for minutes. Days. Years.

She had on the same sweater she'd been wearing the first day they met. The neckline still drooped over a smooth, creamy shoulder. But he no longer had to wonder what her skin would feel like beneath his hand. He knew, and the knowing was killing him. Holt also knew he had hurt her beyond measure. Beyond repair? While his brain warned him he had come on a fool's errand, his heart insisted that God protected fools and little children. Three days ago he had acted like both.

"Mind if I sit down?" He didn't want to sit down. He wanted to take her into his arms, hold her, feel her next to him, love her. . . .

"Oh. Oh, I'm sorry." Casey gestured toward the sofa. "I forgot my manners." She hadn't forgotten how it felt to be held in his arms, kissed by his lips, loved....

He sat down. Casey swallowed hard and seated herself on the opposite end of the couch. More silence.

Then suddenly Holt got up and walked to her bookcase, crammed his hands into his pockets and stood with his back to her, as though the contents of the shelves were of vital interest.

"Can...would you like some coffee?"

He whipped around. "No. I don't want... No, thanks," he said, shoving his hands even deeper into the pockets.

Casey could see how difficult the visit was for him. Obviously Grace had badgered him into delivering the gift. And just as obviously, he had agreed against his better judgment. He was nervous, and Casey was sure he couldn't wait to leave.

"Holt. This really isn't necessary. I wish you would take the gift back and thank her, but I can't accept."

"It'll break her heart."

And it's breaking mine to have you here so close, yet so very far away. "I'm...sorry."

"Won't you look at the gift before you send it back?"

"I don't think—"

One hand appeared from its hiding place in his jeans pocket; his fingers closed around a small, tissue-wrapped object. He discarded the paper and placed it in Casey's trembling hand.

A dainty, diamond and sapphire brooch winked up at her from the palm of her hand. "I...I can't—"

"There's an inscription on the back."

Gingerly Casey turned the exquisite piece of jewelry over. There, engraved on the smooth back of the brooch were the words, Norah, My Darling, My Life. Forever, Alex.

Casey lifted her gaze to Holt. "The man Norah Tanner loved."

"He gave it to her the night he died. Grace wanted you to have it."

Confused by his words and overwhelmed by his presence, Casey shook her head. Tanner must have given the brooch to Grace when she worked on the estate. Casey was touched by the gift, but still uncertain why Holt seemed to speak as if it held some hidden secret.

"Norah Tanner doesn't exist anymore," Holt said. "She hasn't for years."

Again assuming the obvious, Casey decided the legendary movie star had died. "That's why Grace was pretending," Casey whispered.

"She wasn't pretending."

Casey stared at Holt, her mind refusing to accept the implication his statement provoked. "I don't under—"

"Grace Malone *is* Norah Tanner," Holt said in a voice that sounded amazingly lucid, despite his words. "Or at least, she used to be."

Seeing shocked disbelief in her clear blue eyes, Holt proceeded to explain the unexplainable.

"Norah was nineteen and married when she fell in love with Alex Grant. He was kind, gentle, loving—everything her husband wasn't. Phillip Tanner was insanely jealous. And vindictive. He found out about Norah and Grant and confronted them, but something went wrong and Phillip snapped. He killed Grant, then himself."

The room was deathly quiet, and several minutes passed before Holt cleared his throat and started to speak again.

"Phillip had his will drawn up so his estate would be tied in very tight, neat, legal bows. Everything went to Norah, so long as she lived in Texas for the rest of her life. She couldn't sell the estate, or she forfeited everything, and she couldn't run such a risk, especially after she discovered she was carrying Grant's child. Norah's daughter was born about six months after she arrived in Texas. She named her Rosemary after Alex Grant's mother."

When Holt paused, drawing in a deep breath to continue, Casey glanced down at the sparkling pin in her palm. "Thank you for telling me, Holt. I ... I think I understand now why—"

"You don't understand, because I haven't finished the story. Norah had suffered through enough gossip for a dozen lifetimes, and she didn't want that for her child. So she kept Rosemary isolated on the estate. She had everything; private tutors, beautiful clothes, but it wasn't enough. Two weeks after Rosemary turned sixteen, she took pleasure in informing Norah she was pregnant by the town boy hired to help out the gardener."

His voice softened, lowered as he said, "In her own way, I think she loved me, but couldn't handle the responsibility. One day she walked away and never looked back."

"You?" Casey breathed, still stunned, but slowly beginning to make sense out of all he had told her.

"Grace isn't my aunt. She's my grandmother."

"I thought she was pretending to help me," Casey said, more to herself than to him.

"In a way she was. After my mother left, Norah swore her grandson would have the one thing her daughter didn't— freedom. In the beginning, when she went to work at the diner, she used old clothes and a wig to create Grace. Later it wasn't necessary. Finally Norah became the fantasy and Grace the reality."

"I ... I don't know what to say—"

"Say you'll keep the brooch." He reached out and took her hand, closing her fingers over the glittering pin. "Say you'll keep me."

Casey's eyes flew to his.

"I wanted you the first minute I saw you, Casey. Then I started loving you and I don't know how to stop. Don't ask me to. Until you came along, I was convinced I'd never find a woman I could trust enough to love me and my secrets. I just didn't understand you can't have trust without giving it. I love you, Casey, and I'll spend the rest of my life trying to make up for the pain I've caused you."

Casey's knees threatened to buckle. She closed her eyes and whispered, "Oh, please, God, don't let this be a dream."

"Open your eyes, darlin'."

She opened her eyes and looked at him.

"I made a sobering discovery after you left. There's no me without you. I'm only half a man with half a heart. Please, forgive me. I love you, love you, love—"

His kiss ended the conversation. Ended their pain.

"Don't..." He kissed her mouth, chin, cheeks. "...ever..." He kissed her eyes, forehead. "...leave me."

"Never. Hold me...Holt, hold me."

"Always...always."

Much later, whispered endearments and promises mingled with the last gold of the day spilling through Casey's bedroom window.

"Does this mean you intend to keep my grandmother's gift?" Holt stroked her soft, smooth tummy, just above her nest of dark curls.

"Yes." Casey smiled. "Remind me to write her a thank-you note."

"You could tell her in person."

"But I would have to go to Texas to do that, wouldn't I?"

His hand stilled. "A few days ago I asked you to stay with me. I was a coward and didn't say what was really on my mind, in my heart."

"What did you want to say?"

"Marry me. Love me and let me love you." Holt held his breath.

Casey's eyes pooled with tears. "I'll marry you, live with you, love you until there's no breath left in my body."

"In Texas?"

Casey smiled. "On the moon, if you want."

"A few acres just outside Crescent Bay will do nicely."

"Yes," she whispered as his mouth claimed hers. "Nicely."

Epilogue

"This is Marla Thompson in Los Angeles. And it is indeed a sad day for movie fans the world over, as we mourn the passing of one of Hollywood's great legends—Norah Tanner.

"Sometime shortly after noon yesterday, the legendary movie star passed away at her estate in Texas. Sources close to the seventy-year-old Tanner said she had been in failing health for some time and had, in fact, been bedridden for the last several years.

"'Notorious Norah,' as she was referred to by the press during her heyday, was a major participant in one of the biggest scandals to ever rock Hollywood—the murder-suicide of her then lover, actor Alex Grant, and her husband, the noted director, Phillip Tanner. According to the legal firm that oversees the estate, Ms. Tanner's will specifies that her twenty-three-room Texas mansion is to be refurbished to serve as a halfway house for runaway teenagers, with an accompanying trust fund to provide the necessary operating expenses.

"No services have been set, as the legendary star requested her body be cremated. Later on this week we will offer a look back at Norah Tanner, her films, her triumphs and tragedies—"

Holt snapped off the television set, and the brightly smiling newswoman on the screen faded to a dot, then disappeared. Naked as the day he was born, he padded back to the bed, quickly slipping under the cover to snuggle next to the soft, warm woman patiently waiting for his return. He gathered her into his arms, nestling her head into the hollow of his shoulder.

"Wonder how long it took Grace to come up with that idea," Casey murmured against his throat.

"Hmm," he said, enjoying the deliciously provocative feel of her mouth. "She's probably had it in the back of her head for years, just waiting for the right time."

"You think so?"

"I think..." He kissed the top of her head as he caressed her bare back beneath the sheet. "...At this very moment, Gracie is the last thing on my mind."

"So, tell me, C-h-i-e-f, what *is* on your mind?"

"I was just thinking about my wife."

Casey pulled back until she could look into his eyes, into the teasing sparkle. "This is a minor point, but I don't believe you have a wife."

"I know, and it's a sorry state of affairs," Holt said, his fingers gently toying with the soft underside of her breast. "No pun intended."

"None taken," she replied, loving the way he treasured her body.

"I'd say the situation calls for immediate action."

"Do you?"

"I do." He pushed her breast up far enough to take a dusky nipple into his mouth.

"That's..." Casey sighed. "Oh...I, Holt..."

"Don't you?" he asked around the other nipple.

"Don't I what?" She gasped as his teeth nipped lovingly at tender flesh.

"Think the situation needs correcting."

"I . . . do," she breathed as he stretched his body the full length of hers and held her close.

"Then we're married," Holt said, wearing the crooked grin she loved so much. "I said, 'I do,' and you said, 'I do,' so that means we're married."

"Didn't we skip a step, like a church, flowers—?"

"Details," he teased, then suddenly became sober, gazing deeply into Casey's eyes. "Important details and ones I want to take care of as soon as possible, but in my heart we're already man and wife." His fingers threaded through the hair at her temples, and his hands held her fast. "I want you by my side for the rest of our lives. I love you, Casey."

"And I love you," she whispered as his lips touched hers, sealing their vows with sweet promises of forever.

The day surrendered to night's timeless seduction as they held each other, held fast to the future. Sunrise, sunset. Hope, peace. And always, always, love.

*   *   *   *   *

FOUR UNIQUE SERIES
FOR EVERY WOMAN YOU ARE ...

Silhouette Romance®

Love, at its most tender, provocative,
emotional ... in stories that will make you laugh and
cry while bringing you the magic of falling in love.

6 titles per month

Silhouette Special Edition®

Sophisticated, substantial and packed with
emotion, these powerful novels of life and love will
capture your imagination and steal your heart.

6 titles per month

SILHOUETTE *Desire*®

Open the door to romance and passion. Humorous,
emotional, compelling—yet always a believable
and sensuous story—Silhouette Desire never
fails to deliver on the promise of love.

6 titles per month

SILHOUETTE·INTIMATE·MOMENTS®

Enter a world of excitement, of romance
heightened by suspense, adventure and the
passions every woman dreams of. Let us
sweep you away.

4 titles per month

SILG-1RRR